SHOT
CALLER

By Jen J. Danna

Exit Strategy

Shot Caller

As Sara Driscoll

Lone Wolf

Before It's Too Late

Storm Rising

No Man's Land

Leave No Trace

Under Pressure

SHOT CALLER

JEN J. DANNA

PINNACLE BOOKS
Kensington Publishing Corp.
www.kensingtonbooks.com

This book is a work of fiction. Names, characters, businesses, organizations, places, events, and incidents either are the product of the author's imagination or are used fictitiously. Any resemblance to actual persons, living or dead, events, or locales is entirely coincidental.

To the extent that the image or images on the cover of this book depict a person or persons, such person or persons are merely models, and are not intended to portray any character or characters featured in the book.

PINNACLE BOOKS are published by

Kensington Publishing Corp.
119 West 40th Street
New York, NY 10018

Copyright © 2021 by Jen J. Danna

If you purchased this book without a cover, you should be aware that this book is stolen property. It was reported as "unsold and destroyed" to the Publisher and neither the Author nor the Publisher has received any payment for this "stripped book."

All rights reserved. No part of this book may be reproduced in any form or by any means without the prior written consent of the Publisher, excepting brief quotes used in reviews.

All Kensington titles, imprints and distributed lines are available at special quantity discounts for bulk purchases for sales promotion, premiums, fund-raising, educational or institutional use.

Special book excerpts or customized printings can also be created to fit specific needs. For details, write or phone the office of the Kensington Special Sales Manager: Kensington Publishing Corp., 119 West 40th Street, New York, NY, 10018. Attn. Special Sales Department. Phone: 1-800-221-2647.

PINNACLE BOOKS and the Pinnacle logo are Reg. U.S. Pat. & TM Off.

ISBN: 978-0-7860-4662-1
First Kensington Hardcover Edition: September 2021
First Pinnacle Paperback Edition: August 2022

ISBN: 978-1-4967-2793-0 (ebook)

10 9 8 7 6 5 4 3 2 1
Printed in the United States of America

For Jess
You've always stood behind me, using your talents to enhance my writing in every way you could. From your artistic eye, to your outstanding photography skills, to your enthusiastic beta reading, you've helped bring my books to life. Thank you!
Also . . . commas!

CHAPTER 1

*T*he bridge stretched far into the East River, rising slowly into a steel-gray sky roiling with dark clouds. Railings flashed by in a matching shade of grimy gunmetal, broken only by ragged wheals of rust where industrial paint had long ago been stripped by wind and weather as rot took hold.

They called it the "Bridge of Pain" and said it led only to violence, misery, and isolation.

Those destined to stay within its walls emerged changed. Broken. Having left an integral part of themselves behind in a desperate bid to survive.

Gemma Capello's time there would be short compared to many, but a part of her dreaded not only what brought her there, but what would keep her.

Rikers Island.

Widely known as one of the worst jails in America,

Rikers was considered a blight on New York City. So much so, the city had committed to shuttering it in 2026.

Many said the closure couldn't come fast enough.

Some NYPD and Department of Corrections officers disagreed. In their minds, inmates were incarcerated because they'd broken the law, and Rikers was part of the justice system's effort to right that wrong. Maybe it was in part because of Gemma's calling and her innate ability to burrow inside the mindset of others, but she saw those inmates more clearly as fallible human beings than many of her fellow officers. She also recognized that sometimes justice rolled roughshod over human rights. In her mind, Rikers was a very public example of that abuse.

Moments before, she'd pulled up to the security booth on the Queens side of the Francis R. Buono Memorial Bridge. Immediately, an extra show of force was evident in the additional correction officers stationed there to thoroughly question anyone wishing to gain access to the island and to turn back those found unacceptable. The island was on lockdown and visitation rights would have to wait for another day. The Otis Bantum Correctional Center was in crisis and every available man was on-site, leaving the other buildings potentially short-staffed in case of emergency.

Gemma had waited patiently as they examined her ID and then waved her through with calls of "Good luck!" She could practically hear the silent *You're going to need it* as she drove away, the grim tone chasing her onto the bridge.

She glanced over the right railing, across the wind-tossed choppy waters of the East River to the eastern side of the island. On the southern edge, a low, multicolored smear marked the visitor and employee parking lot, with the pale streak of the Control Building—the administrative facility where visitors and most employees entered the island and then boarded buses to travel to any of the ten jails—behind it. In the distance, taller detention centers rose into the sky.

Gemma had been to Rikers before, but each time it was like entering a war zone. She never felt like she could draw an easy breath until she was back on terra firma in Queens. It was said Rikers Island was sinking; geologists meant that literally, but in her mind, it was sinking straight into the blackness of despair.

Now she was called to report in at the Otis Bantum Correctional Center where, a little over an hour before, a riot had erupted and a group of inmates had taken control of one of the secured units. That was bad enough, but the eight correction officers they'd taken hostage had called for the big guns: the NYPD HNT—the Hostage Negotiation Team. Lieutenant Garcia, the commander of the team, had called her in, but even with lights and sirens, it had taken her nearly a half hour to fight her way through midafternoon traffic to the island.

In a few more minutes she'd be over the bridge and faced with additional layers of security—some standard, some likely extra layers in response to the crisis—to get onto the island proper. Then it was just a matter of finding the right jail and getting to work.

A low roar drew her gaze out the passenger window and her heart lurched into her throat at the sight of a massive jet speeding directly toward her on one of La-Guardia's two runways, less than a half mile to the east. The plane left the runway, banking upward at a steep angle to rumble ferociously overhead. Heavy vibrations rattled Gemma's breastbone as it jetted away from New York City and into the overcast sky.

She crossed the apex of the bridge and coasted down toward land. Spread out before her, Rikers covered the entire breadth of the island in clusters of buildings, each contained behind rows of chain link and razor wire. On the far side of the island, a quintet of stacks from the power plant pumped out billows of charcoal smoke to meld into the low-lying cloud cover.

Coming off the bridge, she joined a short line at the next set of security booths. When it was her turn, she pulled up to the booth, put down her window, and extended her identification. "Detective Gemma Capello, NYPD Hostage Negotiation Team."

The burly corrections officer leaned in to inspect the picture on her ID, then her face, and then the ID again. He gave a curt nod. "Go on through to the next booth."

One more round of identification and inspection and then Gemma had her directions—stay on Hazen Street straight ahead and follow the road as it curved to the left into Hillside Avenue. The Otis Bantum Correctional Center, or OBCC in officer shorthand, would be on the left. But as Gemma closed in on the OBCC, she realized directions weren't required. All she needed to do was follow the emergency vehicles and flashing lights. It felt like every Department of Corrections worker and NYPD cop not already on duty had converged on the site.

The OBCC was a frenzy of activity—people streamed across the front parking lot, and emergency vehicles, both Department of Corrections and NYPD, lined the roadway. Gemma overshot the facility and found a parking spot on the far side of the road near the western edge of the island next to a small storage building. Getting out of the car, she buttoned her blazer and jogged back down the road, thankful for the flat-soled boots she paired with her tailored suits for just this reason.

She ran along the fence line where it towered ten feet overhead, curls of vicious razor wire twisted in loops over the top. Fifteen feet away, a second line of fencing ran parallel to the outer ring to dissuade anyone with hopes of escape—if the inner fence didn't tear their flesh to shreds, the outer one would. High-tech security could be hacked, but there was nothing like good, old-fashioned agony to dash the hopes of anyone wishing for freedom outside the walls of the jail.

Abandon hope, all ye who enter here.

Gemma dropped into a walk as she arrived at the parking lot. She scanned the buzzing activity, searching for Garcia's salt-and-pepper hair among mostly younger officers, her ears attuned for any familiar voice, but the surrounding furor had an edge of unfamiliar desperation to it. To save time, she pulled out her cell phone and texted her lieutenant of her arrival. Seconds later, she received instructions to meet him under the trees just north of the main entrance. She cut to her right and, pushing past a cluster of correction officers, spotted Garcia standing with three other men with their backs to her.

She didn't need to see his face to identify Trevor McFarland—his boxy charcoal suit hanging drunkenly as if he'd recently shed weight too quickly gave him away, as did the bulky equipment bag on his shoulder. He hadn't suffered a drastic weight loss; he just never seemed to care that the off-the-rack suits he wore on the job didn't actually fit him. It was the same reason he kept his fair hair buzzed short—so he didn't need to fuss with it or worry about departmental regulations. McFarland was always more concerned with the job than the trappings of it, a sentiment with which Gemma wholeheartedly agreed.

At a word from Garcia, all three men glanced back toward her, allowing Gemma to quickly identify the rest of the team. Fresh-faced and with a cheerful grin as he pushed his bone-straight black hair out of his eyes, Jimmy Chen wore a suit and tie in an identical shade of navy blue. He was one of the newer members of the team, but even HNT rookies had at least a dozen years on the force. In the months since he'd joined the HNT, he'd shown himself to be intuitive, a quick thinker, and, thanks to his Asian-American roots, an asset in situations dealing with sensitive racial issues when a suspect didn't want to deal with yet another white guy who didn't understand his specific problem. The third man was Kurt Williams, a senior member of the team, his neatly trimmed beard liberally sprinkled with gray, his hazel eyes behind his boxy, wire-rimmed glasses serious and steady. He'd paired a subtle hunter green and navy blazer with dark trousers, giving him an elder statesman/professorial air.

Garcia's put together a solid team for this.

Once again, Gemma was the only woman on the team. When under twenty percent of the entire NYPD force was female, this wasn't a surprise. Unlike some of the women on the force who tried to blend into the male background, Gemma never tried to hide her gender. She might wear simple, tailored suits and sensible footwear like the guys, but she let her curly hair tumble to her shoulders, and she wouldn't think of walking out of her apartment before framing her brown eyes with a swoop of eyeliner and a few flicks of mascara.

Of only medium stature, but with serious muscle behind his bulk, Garcia stepped out from the group and motioned Gemma over.

Gemma sidestepped around a bench where a uniformed correction officer was seated, attended by a paramedic who held a wad of gauze over his left eye while blood oozed down his cheek. "Sorry I'm late. I got here as fast as I could." She nodded at the other detectives in greeting.

"We're still waiting," McFarland said. "DOC admin wants to be in on the briefing."

The Department of Corrections was ultimately responsible for all activity on Rikers Island, so this wasn't a surprise. "The commissioner's on her way?"

"Expected shortly. Your father's already inside."

Tony Capello, a forty-year veteran of the NYPD, was the current Chief of Special Operations. As such, he oversaw the many units inside the division requiring specific training to respond by land, air, water, horseback, or for crisis situations requiring specialized skills or equipment. Considering the Emergency Services Unit and the HNT were under his purview, it was no surprise he'd want to be here to help establish the NYPD's presence within Rikers.

Gemma glanced toward the main entrance. "I should have known."

"Considering the media circus this could become, he'd want in on this from the beginning to help steer the story." Garcia's gaze shifted abruptly to focus on something over Gemma's shoulder.

She turned to find the Apprehension Tactical Team had arrived. The A-Team, as they were more commonly called, was the NYPD Emergency Services Unit's tactical outfit, and were often called into hostage situations. As usual, they looked ready for a siege, suited up in unrelieved black with heavy body armor, boots, helmets, and safety glasses. Each officer carried not only a handgun at his hip but an M4 carbine on a sling strap against his chest. "Who's leading the team?" Gemma asked.

"Cartwright."

"Good." When Garcia turned to fix her with a pointed stare, she shrugged. "Sometimes Sanders can be a little hotheaded." *They don't call him Shoot-'em-up Sanders for nothing.* "Cartwright's a slower burn, which is what this situation is going to need, especially if there might be a clash with Rikers's own emergency team."

"That's for Cartwright to manage. Rikers ERSU can't be occupied with this situation for days." Rikers's Emergency Response Service Unit—the ERSU—was the DOC's tactical team. "They need to be available in case of crisis anywhere else on the island. If their people get spread too thin because of this situation, they're going to end up with another crisis."

Gemma scanned the A-Team officers, but at this distance and with helmets on, she couldn't distinguish one officer from another.

If Logan was part of the team, she couldn't tell.

Detective Sean Logan, who'd gone through the academy with her. Who'd been always a rival, sometimes a friend, usually a pain in the ass, and, for a single night about fifteen years ago, her lover. Who'd been ordered to the rooftop across the street from Saint Patrick's Old Cathedral two months earlier and had ignored her personal plea to save the life of John Boyle, the retired cop who'd vented his grief after losing his son by taking hostages at New York City Hall.

Who'd fired the fatal shot.

Logan had followed Sanders's orders to take the shot if he felt Gemma or her brother Alex had been threatened by Boyle. But she understood with that kind of order, Logan relied on his own judgment of the situation to decide whether to take a life.

It was unreasonable to still be angry over what had happened in the cemetery, but months later she still couldn't shake it off. In her heart, she knew Boyle was trying for suicide by cop, but there hadn't been enough time to convince Logan that Boyle wasn't a threat to anyone but himself. She'd depended on their history for Logan to trust her implicitly.

A man had lost his life because, clearly, Logan didn't trust her judgment over his own, even when she'd spent hours with the suspect, getting to know how he ticked.

She hadn't worked with Logan since that night. But sooner or later, he was going to circle back into her orbit. And with a situation of this size, unless he'd recently gone off shift, as one of the A-Team's most competent officers, he'd be here.

She'd just have to deal with it.

She turned away from the A-Team and toward Garcia. "When's the briefing?"

"In ten." Garcia shot back his cuff and checked the time on his watch. "Whether the commissioner is here or not. They're giving her time, but they can only afford so much." He pointed at the industrial cement steps leading to a door where the parking lot curved around the building. "We still have to get through another round of security, so let's move or we'll be late."

It was time to find out how bad the situation was.

They'd know soon whether this would be a standoff that could be negotiated in a single day, or whether this would take over their lives for days, or maybe a week, or more.

Negotiating was already hard enough, but when it was with inmates already looking at life sentences with absolutely nothing to lose, the cost of a team's lack of success might be paid in human lives.

CHAPTER 2

Single file, they made their way through the OBCC's heavy security—a room labeled ARSENAL—where they had to relinquish their service weapons, pass through metal detectors, endure ID scrutiny for the fourth time, and then wait for a laborious bag check that made Gemma grateful she never carried one on duty. She preferred instead to wear her Glock 19 in a holster on her belt and her gold shield clipped onto her waistband, where it was visible through her open blazer. McFarland, however, wasn't so lucky, and the search of his jam-packed communications equipment bag held up the group temporarily.

The inside of the OBCC was equally as dreary as the outside. Industrial gray concrete block walls rose above what was probably originally a beige tile floor, now discolored with age and constant use into a nondescript mud brown. Fluorescent lights lined the ceiling, a random scattering of panels dark from an absence of maintenance. The air was stale, heavy with a lack of circulation, and tainted with the sour odors of sweat, mildew, and fear.

Correction officers filled the hallways, clearing people through security and pointing them toward a meeting room near the warden's office. Most of the officers were men, almost all were people of color, and, universally, their expressions reflected their fury at the deadly nature of the situation. Chaos had entered their house and they weren't going to stand for it.

They wore uniforms of navy blue or powder blue and navy, except for the captains, deputies, and warden who each wore a navy tie over a crisp white shirt. Each officer wore a DOC badge over the left breast pocket engraved with their name and a heavy utility belt that carried the tools of their trade, including a collapsible baton and a can of pepper spray.

Firearms were strictly forbidden in all prisoner areas to avoid a situation where an officer could lose his gun to an inmate. The only exception to this rule would be the A-Team officers—if they were forced to go into the facility because correction officer lives were at stake, the situation was far past the point of nonlethal enforcement. They would avoid lethal force, but it had to remain an option for them.

Gemma and the rest of the HNT were shepherded into a modest meeting room already filled to standing room only. They lined up against the rear wall, waiting as more people crammed in. Heat prickling up the back of her neck, Gemma unbuttoned her jacket; the temperature in the room was already climbing with the crowded conditions and lack of air flow, and they were likely going to be trapped inside for a while. Conversation was a grim hum.

She caught sight of her father standing at the front of the room, talking to an older man in a white shirt and navy tie.

Bet that's the warden.

Even at sixty, Tony Capello was still a commanding figure. He'd never cracked six feet, but he more than made up for his shorter physical stature in calm, logic, and decisive choices, especially during crises. His dark hair had long gone to gray—he told his children it was from raising them as teenagers after they lost their mother—but he still moved with the ease of a much younger man. Gemma smiled as she watched him talk, his hands expressively accompanying his point. *You just can't take the Sicilian out of the cop.*

McFarland dropped his bag between his feet and leaned sideways, cocking his head toward her. "Ever done a prison standoff before?"

Gemma glanced sideways at him to find his eyes facing ahead. "No. You?"

"Nope. I also haven't done anything longer than a day or two. Mostly they're only hours long. This one though . . . probably not so much."

"I have a feeling this one's going to be a test of our endurance."

A dark-skinned, middle-aged woman wearing upper-rank white entered the room with DOC Commissioner Frye, a tall brunette in heels and a stylish skirt suit. The man talking to Tony excused himself, moved to shake the woman's hand, and then waited as she and Tony took two seats in the front row before moving to stand in front of a smeared whiteboard badly in need of a good cleaning.

"Good afternoon." The older man, whose receding white hair was balanced with a bristly white mustache, stood with his feet braced apart and his hands on his hips as he scanned the room. "Thank you for coming out to assist. I'm OBCC Warden Carl Davis." He gestured to the tall, thick-set woman beside him who wore her hair pulled back tightly into a simple bun. "This is Deputy Warden Nya Coleman."

A motion off to one side drew Gemma's gaze. Lieutenant Cartwright stood framed in the doorway; he and his officers were still out in the corridor, unable to squeeze into the overpacked room with their bulky equipment and weapons.

"About ninety minutes ago," continued Davis, "an incident occurred in one of our two Enhanced Supervision Housing units. What started off as a prisoner escaping his shackles inside ESH1 became a fight, which then escalated to a hostage situation. For those of you unfamiliar with the ESHs, these are relatively new units, opened only a few years ago as an alternative to the Central Punitive Segregation units—solitary confinement—especially for inmates twenty-two and under, as per current DOC regulations. In solitary, inmates are in their cells for twenty-three hours a day with one hour of outside recreation time, if the inmate wants it. In an ESH, except for periods of lockdown when all inmates are in their cells twenty-four/seven, these inmates are out of their cells for a minimum of seven hours a day for interpersonal interaction. They're also offered social programs and mental health assessments.

"Ideally, it sounds like a great program. In practice, we've had significant difficulties. Part of the problem is the inmate populations in general and, specifically, in those units. The DOC is trying to decrease the inmate population by keeping more pretrial detainees in neighborhood facilities or out on bail pending their trials. They've been successful, but that means the population at Rikers, while smaller, is now a more dangerous group charged with more serious offenses. Those are the inmates we have in the ESHs. Most of them are gang members, and almost all of them have violent pasts. And violence is their go-to method to solve any problem, whether with an officer or with another inmate." He tossed a glance in Cartwright's direction that Gemma read as *You know the kind . . .*

"What gangs are in ESH1?" The unseen voice came from the front of the room.

"You name it, we have it. And all in very close quarters. It's one of the reasons for the larger officer contingents in those cell blocks. It's the only way to keep them under control. They don't respond to reasoning, only to force."

On the other side of McFarland, Chen let out a low grumble of dissent.

"This particular clash was between the Filero Kings and the Gutta Boys." Davis beckoned someone in through the door. "I'd rather you hear what happened from a witness. Officer Neubeck, please come in."

A man squeezed past Cartwright, and Gemma recognized the correction officer she'd seen receiving medical treatment on the bench outside. His left eye was covered by a gauze dressing, and while his face was now clean, blood soaked the collar of his wrinkled, dirt-smudged shirt. He walked with a slight limp, and his knuckles were bloody and puffy. It looked like he'd given as good as he got.

Neubeck came to stand beside Davis, glancing around the room and nervously shifting his weight from side to side. "Afternoon." The word came out as a mumble, so he cleared his throat and tried again. "Afternoon."

Gemma could hear the correction officer in his tone.

"We had an incident in ESH1 this afternoon. Following lunch, some of the inmates were out of their cells and shackled to the tables on the mezzanine, which is protocol for when they're out of their cells. Rivas got free."

"How?" The question came from near the door.

"A lot of the inmates, they learn how to get out of restraints. Some of the equipment, it's not in the best shape. They know how to get loose. Rivas did and went after Burk, who was shackled a few tables over. He got Burk in a headlock, pulled out a switchblade, and started slicing the skin off his face."

A murmur of shock rippled through the room. What was a prisoner doing with a weapon like that inside a high-security unit? Sure, prisoners created their own shanks out of whatever was handy, but an actual switchblade?

"It was a nightmare. There was blood everywhere and Burk was screaming and Rivas was yelling he was going to kill him slowly, starting with skinning him alive."

Gemma shuddered at the mental picture Neubeck was drawing in her mind. Rikers was rough, but this story was shining a spotlight on the brutality of inmate interactions.

"The observing CO hit the alarm and we waded in to break it up. What we didn't know was four other guys were also free and they went after us so Rivas could keep working. A skills class was running in the classroom. Those inmates weren't restrained, and they ran in to stop Rivas. It was total chaos and it all happened so fast." He reached up and touched the gauze covering his eye. "It was a shit show. COs came from outside the unit. We would have gotten it under control, but then Rivas got Officer Evans in a choke hold with the switchblade to his throat right as the ERSU showed up."

Neubeck had to stop and take a breath. "Rivas told us to back off or he'd end Evans. And then if that didn't get the point through, he'd move on to Officer Montgomery. And then Officer Garvey. Other guys also had homemade weapons. A shank from a fork. A blade from a bit of radiator they'd ripped off. So we backed off, but had to leave eight COs behind. Some of the inmates begged to go with us, so we took anyone close who wanted to stay out of that powder keg. Then the inmates took over the control room and locked the door behind us."

Davis clapped a hand on his shoulder. "You did what you had to. We'll go in and get our officers out. We won't leave them in there with those . . ." His voice trailed off and Gemma could see him clamping down on the word he wanted to use—*animals*—and searching for a more acceptable term. "Inmates," he finished.

Neubeck tossed him a disgruntled look and stepped away, moving toward the door as if hoping for escape, but stopped short to stand against the side wall.

Gemma studied the interaction with interest. *Davis comes across as a magnanimous leader, but his own men don't seem too fond of him.*

She glanced over at her own team to see if anyone else

had picked up on it. McFarland's eyes were fixed on the front of the room, as were Williams's, but Chen raised a single eyebrow at her as if to say *Did you catch that?*

"That's where we are now," Davis continued. "We're still confirming head counts of both staff and inmates, but it looks like forty-two out of the original fifty inmates are still inside. Only inmates near the door were able to be escorted by the COs if they wanted out, so we're not sure how many are there unwillingly. And they have eight COs. The building's on lockdown—hell, the entire island's on lockdown—and there's an ERSU team stationed right outside the door, ready to move in if we give them the go-ahead. Or in case someone comes out, which doesn't seem likely, but we're prepared no matter what."

"We'll replace that team with my A-Team officers," Cartwright said from where he leaned against the door frame. "That way we're ready to go right away. Then your men can assist with this and other facilities on lockdown."

The twist of Davis's lips telegraphed he wasn't happy with his decreasing control of this situation as the NYPD came in and took over, but he remained silent.

"What kind of communication do you have into the unit?" Garcia asked, raising his voice to be heard at the front of the room.

"We had security cameras in there, but the first thing the inmates did was rip them down or destroy them, so we don't have eyes anymore. There's phone communication into the control room. Each CO has a radio, but we've heard nothing from them, so they probably don't have them anymore."

"What are our tactical options?" Cartwright asked.

"Correction units are designed to be hard to escape

from, but in this case, it makes it hard for us to get access to that same space. There are only three entrances to the unit—the main door from the corridor, and the emergency exit doors at the back of each of the two levels that lead to a stairwell and emergency exit. They're all controlled from inside the unit, but we have alternate controls outside each door in case something like this ever happens. They're usually locked out, but we have access to them. We can get you in as soon as you're ready. I'd like to see my guys home for dinner tonight."

"It's way too early to jump to that option," Garcia said. "You're going to need to moderate your expectations. A tactical entry at this time isn't advised."

"You don't know who you're dealing with. These men are brutal. They won't hesitate to kill or maim to get what they want. You need to get in there and get my officers out."

"I've been a negotiator for nearly fifteen years and a cop for more than a decade before that. I know exactly who I'm dealing with. And I've seen situations like this before. You go in with force, you're going to lose lives, including your officers. Let the negotiators get in there. Give us a chance to talk them down."

"I agree," said Deputy Warden Coleman, pinning the warden with a hard stare. "We don't know who's in charge up there or what kind of hold he has on the rest of the inmates. We might be able to talk to someone who understands the bind they're now in."

Davis shot an acidic glance at Coleman.

This guy doesn't seem to be anyone's favorite.

"What do we know about the hostages?" Garcia asked. "Where are they holding them? Are they together, split up?"

"The little we got before we lost visuals showed the

inner doors all open and COs being held inside a couple of the central cells. But that was nearly an hour ago."

"That's smart," said Cartwright. "That gives the inmates plenty of time to get to the COs and kill them at the first sign of a perimeter breach. Someone is thinking rationally."

"What about injuries to our people?" asked a man in doctor's scrubs. "As we can see from Officer Neubeck, there are injuries from the riot itself, not to mention anything that came after. If any of our officers are injured, we need to tend to them."

"That will be a negotiating tactic," Garcia said. "We'll negotiate for care for both the inmates and the correction officers. If they want the one, they'll have to allow the other. That will let us get a real feel for the situation."

"We need to be careful of the mix of inmates we've got in there," Deputy Warden Coleman said. "Warden Davis mentioned the gang issue, which is a problem anywhere on Rikers, but in ESH1, it's going to be particularly problematic. It's a pressure cooker at the best of times, but now . . . now it's going to be a war zone because of the rival gangs." She glanced over to Neubeck, who nodded in agreement.

"We need to know whatever information you have," said Garcia. "Once we make contact, it will help us know who we're dealing with, and who's at risk. We'll need to find leverage over whoever is calling the shots . . . for everyone's safety."

"There's a wide range of gang members in there," Coleman continued. "And different allegiances have formed between them because when you're inside, you do what's necessary to survive, even if it means calling a cease-fire with someone who'd be an enemy outside these walls.

But there are those labeled as snitches by gang members. And 'snitches get stitches' doesn't even begin to describe what these inmates will do to each other if they feel they've been wronged and have a chance at retribution. As it is, I'm afraid we may be about ninety minutes late there."

Davis jammed his hands in his pockets, his hunched shoulders stiff. "The first few minutes after an incident like this, it's chaos. And it's likely that following the retreat of the ERSU and the COs, vendettas were carried out while there was no hierarchy in place and no one in charge. At the beginning, it will be every man for himself."

"The first thing we need to do then is establish if anyone is injured. Or worse, dead," Garcia stated. "Where would you like us?"

"We've cleared an office for you." Coleman pointed out the door diagonally across the hall. "They're setting up the communication equipment you requested. If you'll follow me, I'll take you there."

Garcia led the team as they wound along the outskirts of the room and to the door, where they had to sidestep around Cartwright and his bulky gear to step from the stuffy heat of the meeting room into the cooler corridor air. Garcia stopped momentarily to talk to Coleman, and Gemma halted right behind him.

She closed her eyes for a second and drew in a relieved breath as cool air washed over her. It had been uncomfortably warm in the meeting room, and the stress and fury from many of its occupants had raised both the temperature of the room and her own tension. She needed to let go of the absorbed stress to prepare to make contact with the inmates. A negotiator had to be calm at all times, so starting with stress only made a hard job immensely more difficult. She blew out a long breath and opened her eyes.

And met Sean Logan's gaze.

Standing six feet away, he was dressed all in black, his bulletproof vest stamped with NYPD ESU and his heavy helmet in place, hiding his blond hair. He stood at rest, his hands layered over the butt of his rifle where it hung from its sling with the barrel pointed at the floor. She held his gaze without flinching—*You didn't have to take that shot*—and then purposely turned away from him and fixed her gaze on Garcia as he finished his conversation.

Garcia turned back to his team. "We're in here." He led the way down the hallway and through a doorway marked CONFERENCE ROOM 2.

Gemma shoved down her irritation at Logan. Now was not the time for her head to be somewhere other than in the game.

It was time to see who was still alive in ESH1.

And who they could keep alive.

CHAPTER 3

*T*he conference room was small, but it would be more than sufficient for their needs, even for a protracted negotiation. No fancy presentation equipment, glossy table, or cushy chairs; this room was strictly bare bones—a narrow table that sat six, held up by paired collapsible legs at each end, and surrounded by scratched black plastic chairs. But the phone equipment Garcia had requested sat in the middle of the table, even if it did look straight out of the 1970s.

Garcia frowned at the basic equipment. "McFarland?"

McFarland, a natural-born tech whiz, though it wasn't his official role on the team, always seemed to be able to work wonders with almost nothing. "I've got it, sir. We'll be ready for full communications in a few minutes."

As McFarland got busy setting up the equipment they'd need, liberally adding pieces from his bag of tricks, Garcia turned to the rest of the team. "We've lost a lot of time already and we need to make contact as soon as communications are ready, so let's get organized." He pulled two chairs away from the table, skirting McFarland as he sidestepped to drop a set of miked headphones on the far end of the table and pulled three more unmiked sets from his bag. Garcia pointed to the chair on the far side, farthest from the door. "I'm going to make a calculation about suspect response, and put you, Capello, as primary negotiator."

"What's your calculation?" Gemma's gaze swept her three male colleagues. "I'm happy to do it, but I'd like to know your strategy so I can play into it."

"We already know there's bad blood between the inmates and the COs, and more between the inmates themselves. Because of the all-male population in OBCC, and the decreased proportion of female representation in the CO ranks, I bet almost all of the inmate-CO aggression is male-to-male."

"You think putting a female on the other end of the line will make the inmates more cooperative," suggested Williams. "And possibly more communicative."

"Some hostage takers respond to authority," Garcia began.

McFarland's cynical laugh cut Garcia off. "Not this group. This is a group that got here by challenging authority."

"And a group that now lives under the fist of authority," Chen finished. "You're betting Capello will be less threatening because of her sex."

"It's a possibility I'd like to explore in this situation," Garcia said. He met Gemma's eyes. "I know you can also lay down the law if needed. Play it by ear, see whether it's the soft touch or firm hand that connects with them. I suspect you'll figure out pretty fast which one will work. And either way, I think you'll have the greater ability to naturally play either card." He pointed at the chair beside Gemma's. "McFarland, you're coach." Then the two chairs in front of him. "Chen, you're scribe. Williams, I need you to coordinate and liaise. There are a lot of people who will want to steer this situation, from Commissioner Frye, to Warden Davis, to Cartwright, to Chief Capello. And from there to Chief Phillips, because there's no way reporters aren't going to be all over the head of the department on this, which means he'll also be looking for results. Basically, I'm going to need you to stand in between all the external forces and the team to allow them to get their job done."

Williams gave him a curt nod. "Understood. You won't be part of the team?"

"I'll be overseeing the entire process and will be coordinating at the upper levels. This is going to be a PR and media circus, and I anticipate everyone from the *New York Times* to the mayor will be looking for answers and information, so I'm going to be the voice of the HNT. But we're going to need twenty-four/seven coverage in here while this is going on, so we're going to work this as two twelve-hour shifts from eight to eight."

Gemma sat down in her chair and picked up her headset, looping it around her neck. "Who are you picking for the other team?"

"Elijah Taylor as primary negotiator. And then Graham, Corbitt, and Shelby to round out the team. I've already got them on standby."

"Good choice." Gemma knew Taylor well, having worked with him on the team that had freed the hostages in the City Hall situation, as well as on a handful of other cases. "Taylor will strike the right tone for this and that team will work well together."

"And in case using a woman as primary on this shift doesn't play well with the inmates, we'll balance it off with a male primary on the night shift. If only a woman plays, then Shelby steps in to negotiate on the night shift. They'll be here at seven-thirty tonight for the pass off. Now, since I won't always be here and you may have to make judgment calls on the fly, let's lay out the ground rules. This one's going to be tricky because of the number of inmates involved and the number of hostages. Obviously, goal number one is to free every one of the hostages. But our hands will be tied when it comes to trades. We can't offer to commute anyone's sentence. We aren't going to offer to bring in family members to talk to the inmates because it's simply too risky to bring in anyone untrained to negotiate for us. But we will offer whatever's in our power to provide them that the DOC will allow. Food, medical care, whatever they need for their comfort."

Williams glanced through the partially open doorway to the bustling hallway beyond. "Based on what we heard from Davis, what the DOC will allow may be our biggest stumbling block."

"Possibly, but we'll be going over Davis's head on this one. I'll try to be here as much as I can, but I can always be reached. Use your judgment, and if the call is too risky, make contact and we'll work through it together. Or, if you need upper level sign-off, I'll get that for you. Is the tech ready to roll, McFarland?"

McFarland held up a single finger, plugged in the last set of headphones, hit a few buttons, slipped the headset on, and nodded his satisfaction before setting it down and stepping away. "Ready."

"Good. I'm going to go find Davis. We need to know who we're dealing with—they have to give us something. Going into this blind would be a mistake." Garcia stepped out into the hallway.

McFarland circled the table to take the chair beside Gemma. "Did you catch the interaction between the warden and his CO?" He tipped his bag against the legs of his chair and rooted around for a moment before pulling out a stack of yellow legal pads and a handful of pens, keeping one set for himself and pushing the rest into the middle of the table.

"I did. I was wondering if anyone else had." Gemma reached for both paper and pen. "He certainly made it look like he was sticking up for his officers. But it makes you wonder why there's bad blood between him and Neubeck, because that part came through loud and clear."

"And then more bad blood between him and his deputy. I don't know if she rubs him the wrong way because she's a woman, or because she's black, or because she challenges his command, but there's definitely friction there. I also got the vibe that Coleman is a lot more reticent to harm the inmates than Davis, which could also be a source of tension. Davis seems hard-core old school when it comes to how to treat the inmates." McFarland glanced up at the analog wall clock hanging at the head of the table. "We need to get this moving. We're going to be pushing two hours before we make contact. God only knows what's happened in that time. And we don't have a briefing book or anything yet."

"No, and it's going to be more important than usual because of the complexity of the situation, and because we'll be passing off negotiating with a second team. The only good thing is once the briefing book is compiled, it's going to be the most complete we've ever had."

Every hostage situation was different, but a negotiator's tools of the trade were constant, and the briefing book, or sometimes a situation board, was the heart of the negotiation team's efforts. It contained all the relevant information the team would need to deal with the hostage taker, and to plan a tactical assault, if needed. It would contain details on the suspect—his name, race, criminal history, details about his family and/or relationships, his mental health status, medical and/or addiction issues etc.— as well as similar information on the hostage or hostages. It would also contain any information about the physical locations of the situation, including maps, floor plans, and photos. Basically, it was the negotiation bible, and allowed the negotiator every bit of information that could assist in the process at his or her fingertips.

A negative about a prison riot, which was certainly relevant here, was the sheer number of people involved, both hostages and hostage takers. However, a positive in this case was that most of that information would be at their fingertips, or at least at the fingertips of the warden and the Department of Corrections, which would give them a significant advantage. They'd know who was still inside the unit, and would have up-to-date records on their crimes, gang affiliations, and mental and physical health statuses. This would give them a leg up and would allow them to leap into the negotiation with an unusual amount of insight.

Which was good, because, in many other ways, the deck was stacked against them. Rikers was not only a jail for sentences under a year, but was also a holding facility for those charged with serious crimes pending significant sentences, and some inmates knew life imprisonment already awaited them.

When the rest of your life was already spoken for, where was the cost in acting out?

Garcia came through the doorway, but he was alone.

"No warden?" Williams asked.

"He's coming. He knows what we need, and knows we need it now, so he's grabbing some initial information and will be right behind me."

True to his word, Davis strode into the room only minutes later, a large sheet rolled under his arm and a short stack of photos and papers in his hands.

"Are those the blueprints?" Garcia asked.

Davis placed the photos onto a clear section of the table. "Yes, but we have something else to deal with first. The mayor is on line two. He wants to talk to the negotiating team."

Gemma and Garcia locked gazes, and McFarland groaned.

Kevin Rowland, the man whose campaign to end stop-and-frisk had cost him his closest friend during the City Hall standoff. Another high-profile hostage situation in his town only months after the death of Charles Willan was sure to push buttons with the mayor, and he'd likely pressure to end the standoff quickly. But in a situation like this, a quick resolution could be an unmitigated disaster.

"Do you want me to talk to him as primary negotiator?" she asked.

"I don't want him talking to the team," said Garcia. "I'll take this. If he wants updates, they can come through me. This is how we'll work this whole situation, so let's get him used to it now. I won't have him interfering with your process and distracting you. Hand me your headset. I want you all to listen in so you have the full picture of the pressure surrounding this standoff."

Chen and Williams slipped on their headsets. McFarland grabbed his and leaned toward Gemma, holding the headset between them so they could both follow along.

Garcia took a deep breath, casting his eyes heavenward as if asking for patience, and nodded at Gemma to connect him to line two. "Mayor Rowland, Lieutenant Tomás Garcia. What can I do for you?"

"Garcia!" The mayor's greeting was practically a bark. "Have you made contact?"

"This is a complex situation, sir, and we're only getting started. We've been briefed and have set up our equipment. You called just as we're about to reach out to the inmates."

"So you can't tell me anything."

"Not yet, sir. But I'd be happy to keep you updated as we learn additional information. There will be teams here, twenty-four/seven, until the situation is resolved."

"Twenty-four/seven . . . so you're not leading the team."

"I'm leading the *teams*." Garcia leaned on the final word. "We'll have two groups, both made up of my best detectives, each taking twelve-hour shifts."

There were several seconds of silence during which the detectives in the room exchanged questioning glances.

"You think it's going to take so long it's going to need shifts," Rowland stated flatly.

"Sir, you need to be realistic about this. This is not a quickly resolved crisis, at least not without bloodshed. And we have eight officers in there, eight of our men and women, whose families are waiting for them to come home. We're going to get them there, which means we can't use force as our first option."

"You may need to use force eventually."

"We may. But not now, and quite likely not for days. We'll use that time to our advantage. We'll be switching off shifts, and getting rest, and bringing in food and coffee as we need it. They'll have none of that, which will put them in a position of weakness and will give us leverage."

"So you'll use food as a means of manipulation?"

"We don't consider it manipulation. It's a negotiation tool. We give them something—like food—and they give us something—like information or a hostage."

"What if they won't do that? You're in control. What about turning off their power and heat? It's not January, but the nights are cool. How would they like to be cold and in the dark?"

Unseen by the mayor, Garcia rolled his eyes and mouthed, "God help us" to his officers. "I wouldn't recommend that, sir." This was the experienced negotiator; his voice conveyed none of his frustration. "Definitely not now, and maybe not at all. We have to walk a fine line. We want to pressure them into releasing the hostages and ending the siege, but not at the expense of the hostages themselves. This is where prison negotiation is tricky. Some of these men are already charged with crimes that could net them a life sentence. So, what's one more sentence to add to it? If they think they're never going to get out, what's holding them back from violence? That's what we have to deal with. Our number one priority is getting our officers out alive and preferably unharmed. If we're too heavy-handed and do something like cut their power and heat, they'll take out their anger on the hostages. That's unacceptable. Better chances of success lie in finding out if the inmates have demands we can meet to end the situation peacefully. You need to be patient, sir, and manage your expectations, as well of that of the citizens. Given enough time, we have an excellent chance of bringing everyone out alive."

"I want to be kept in the loop."

"Understood, sir. I'll be in contact as soon as I know more." He tapped the button and disconnected the call. Sliding off the headset, he handed it to Gemma. "That went better than expected."

"This time," McFarland said. "We know what he's like when he gets impatient and wants to show who's in charge." He sat down in his chair, the plastic creaking ominously. "You didn't tell him that Capello and Taylor were the primary negotiators."

"I don't want him to make any connections to last August past me. It's only going to rile him and keep him on our backs. We don't need that." He drilled an index finger into the table in front of Williams. "Rowland may be one of the external forces I'm going to need you to stand in front of. He's given us trouble before. He's not patient in these situations."

Williams knit his fingers together on the table in front of him. "I'll handle him." Williams's tone was mild, but there was surety and experience backing them. Williams was known in the department for his patience in almost any situation, and for his ability to smooth ruffled feathers in hostage takers and external forces alike.

Garcia picked up the roll of paper, spreading it wide and turning it toward the table. "I requested the floor plan of ESH1." He nudged the bag beside McFarland's chair. "Got any tape in there?"

"Duct tape. You can't MacGyver a fix for any situation without it." McFarland rooted around at the bottom of the bag and then extracted a compact roll of duct tape. He plucked the map out of Garcia's fingers. "On the wall for easy reference?"

"Yes."

McFarland moved to the head of the table and proceeded to tape the blueprints to the wall under the clock where everyone could see it clearly, especially Gemma.

The Enhanced Supervision Housing unit occupied two floors encompassing an entire wing of the building. The blueprints sketched out the space both from above and from the side. The main entrance, a single sliding reinforced door, led to the ground floor. A small office was located just inside the main door. Inside the facility, two corridors ran down either side of the first floor in front of a row of paired, numbered doors. Stairs rose from the main entrance to an open, raised mezzanine that ran nearly the full length of the unit. From the mezzanine, stairs climbed to the second level to both the left and the right to connect with the narrow platform that ran around the upper level, fronting a second run of paired, heavy cell doors. At the far end of the mezzanine, another set of stairs led down to the ground floor and a large, open-ceilinged room surrounded by windows. The back wall of the unit on each floor was taken up by five tall windows, broken by a series of thick security bars.

Davis extended a quartet of 8" x 10" photos. "Take these too. This will give you a better mental picture. These are promo photos taken before we opened the facility in 2015." His tone took on a hard edge. "Back when we had high hopes about how well it would work." He handed them to McFarland to hang on the wall flanking the blueprints.

In the photos, the ESH was depicted in full color. Despite the barred windows, sunlight poured into the unit, brightening the space. The walls were a clean, pale yellow, contrasting the navy cell doors with their large, white, block numbers. Heavy support columns bearing large flat-screen TVs marched down the outer edge of the beige-tiled mezzanine floor in navy and yellow, parallel to two neat rows of steel tables. Along the edge of the second-floor walkway, large blue letters decreed POSITIVE ANYTHING IS BETTER THAN NEGATIVE NOTHING. Tables and chairs filled a classroom on the far side of the unit. At the end of the unit on each floor, a bright red door led to an emergency staircase behind glowing exit signs.

The last photo showed one of the modular cells, a cramped space in bright white with an inset bunk at the far end topped by a thin mattress and pillow. A metal sink and toilet were installed opposite the bed on a short, diagonal wall. A small table, built into the wall, was positioned close enough to the bed that the mattress could double as a chair. Two large plastic storage containers sat on the table for the inmate's possessions. A small, barred window let light into the cell. It looked clean and efficient . . . if you forgot that those four walls were the occupant's entire life in about eighty square feet for a minimum of seventeen hours a day. Gemma couldn't imagine how claustrophobic and lonely it would be within those walls. And this image came from when the unit was new. This many years later, it would be dingy and scarred. Before long, the occupant would likely be equally scarred.

Eye on the ball. That's where the hostages are now

being held. But remember the state of the mind who's been kept in that cell and who will now be on the other end of the phone line.

"That's helpful," Garcia said. "If we can get them on the phone, where will they be?"

"Here." Davis tapped the office by the main entrance. "That's the security and control room. It looks out over the entire facility and also contains the controls for opening the front door, rear emergency doors, and cell doors."

Chen studied the blueprints intently. "Any controls for the main door on the outside?"

"Of course. For exactly this reason. So we can walk in at any moment."

"Surely they know that," Williams stated. "And will have someone ready at all times to take out the first hostage the moment you do."

His jaw locked, Davis nodded. "That's what I thought so I didn't want to make a move until you got here. They're entirely capable of killing hostages on a whim. That's why I think you need to get in there. You're banking on them responding to logic. They don't. They only respond to force. You want to get through to them, that's the only way. You give them an inch, they'll take a mile."

"I disagree." Garcia's tone brooked no argument. "And for now, Cartwright is on board with a negotiated solution, so that's our direction."

"I think you're making a mistake. But if that's your plan, you'll need this." Davis walked to the table to pick up the remaining papers. "The list of who's in there—the COs who didn't make it out and the inmates who stayed in. But so far, it's bare bones."

"We need more than that," Garcia said. "We need anything you have on every inmate in there. Their background, medical and psychiatric history here at Rikers, and relationships with other men in the unit."

"Coleman's already working on that. She'll be in as soon as she has something for you. But at least you can start with this."

Gemma reached across the table and snagged the list. She laid the two pieces of paper—one with the names of the inmates, one with the names of the COs—out in front of her. "Then let's get started. We have our lists. Let's see who will answer the phone."

"And if they don't?" Davis asked.

"Then we'll move on to Plan B."

Gemma turned toward the phone. Time to make the first call before Davis asked what Plan B was.

There was no Plan B, at least not yet. Welcome to the world of negotiations, where strategy was a moving target and action plans were crafted on the fly. Negotiators not only had to be calm, patient, and great listeners, they also needed to be crafty, flexible, and able to think on their feet.

Because when lives were on the line, sometimes fancy footwork could keep blood from flowing.

CHAPTER 4

As McFarland, Chen, and Williams watched from their seats around the table, with Garcia and Davis standing behind her, Gemma dialed the extension for the ESH1 control room.

The phone rang in their headsets. Gemma looked up at Garcia and nodded.

The phone continued to ring.

After a dozen rings, she disconnected, waited for a slow count of ten, and dialed again.

No response.

They did six rounds with no one answering.

"What do you think?" Chen asked. "They don't want to pick up, they can't pick up, or they've destroyed all methods of communication and can't hear us call in?"

"My money's on them not wanting to pick up," Mc-Farland said. "I don't think they'd be stupid enough to

destroy their only method of communication to the outside world."

"Getting them to talk to us will be tough." Williams
met Gemma's eyes over the top of his glasses. "They're
not going to want to trust anyone in a position of authority. They're probably whooping it up in there because of
that lack of authority."

It wasn't hard to imagine the euphoria those inmates
must be feeling at the autonomy and sheer freedom of
choice after life in that cramped space with every moment of their lives regulated by someone else. No one to
lock them in their cells for the majority of the day, or tell
them when to wake up, eat, go to bed, and how to behave.
Especially for men who'd been incarcerated for months
or even years, the riot provided a freedom that must be
nearly foreign to them by this point. But it made Gemma
wonder how the lesser prisoners were doing—those who
may have moved from one faction's authoritarian rule directly to another. Moreover, she thought of the hostages,
the COs used to being in charge, now at the mercy of men
who were celebrating their exchange of power. And who
might feel tempted to use that power on those who were
now powerless.

Through the celebration, there would also be a struggle for superiority. And for gang members used to solving
problems with violence, they would simply fall back on
old habits.

Who'd be at the receiving end of that violence?

"This isn't working." Gemma swiveled in her chair to
face Davis. "Warden, you mentioned in the briefing that
you have a team outside ESH1. Can we check with them
to see if they could hear the phone ring?"

"I can." Davis pulled a chunky handheld radio from

his utility belt, set the channel, and raised it to his mouth. "Davis to Response Team One."

"Response Team One." The voice was male and tinny.

"Status update."

"We're about to pass off to Lieutenant Cartwright and the A-Team. But so far, the inmates have made no attempt to leave the facility."

"Can you hear what's going on inside the unit?"

"A lot of yelling. They sound victorious, not angry. If anyone's being hurt in there right now, it's being drowned out."

"Did you hear a phone ringing?"

"Over the noise and through the wall or security door? No, nothing like that."

Davis's lips twisted into a frown. "Roger that. Davis out." He lowered the radio and then clipped it onto his belt. "I don't know if we're getting through or not."

"My bet is we are," Williams said. "But either they don't want to talk to us because they're high on their newfound freedom and don't want to think about the compromise required by negotiation, or they're struggling over hierarchy, who's in charge, and who will speak for the group. Either way, the question is: How do we get through without opening the door?"

"We aren't there yet, but if that happens, we're doing it with Cartwright and his men standing in the entryway." Garcia strode over to the blueprints and indicated the small room by the main entrance. "This is the office with the phone?"

"Yes." Davis circled the table to stand opposite Garcia so the negotiating team had a clear view of the floor plan.

"You said the hostages were in two of the internal cells. Which ones and on what floor?"

"These ones." Davis pointed to a pair of cells, numbered 5 and 20, located in the middle of the cell block on the lower level, on either side of the mezzanine. "At least that's what we could see before they pulled down the cameras. It's possible they've moved them by now."

"Possible, but we'll work with the information we have."

"Sir, heads up."

Garcia turned around just in time to catch the red marker McFarland tossed. "Thanks."

With Davis clarifying a few details, Garcia marked the location of the phone, the cells where the COs were being held hostage, and all points of egress from the unit. Then he stepped back and studied the layout. "Are there windows in the security door? Can the team stationed in the hallway see what's going on inside?"

"Yes, the door has horizontal bars of security glass from the bottom to the top. In case of an incident, someone outside can get a nearly full view of what's happening inside, but the door's made of steel and there isn't a single opening big enough for escape if they got through the reinforced glass. I told my guys not to move up and look through the door because I thought the inmates might see that as encroachment."

Swiveling in her chair, Gemma studied the layout, looking for any aspect of the floor plan that might give them the upper hand. Or at least a way to start a conversation, but, as Davis noted, the security that kept the men in, also kept the DOC and NYPD teams out.

She was shifting back in her chair when her gaze skimmed past Davis. She froze midway, and then her gaze snapped to the radio on Davis's utility belt. She reached a hand out a few inches, checked herself, and pulled back. "Warden, you used your radio to talk to your response team. Is that how you talk to the COs?"

Davis's hand instinctively reached down for his radio. "The COs on the floor? Yes."

"And the COs on duty in the unit would have had radios?"

"Yes."

"And where would those radios be now?"

"In the . . ." Davis trailed off, his head cocking slightly to the side as he stared at her. "Somewhere in the unit. I can't see them being on the COs because they'd never give the hostages a way to reach out to us."

"But unless they tossed them out the door—and your team would have mentioned it if they did—they're still in there somewhere. And if we're lucky, at least one of them is still on. Are they on a specific channel?"

"Yes." He yanked the radio off his belt again, adjusted the channel, and extended it to her. "You want to try to contact them through the radio?"

She took the radio, turning it over in her hand to stare down at it. "The phone can ring and ring and no message gets through. But if the radios are on, I'll be able to talk to them. They may not answer, but I can tell them who we are and that we want to listen to what they have to say."

Davis's brows snapped together. "What they have to say? Some of these guys are killers. If you mollycoddle them, you'll get nowhere and you may get my guys killed."

"On the contrary, Warden, this is the heart of a negotiation. Less talking and a lot more listening. Only once the inmates feel they're being heard will we be able to make any progress. The key to this working is that we need to respect those at the other end of the line—"

"They're criminals." Davis's voice whipped out like

the parry of a blade. "They're antisocial personalities who can't get along in society. *That's why they're here.*" Fury shimmered through his hard-bitten words.

Gemma took a moment to let Davis's message sink in, giving him time to recognize what he'd said before she set him straight. "If I treat them like low-life scum, we might as well pack our bags and go home. If I talk to them like that, express any disgust I have for them, what's going to happen to your COs? Nothing good." Davis took a step forward, started to interject, and she ruthlessly cut him off. " We work by actively listening to whoever we're negotiating with, showing them respect, making a connection, and starting a dialog. We'll lower the emotion, let their anger defuse, and when that happens, they'll become more rational. Only then do we have a chance to negotiate an end to this standoff. *That's* how we'll save the lives of both your COs and the inmates. Remember, some of the inmates are also essentially hostages. They didn't ask for this crisis. They just couldn't get out before the walls closed in. We need to think of them as well."

Davis stared at her silently, his jaw squared into a mulish clench and his cheeks flushed.

Doesn't like to be checked by a lowly detective.

"I like your plan with the radios," said Garcia, drawing their attention and breaking the moment, pushing them forward. "Give it a try."

She nodded and keyed the radio. "Hello, men of ESH1. My name is Gemma Capello. I'd like to talk to you to resolve this situation. I've been calling. Perhaps you haven't heard the phone ring, or you've been unable to answer. But I'll call again in"—she glanced at the clock on the wall—"fifteen minutes. I'll call the phone in the control room by the front entrance. Please answer. I can't help you unless you talk to me. Talk to me, and I can keep officers out of the ESH. Talk to me, so I can understand the situation from your point of view. I'll call in fifteen minutes. Please pick up." She ended contact and set the radio on the table. "If we're lucky, someone heard it through the party going on in there and is conveying the message to whoever is now in charge or will answer the phone himself. But I'm going to radio in again every five minutes until it's time to call them and maybe we'll get through."

"You didn't tell them who you are," Davis stated. "You just gave your name."

"Consider the group we're dealing with." Gemma ran her index finger down the list of inmate names. "Many of these are career criminals. You mention the term 'detective' around them, and their backs go up. By leaving my rank out of the discussion, they have no idea who I am, or how much experience I have. So they can't push back with whatever story they might make up around me. They may not know the NYPD is involved. They may assume I'm DOC."

"And you think that gives us an advantage?"

"It might, so it's worth taking. The NYPD put them here, the DOC is only tasked with keeping them here. Depending on their relationship with the COs, they might hold less of a grudge against Corrections. That might also play against us, depending on how many of the stories leaking out are true."

"Stories?"

"Come on, Warden, you know stories of the treatment that goes on around here get out. I'm not saying it happens on your orders or even how much it happens in this house, but you know what they say about Rikers. The mistreatment. The beatings. COs turning their backs on inmate-on-inmate retaliation. Anyone who reads the *Times* knows about it. Leaving my affiliation out of the picture opens the door to them not assuming I'm from whichever group they hate more. And since we don't know who we're going to be talking to or if it will be a spokesman or a round of inmates, it's the safest way to start."

Movement drew her attention and she turned to find Deputy Warden Coleman standing in the doorway.

Coleman paused, one hand on the jamb, the other holding a black binder to her chest. Her gaze shot from Davis to Gemma to Garcia. "Am I interrupting?"

"Not at all." Happy for the break in the tension, Gemma pushed back her chair and stood, extending her hand. "Detective Gemma Capello."

"Deputy Warden Nya Coleman. I—" She cut off abruptly as Davis suddenly turned, muttered something about checking on an update, and cut around the table and out the door, forcing Coleman back a step into the hallway. Shaking her head, she watched him stride down the corridor before facing the negotiation team. "I'm sorry. Clearly I did interrupt something."

"Please don't apologize, Deputy Warden. We're just explaining our process to the warden."

"First of all, there's no chain of command between us, and we could be working together for at least a few days, so, please, call me Nya. And I suspect that if your process doesn't include storming the facility sooner rather than later, Warden Davis might have considerably less patience for it." She looked down at the binder she was carrying and seemed to remember her purpose. "This is for you." She extended the binder and McFarland took it. "I'm in the process of pulling the complete records of the inmates still in ESH1."

McFarland opened the binder out on the table where everyone could see. Inside was a stack of printed records, each with a black-and-white photo in the upper right corner of the inmate from their intake into the jail.

Gemma scanned the information: name, inmate number, charges, gang affiliation, street name, medical issues at intake, any violations of prison protocol and, if so, what if any punishment was assigned. She flipped through the pages. Almost every inmate had an extended list of infractions.

No wonder no one answered the phone. This was a group that bucked authority as a matter of course.

She glanced at the clock. Time to contact them again.

She picked up the radio Davis had abandoned when he left and looked over at Coleman. "We need to contact the ESH again."

She repeated the same message as the last time, telling the inmates she'd call in ten minutes and to please make contact so they could start to work toward a resolution. She ended the transmission and turned back to Coleman. "This binder . . . Is there more information to come?"

"Yeah, quite a bit, but I wanted to get you something to get started with in case you can make contact. The inmates are listed in alphabetical order by their birth surname. But if you need to look someone up by their street name, which is often how they refer to themselves in here, we can help there. I've got a couple of our admin staff pulling together the rest of the information for you and we'll get it in here as soon as possible." Coleman looked from Gemma to the other faces around the table and then to Garcia. "These guys aren't going down without a fight. Are you prepared for the long haul?"

"Yes," Garcia replied. "This isn't our first standoff of this size and complexity. *Patience* is going to be the watchword. They have nowhere to go, and we can outlast them. Hopefully we can get them to talk to us today."

"You think they might not?"

"We haven't had any luck so far."

"And, truthfully," Gemma interjected, "we don't know that our message is getting through to them. If we call again in"—she checked the clock—"seven more minutes and no one picks up, it might be because they've turned off the CO radios or changed the channel so they don't know we've been trying to contact them. But it's a place to start."

"I'm going to leave you to it then, so you can get to work. I'll be back when there's more to add to the book. And if anyone needs us, we're down the hall to the right. Send someone and we'll come running."

"Thank you, Nya," said Garcia. "You've been very helpful."

She stood in the doorway, her arms empty, shifting her weight uneasily from foot to foot. "I just want . . . Those men . . ." She blew out a breath. "Pull it together, girl," she muttered to the floor before looking up. "Not everyone in there is a career criminal. Some of the guys in there haven't been sentenced yet and still say they're innocent. But they couldn't pay the five-hundred-dollar bail fee, so they're here. They just want their day in court and to get home to their families. But to do that, they've got to stay alive. And I'm scared about what's going on in there. If I pop by occasionally for an update . . . is that okay?"

"Of course." Gemma pulled the binder closer and smiled her thanks. "If the door's closed, we're talking to them or can't be disturbed. Otherwise, feel free to come in. And it sounds like you know the men in there."

"Not all, but I came up the ranks as a CO, and then a captain. I'm the first female deputy warden at OBCC, even though I suspect the reason I got it is because none of the men wanted it. But that's fine, because maybe I can do some good here. Some of the inmates I know personally, but more than that, I know the type of guy who ends up here. So if I can help, let me know."

"We will. Thank you."

With a nod, she disappeared out the door and down the hallway.

McFarland stared out the door after her. "Lots of politicking going on around here. You have to wonder if that's going to affect what we need to do."

Garcia waved it away. "That's my problem. You guys keep your heads down in here and let me take the heat outside this room."

Gemma made one more appeal via radio, and spent the intervening minutes scanning the inmate sheets, trying to get a handle on the men inside the ESH.

She kept her eye on the clock as it ticked toward the appointed time. "It's time. Let's call again and see if we get someone." She dialed the number and sat back in her chair as it rang in her headset.

The phone was picked up after the second ring. Background noise exploded across the line, shouts and laughter, for a full second.

Gemma was drawing breath to speak when the line went dead without anyone speaking. She jerked upright in her chair, her gaze shooting across the table to Chen.

Chen shrugged. "Guess they didn't want to talk."

"I guess not." She drummed her fingers on the table. "I don't think there's any point calling again right away. I think we just got our answer. They're not ready to talk yet."

"But I'd read that as they got your radio transmission," Williams said. "So at least we have a way to contact them, even if they aren't talking to us."

"And this could give us a little more time to fill this out." McFarland ran his thumb over the pile of records.

It wasn't exactly great progress, but there was a base level of messaging going on, which was better than they had twenty minutes before. And forward motion was progress, no matter how small.

She'd take it.

CHAPTER 5

Gemma was the first of her team to report for duty the next morning, arriving at the OBCC HNT command center at 7:15 a.m. She found four detectives inside the room, awake, but looking more than a little haggard around the edges.

"Good morning."

Elijah Taylor looked up with a welcoming flash of white teeth in his dark face. Impeccably dressed as always in a stylish dark suit set off with an electric-blue tie, the night was wearing on him—his eyes were slightly bloodshot from exhaustion and drooped at the corners, his tie was loosened and askew, and a large disposable coffee cup sat half-full on the table in front of him beside two empty cups. "Morning." His gaze dropped from her face to the large thermos she carried. "If you brought your own coffee, that may be the wisest judgment call you'll make all day." He rubbed a hand over his belly. "What they brew here is worse than any cop coffee I've ever had. Which is saying something."

"I know, I had a cup of it last night. I'm pretty sure it could be used to strip rust off the Brooklyn Bridge." She lifted the thermos. "Thus, enough coffee to last me hopefully the whole day." She scanned the room. She knew all the detectives, had worked with them on various standoffs, and could identify the roles Garcia had assigned from their seating position. Taylor was the primary negotiator. Next to him as coach, Burt Corbitt, one of the longest standing members of the HNT, sat with his coat tossed over the back of his chair, his tie trailing out of its breast pocket, and his shirt sleeves rolled nearly to his elbow. Across from him, Gina Shelby, dressed in a black suit and ballerina flats with her blond hair spilling over her shoulders, sat in the coordinator's chair, and Steve Graham, a detective who'd come through the academy the year before her, grinned at her and gave her a broad wave from the scribe chair. "How did it go last night?" she asked. "Any progress? Did you make contact?"

"No. We tried until nearly midnight, and then made the executive decision to stop calling before we made them angry and that rained down on the hostages." Taylor straightened in his chair, tugged on his shirt collar to straighten it, and tightened his tie, running a hand down its length to ensure it lay flat. "We figured if they really wanted to talk"—he had to stop to hide a yawn behind a beefy palm—"they'd call out and any outgoing call would get routed directly to us. Or they use a radio. But apparently the inmates have a standard four a.m. wake-up time for breakfast so we thought letting them have some quiet time might help to calm things down since they'd been up for twenty straight hours at that point."

"So you had a quiet night."

"Not that quiet. We spent the time working with the warden's office compiling this." Taylor laid his hand on the binder that Coleman had delivered the night before. But now, instead of a small stack of records, the binder was close to overflowing and organized with tabs to separate relevant information. "This is what we'll need over the long haul. All the inmate records, including medical and mental health—and it's going to be important that you have a look at that because we have some significant mental illness in there."

"What kind of mental illness? Give me a snapshot."

"You name it, the ESH has it. Clinical depression, bipolar disorder, anxiety disorders, schizophrenia, antisocial personality disorder. But the biggest problem is substance abuse. Many inmates are significantly addicted and are in programs to manage that. Overall, as a group, they're violent and extremely unstable. Especially now, because no one is overseeing their medications. We have to be prepared that the stability provided by the meds will end as their last dose runs out."

"Administering them, or taking them?"

"Both. And from what I understand about those kinds of medications, you don't quit them cold turkey. If you mean to stop a medication, you ease off it gradually. We have a large number of men who are abruptly terminating treatment."

"And crashing out of treatment like that could produce some radical mood changes."

"The other new information is the staff records of the

hostage COs, including any inmate and lawyer complaints, and any disciplinary action taken after incidents with inmates. And we also have this . . ."

He swiveled to face the rear wall and Gemma realized they'd turned the entire area into a giant situation board that would last for the whole standoff. A piece of paper directly under the clock decreed DAY 2, handwritten in black marker. Large lists of inmates along with their gang names and affiliations, easily readable at a glance from the table. A list of the hostages. A list of Rikers phone numbers for instant communication with jail personnel if needed. Radio frequencies, if they needed to continue to use the radio for communication. A spot to note demands once they came in. A list of DOC personnel who'd be involved in the standoff, including administration and the Emergency Response Service Unit. A note of which NYPD teams were involved and their rotating shifts.

Like the HNT, the ESU had assigned two A-Team shifts for the standoff to maintain continuity. A quick glance told her that Logan was assigned to the same eight-to-eight shift as her own team. If she was lucky, she'd be in the negotiation office and he'd be outside the ESH and she wouldn't run into him during the whole standoff.

"Great work." Gemma circled the table to look closer at the posted information. "This will be invaluable for keeping the entire team on the same page at a glance."

"That's what we thought," Corbitt said. "This isn't like a typical situation where you've only got one hostage taker. We have multiple hostage takers, multiple hostages including both COs and inmates, and probably a number of people who are just trying to lay low and survive the next few days."

"That's going to be tricky, because, by this point, turf lines are being drawn and inmates are likely being forced to take sides."

At the sound of his voice, Gemma turned around to find McFarland standing in the doorway. He carried his equipment bag over his shoulder and, in the lee of one arm, the most obscenely large thermos she'd ever seen. "What the hell is *that?*"

He patted the thermos. "Manna from heaven. Or, more realistically, it's over a gallon of actually drinkable coffee that will stay warm for forty-eight hours. I tried the coffee here yesterday and just about puked. And I think it ate a hole in my gut." He sneered at the three coffee cups in front of Taylor. "How has that not killed you?"

Taylor's lip curled as he stared down at the half-full cup. "Trust me, it's trying."

Gemma pointed at McFarland's monster thermos. "You drink all that coffee by yourself, you'll be wired for sound."

"Depending on how today goes, that might not be a bad thing."

Shelby side-eyed the thermos and then rolled her eyes in Gemma's direction. "I think he's overcompensating. It's the cop version of a flashy red sports car."

"Hey! I'll have you know my girlfriend bought me this thermos." McFarland's put-on affront fell away and he chuckled. "Though I have to admit I've never used it before now because it really is ridiculous. But this time it might come in handy. It'll do for the whole team."

"In that case," Shelby corrected, "have your girlfriend buy another one and send it in to us tonight. We could use it." She wilted back into her chair. "Hopefully tonight will be better. We got this assignment so late, no one had time to take more than an hour-long nap to power up for the night shift. I'm going to go home and sleep until I need to catch the train for our shift."

Taylor shook his head emphatically. "Absolutely not. Getting here by public transit is an exercise in frustration. Just get to One Police Plaza by seven. I'll pick everyone up and we'll drive onto the island together. That's an extra hour minimum you can sleep. We're going to need all the rest and patience we can get. I have a feeling negotiations are going to progress today so we may have a busy shift tonight."

Over the next half hour, the rest of Gemma's team arrived, got settled in, and Taylor and his team gratefully headed out, looking forward to a decent breakfast and a solid eight hours in bed before they needed to turn around and come back in.

Taylor paused in the doorway. "One more thing. Garcia wanted me to pass on that he'll be in later this morning. He has a meeting with Chiefs Phillips and Capello, Commissioner Frye, and Mayor Rowland."

"He's making sure everyone knows how long this could take."

"Phillips and Capello already know, Frye possibly suspects, but Rowland will need it repeated over and over to him. Even then it might not be enough. Frye will worry about how it makes the DOC look. Rowland will be concerned because it's a municipal facility."

"He'll be a lot more concerned about how it'll look if people die," Chen pointed out.

"Which is exactly what Garcia will say. He'll come in after that."

"Have a good rest. See you tonight."

With a brief nod, Taylor disappeared.

McFarland dragged a set of headphones toward him. "So, are we starting off the morning with a wake-up call? Not that I think many of them slept much last night. They'd be either too hyped up or terrified to sleep, depending on how the hierarchy is shaking out."

"Making contact is where I want to begin. But something else occurred to me on the drive in this morning and I want to make a phone call before we dive in. Give me a few minutes."

Gemma slipped out of the conference room, closing the door behind her as she looked around for a quiet spot. Just like yesterday, the hallways were a beehive of activity as COs, ERSU officers—called "Ninja Turtles" by the Rikers inmates because of their heavy helmets and body armor, the color of dirty pond water—and admin staff hurried up and down the corridor. It was only 8 a.m., but it was midmorning in a facility that had been awake and moving since 4 a.m.

There was no chance of a quiet spot in the hallway, and she didn't want to go outside, which would mean going through security all over again, but then the dark doorway of the meeting room they'd used for the briefing the day before caught her eye. Slipping between a pair of COs and a maintenance worker pushing a cart loaded with tools, she ducked into the room, sliding her hand along the wall to find the light switch and flipping it on, flooding the room with harsh fluorescent lighting. She moved to the back corner where it was infinitesimally quieter, pulled her cell phone from the pocket of her blazer, and speed-dialed a familiar number.

The Capello family was spread far and wide through New York City's first-response network, all following in their father's footsteps. Gemma was the fourth of Maria and Tony Capello's five children, and the only female in the family following Maria's murder during a bank robbery and the ensuing hostage situation. A bank robbery that had trapped Maria and her only daughter with the other hostages.

Gemma had been ten when her mother had climbed to her feet from their spot together on the floor of the bank and tried to talk one of the two hostage takers into letting the hostages go. They'd silenced her forever with a bullet to the forehead, leaving her lifeless body sprawled on the floor beside her terrified and blood-spattered daughter. The NYPD, with her father following the initial assault team, had killed one hostage taker and captured the other, but it was too late for Maria and the rest of the Capello family. Their world would never be the same.

Whether it was that pivotal experience that had pulled them into first-response work or it was simply in their blood through their father, they'd never know. But twenty-five years later, the Capellos had truly found their calling. With the exception of Matteo, the third Capello son and the only one to join the FDNY, the Capello children were all NYPD officers.

The youngest, Alex, was a member of the NYPD Internal Affairs Bureau, and while many cops looked at him with fear or suspicion, Alex had proved himself to be as fine an officer as any during the takedown of the City Hall hostage taker. He'd translated Gemma's coded message to him, and not only brought reinforcements, but stood as her personal backup during the final fight. Marco, the second oldest Capello brother, was a patrol sergeant with the 5th Precinct. But right now, Gemma needed Joe, the oldest sibling and a captain in the gang squad.

Joe answered on the second ring. "Hey."

"Hey."

"You in on the Rikers situation?"

"Calling you from there as we speak. I have a favor to ask."

"Anything."

"I'm primary negotiator on the team and I need some insight into the inmates we're dealing with. They're right up your alley."

"A lot of them there are. What do you know so far?"

Gemma sat down in one of the chairs in the last row. "The riot took place in one of the Enhanced Supervision Housing units. It's Rikers's answer to solitary, but it sounds like it's not successful as far as keeping warring gang members apart, and I understand there are a lot of them in there. They're who started yesterday's riot. I need to know more about the personalities I'm dealing with and wondered if you'd have some insight."

"I might."

"We're still trying to make contact, but the initial altercation was between members from the Filero Kings and the Gutta Boys."

A long whistle came across the line. "You got specific names?"

"Eduardo Rivas from the Filero Kings and Anton Burk from the Gutta Boys."

There was a moment of silence, then "*Merda*. I'm on my way."

"You're . . . what?"

"I think it would be better if I came in. Get as much information as to who's involved as you can. Who started it and how the dynamics may have changed since, if you can find that out. When I get there, I'll help you figure out how to deal with them in real time."

"You can get free?"

"I'm off today, so yeah, I'm free. See you within the hour." Joe hung up.

Gemma was left staring, openmouthed, at her phone.

What the hell was so awful it would bring her brother running?

CHAPTER 6

*M*cFarland looked up as Gemma came in, his head cocking slightly as his eyes narrowed on her face. "Everything okay?"

"I'm honestly not sure."

"Care to expand on that?"

Gemma sat down in her chair and set her phone on the table. "I called Joe, my brother in the gang squad. There are enough gang interactions going on in there that I thought he might have some insight into how to deal with them."

"Good idea. What's his insight?"

"When I told him who started the riot, he swore, and said he was on his way."

"Well, hell . . . that can't be good."

"That's what I thought."

"He thinks he can be of more help if he's here with us?" Williams asked.

"It sounds like he thinks war is going to break out in there and wants to stop a massacre."

"If so," Chen said, "we'll be lucky to have him."

Gemma slipped on her headset. "Now I *really* want to know the status in the ESH. Let's get someone on the line."

McFarland flicked the radio that still sat in the middle of the table so it spun lazily on its belt clip. "Want to radio in first to give them a heads-up?"

Gemma shook her head. "I want to call in. I want to establish *real* communication. Yesterday afternoon and evening were probably pure chaos. I'm hoping that over-night things have calmed down, and more rational minds are looking at the situation and realizing they have a problem and need to find a way to end this."

"The only way things will calm down in there is if a hierarchy forms," Williams said. "Someone needs to be calling the shots and forming an organized structure, but I'm not sure how efficiently that's going to happen. These often aren't organized minds. It's one of the reasons many of them are here."

"If you can't get through," McFarland pointed out, "it may be a sign it's still chaos in there. Or if you do get through, it may be hard to make a connection with who-ever is on the other end of the line."

"Lunchtime yesterday was the last time they had a real meal," Chen said. "They have to be getting hungry and maybe we can use that for leverage."

"It might be a bit early." Williams pointed to the pic-ture of the cell on the wall. "See those plastic tubs? That's for inmate belongings. Inmates are allowed to purchase food from the commissary from wages earned here at Rikers or from family and friends contributing to their account. It's logical to assume they might be storing food in their cells."

"That's not going to last long."

"I agree. All I'm saying is hunger may not be the motivator it could be . . . yet. In the meantime, it's going to be another reason for inmates to go after each other. Anyone who doesn't share his food, or who doesn't simply relinquish it to the reigning power structure, may find himself a target."

Gemma took the short stack of yellow pads from the head of the table and tossed each member of the team the pad they'd been using the day before to continue their own notes. "Then let's get started."

She slid on her headphones, looked across to get the go-ahead nod from Chen that he was ready to transcribe any conversation, dialed the extension, and counted off the rings as the seconds stretched out with no one answering.

Patience. You have all day and can wait them out.

On the fifteenth ring, Gemma stretched out to disconnect the line, her fingers a fraction of an inch away from the button, when someone picked up the phone. She snatched her hand back as if she'd been burned. Background noise echoed in her headset, but whoever it was didn't speak.

But this time the line wasn't immediately disconnected.

Gemma gave him a moment to step into the conversation, taking advantage of the silence to deduce anything she could about his surroundings in the ESH. Closing her eyes, she concentrated on background sounds: Voices echoed in the distance, giving the impression of a wide-open space and bare, unadorned walls to ricochet sound waves. Male voices were raised—excepting the one female CO hostage, everyone in the ESH was male—but there was nothing in their tone that particularly gave her pause. There was jocularity and bravado, but no hatred or fear.

What did you think, they'd be torturing the hostages right by the phone?

When the silence stretched on long enough that she was sure he had no intention of speaking, Gemma stepped into the void. "I'm Gemma Capello. I'd like to talk to whoever is currently in charge of the ESH."

Only the babble of background noise came across the line.

"I'd like to help you resolve this situation."

Still he refused to speak.

"You know and I know some people in the Department of Corrections would love to send armed officers in there to clean up this mess. That's not what I want. I want to resolve this situation, but I can't do that on my own. I can only do that *with* you. Talk to me. Please."

Silence stretched and Gemma drew breath to speak again when a deep male voice spoke. "Whatcha gonna do for us?"

Finally.

"I want to listen to what you have to say. To understand your position. To find a middle ground with you and bring *everyone* out alive."

"That's bullshit."

"Why?"

"Because you some DOC *chica.*" He gave a derogatory snort. "You just holding the phone until The Man gets back?"

Normally Gemma's technique was not to go in heavy-handed, but instead to emphasize that she was an impartial mediator who wanted to listen. She would draw out the hostage taker, letting him express his pain and frustrations, finally finding an approach to end the standoff in a way that kept everyone involved safe but still gave the hostage taker a path to surrender on his terms.

Not this time.

She wasn't dealing with a man who'd lost his job and whose wife was divorcing him, and who, as a result, was losing the house and the kids and was threatening to take them out. This wasn't a sudden, out-of-character crisis. These were men who'd been hard boiled in a brutal system of incarceration. Softness would be seen as a weakness and a chance to move in for the kill. More than that, she needed to make sure he knew she had the power to make things happen at this end or he'd never waste his time with her.

"Not a chance. I *am* The Man."

She raised an eyebrow at McFarland when rough laughter lashed out at her. But after it died away, the voice that came across the line cut like a knife. "I don't got time for this shit."

"I disagree. I think you have all the time in the world for this shit." Her use of profanity seemed to catch him off guard as he remained silent. Perhaps he sensed what was undoubtedly a common verbal crutch for him was less common for her, and she used his momentary hesitation to move in. "I think you and I can meet in the middle. But to do that, I need you to talk to me."

"So you can hand me a load of shit?"

"You tell me." Gemma kept her voice calm in the face of the rage skittering at the edge of his tone. "Do you want me to lie to you to make you feel better, or do you want me to be honest and tell you the truth no matter what?"

"You gonna say whatever you need to get us to open up. Because that's all that matters. You want your COs, but you don't give a fuck about us. Nobody gives a fuck about us."

Time to separate herself from the DOC he thought spawned her. "Not true. First of all, I'm no DOC *chica*. I'm not part of their incarceration system."

"So, who are you then?"

No help for it. Lying is off the table. "I'm NYPD. Detective Gemma Capello."

"Fuck! That's just as bad. You put us here. We done."

"Wait!" Gemma shot out a hand as if he was in front of her and she could grab hold of him to keep him close. "Think this through. You guys committed a crime in there. You assaulted officers and took hostages."

"So what? Time to kick at someone else's rights for a change."

"It sounds like there's a story there. I'd like you to share it with me. Maybe I can help."

"See, there's your bullshit again. Saying what I want to hear."

"Wrong." Gemma let a little more backbone stiffen her tone. This wasn't a man who would respect any kind of weakness, so strength was her only option, even if that meant flat-out disagreeing with him. Not a typical tactic, but every hostage situation was different, and each negotiator needed to adapt on the fly. "That would get me, get us, absolutely nowhere. You hold lives in your hands. You find out partway along that I'm lying to you and you can easily exact revenge. The only way for us to deal with each other is with absolute honesty." She paused for a moment for emphasis. "Unless, you'd like me to lie to you? Spin you a fairy tale?"

"Fuck, no."

"Then the truth it is. I swear I won't lie to you. And I promise to treat you fairly. If you feel I'm not, you need to tell me. I can't read your mind. You have to talk to me. Do you agree?"

There was a moment of silence, then a muttered curse and the connection cut off.

Gemma sagged in her chair and dragged her headset off to lie around her neck. "That went well."

"Not as bad as it could have," Chen said. "You got him to talk to you."

"Not for long. Not even long enough to give him this extension so he can call us instead of us always harassing him. We have no idea who he is and have very little insight so far."

In first interactions, it was crucial to gather as much information as possible from any hostage taker. But the most important aspect was the emotion that conveyed his mindset. Was he depressed? Contemplating taking his own life? Euphoric? Terrified at what he'd done? It varied from situation to situation and suspect to suspect.

This man was clearly angry—at her, at the situation, at the world. More than that, there was no reticence at what happened. He was defiant and had no problem making sure she knew that.

Which was going to make forming a connection harder.

Gemma poured a cup of coffee out of her thermos and took a sip to wet her parched throat. "Let's look at what we know." She pulled her pad of paper toward her and jotted down her thoughts. "He's young, but I'd guess he's not new here. It sounds like he's accumulated some serious resentment."

"Or it's not his first trip to Rikers," McFarland suggested. "Some of these guys are repeat customers, and I don't mean just a second time. He's got some aggression going there, so I suspect he's going to be a challenge to talk into anything he doesn't want to do."

"Agreed."

"I don't think he's black," Chen said.

Gemma looked up sharply. "No?"

Chen shook his head. "He talks like he's from the street, but black guys from the street drop the 'N' word nearly constantly. Nothing like that here." He paused, as if weighing his words. "He may be Latino. He used the term '*chica*' twice. That may be street talk—"

"Or it may be comfortable language for him because of his background," Gemma finished for him. "We'll definitely have to be on the lookout for more language cues if he doesn't voluntarily give us his identity or gang affiliation."

"We have a number of gang groups in there," said Williams. "Maybe this is one way your brother can help us. And it's not quiet in there, but it sounds relatively calm. That's going to make it easier to deal with anyone on the other end of the line."

"Honestly, I'm not sure if that's good or bad. If we think there will be gang interactions once they're out of their cells and the cuffs are off, that might mean too many of those interactions have already taken place and inmates are dead or injured." She took a deep breath and blew it out. "Only one way to find out." She slipped her headphones on. "Let's get back on the horse. Hopefully we'll get the same inmate and we won't be starting from scratch every time we reach out."

CHAPTER 7

*I*t took ten minutes to get through again. Just as Gemma thought she'd have to take a break and give them more space, the phone was picked up.

"Why you bothering us?" Irritation rang loud and clear, but it was definitely the same voice. "We finally get some freedom and you won't stop."

"You never answered my question. I asked if you wanted me to be straight up with you at all times, or if you'd like to hear the lies you think are part of my stock and trade. I want to hear your answer." Silence beat for a few seconds, so she pushed harder. "You can stay in there in your isolation and freedom for now, but you know it can't last forever if you want to resolve this without possible bloodshed. And the longer this goes, the less control I have. You'll have to talk to someone, so why not me?

Let me assure you, I'm a better option than some of the guys, especially the tactical guys."

"On the real, you gonna be straight up?"

"You have my word. Let's start with the basics. I already told you my name. What's yours?"

"Why the fuck would I tell you that?" Outrage was back in his tone.

One step forward, two steps back. "Because it's disrespectful for me not to refer to you by name. You giving me your name is a sign of good faith from you and helps set the tone. It tells me you're willing to work toward a solution." She didn't mention that she had a list in front of her with the names of everyone inside the facility and could narrow down his identity from it. She needed him to take a step toward her, but couched it in terms that showed how she meant to treat him.

He paused for a long moment. Then, "My guys call me Kill Switch."

She'd seen that name listed in the gang member notation of one of the inmate pages. Gemma's hand shot toward the briefing book, but McFarland was already ahead of her, pulling it to him, and flipping through the pages.

He'd taken a step toward her. He hadn't given his real name, but his gang name. It was something she could work with. And an important step, because calling the voice on the other end of the line a name, any name, even one he'd made up, was instrumental in forging the connection that could find them enough middle ground to surrender peacefully.

"Thank you, Kill Switch. Now, the first thing I need to do is ask after the status of the men and woman inside. Does anyone require medical care?"

"You ain't coming in here." There was steel behind his words.

"You're right. I'm not. But we can send in medical assistance for any of your wounded. Or if the hostages are wounded."

"We're good."

"No one needs attention?"

"Not so much that one of the butchers would help."

"The 'butchers'?"

"Jailhouse docs. They don't give a fuck about us. They hope we won't die, that's about it. Probably 'cause of the paperwork they'd have to do. We'd rather deal with it ourselves."

If any of our officers are injured, we need to tend to them.

The words of the man in scrubs in the meeting room floated back to Gemma. Garcia, like herself, hadn't absorbed the nuance of his point, so his answer—*we'll negotiate for care for both the inmates and the correction officers*—had automatically included everyone in the ESH. But that physician had only cared about the officers, negating the possibility that some innocent inmates had also been hurt by the riot and might require care.

In another example of Davis's priorities, he hadn't corrected the physician.

It certainly highlighted Kill Switch's point.

"What if I can bring in someone else? Not one of the OBCC docs?"

"Won't make no difference."

"I don't agree, but keep it in mind. The offer stays open. And what about meds? There must be inmates and hostages on daily meds. You might not mean to harm anyone, but lack of meds could be a killer. Or could make someone unstable."

"Don't need it."

"I'm not sure that's true. Please think about it. We can talk about it again later." Gemma waved at Chen and mouthed, "Make a note."

He nodded and pulled a second notepad close and started an action list.

McFarland nudged her arm and slid the binder toward Gemma, his index finger beside the name "Kill Switch." Gemma quickly scanned the sheet to find the inmate's full name—Eduardo Rivas.

The man who started the riot.

She'd hold on to his name for now. He'd offered her his gang name, hiding his true identity, so she'd use it until she had to reveal that she knew who he was. When she needed a moment of impact to really connect with him.

"I'd like to set some ground rules for us so you understand how this works."

"Like?"

"For starters, I can give you things, but you have to give me something in return. That's fair, right?"

Silence was her answer, so she pushed on.

"For instance, if you need food because you and your men are hungry, we'll bring in food in exchange for the visit of the med team, or for one of the hostages."

"Are you fucking crazy? You think we're going to let anyone go?"

"I think you're going to think about the offer and realize that for us to make concessions, you have to as well."

The door to the conference room opened and Davis

stepped in. Williams quickly jumped out of his chair and slipped out of the room, pushing Davis in front of him into the hallway and closing the door behind him with a quiet *click*.

Gemma and McFarland exchanged questioning glances, and then Gemma turned her attention back to Rivas. "Do you remember how you said you wanted me to be honest?"

"Yeah." The single word had a surly bite to it.

"Then let's call a spade a spade. You haven't taken hostages in a business or in a rural home. You're an inmate at Rikers Island and you've taken correction officers hostage. You know you're in serious trouble. As I said before, there are parties here who'd have no problem turning tactical officers loose in there. I'm standing between you and them. I'll do my best to resolve this situation peacefully, but you know this isn't going to end with you being released from incarceration." She glanced down to Rivas's records, skimming the list of charges that brought him here—possession of a stolen firearm, second-degree murder, and a raft of drug charges. He wasn't convicted of a crime yet, but stayed at Rikers awaiting his trial, after which he'd be moved to a penitentiary upstate.

With those charges on his record, he might already think he had nothing to lose. Which made him a very dangerous man.

"At worst, this hostage situation could add to whatever sentence you already have," she continued. "But the more you cooperate with me, the better it will go for you."

"What if I don't want to deal with you?"

"Then someone else will talk to you. But you, or someone else inside, will have to deal with a voice on the other end of the phone line. Or you know what the response will be."

"You wanna kill these officers? Or should we take care of that for you?"

It was likely just bravado, but she had to take his threat seriously. *That didn't last long. Time to get personal, even though it reveals you know more than you're letting on.* "Eduardo, you know my first concern is the safety of *everyone* in the ESH. The hostages as well as the inmates. And my best way to guarantee your safety is for you and your fellow inmates to do no harm to the hostages. The moment you hurt any of them, I may not be able to maintain control of the negotiations."

"You done your research."

"The best way for me to be able to understand what you need is to understand *you*. So talk to me. Help me understand. Why was this the response to the COs who entered after the attack?"

"You know about that."

"How the riot started? Yes. From what I hear, you kicked it off. Tell me about it."

"No."

It was crucial right now to start a dialog, to get him talking. If she couldn't get him to talk to her in this call or the next, a wall could go up that she'd never be able to scale. And Taylor might not manage it either. "You sound angry. Like you didn't go after him for a petty reason."

Silence.

Silence could be a useful tool in negotiating because it made many hostage takers uncomfortable and they'd talk to fill the void. But Gemma didn't let this silence drag on too long because she already suspected Rivas was the tight-lipped type who could easily wait her out. "Then how about the hostages? That wasn't something you did on a whim. Why did you take them? What do you hope to gain?"

"You have no idea what it's like to be trapped here."

"No, I don't. Tell me about it. Help me understand."

"Tell you 'bout it? 'Bout the COs who look for any excuse to beat on you? 'Bout time spent in the Bing surrounded by screaming all the damned time that nearly makes you lose your mind? 'Bout sewage flooding up through the floor drains to make you sick? Or the fucking lack of medical care where the docs think any complaint is fake so you can spend time in the wards instead of your cell." It was like the cork coming out of a bottle as Rivas's rage overflowed, and Gemma had to write frantically as she tried to note his every point. "Or how 'bout the freezing in winter and sweating in summer? Or the food so bad, you think they're trying to starve or kill you?" His voice rose even higher. "*What part of that d'you wanna understand?*"

He was breathing hard by the time he stopped, and Gemma gave him a moment to collect himself so he'd hear her.

"That sounds terrible. More than that, it sounds like something no one should have to live through." She kept her voice quiet, hoping he could hear her sincerity, because from what she knew about the nightmare that was Rikers, she suspected every complaint was 100 percent true.

"Yeah, but we do. So maybe we took hostages so someone will listen and not think we're full of shit."

"I don't think that. You know, outside, we hear stories. From multiple sources. For years. I know you're not lying to me. Tell me more. I want to hear your personal experience."

"No. I'm done."

"Wait!"

He paused for so long that Gemma was afraid he'd put the phone down and simply walked off. "Why?"

"Because I want this to be a two-way street. I want to make sure you have a way to contact us. Can you write down an extension?"

He hesitated, then, "Yeah."

She read it out to him. "There will be someone here all day, every day while we sort this out. But Eduardo, I need to make something crystal clear for you. I want to help you resolve this, but the moment one of the hostages is hurt, it's over. I won't be able to keep them out. The same goes for the other inmates. Everyone stays safe from now on."

There was a long pause. "From now on . . . gotcha." And with that, he was gone.

Gemma slumped over her braced forearms. "Wasn't sure we weren't going to lose him for a second there."

"Once the rage started to spew, I kind of wondered." McFarland pointed at Chen's pad of paper. "Did you get all that?"

"Yes." Chen slowly recited the neat, bullet point list of complaints, then laid down his pad of paper. "It's quite a list. I've seen articles about this place, but never been here myself."

"That rage was floating close to the surface," Gemma said. "It didn't take much of a push for it to explode outward."

"I think that says something about what it's like to live here." McFarland hoisted his thermos off the floor, cracked it open, and poured out another cup of coffee. "Emotions are running high. And likely impulses too."

"Which tells us more about how a simple fight turned into a riot. It's not just Rivas's rage. It's collective rage."

"Then layer gang rivalry in the unit over top of that abuse," Chen said.

McFarland capped his thermos. "Yesterday's riot was like a match being thrown into a puddle of gasoline. It exploded, and all went to hell from there."

"Now the question is how do we get a hold of that rage?" Gemma asked. "Knowing you have to go back to that way of life, and probably worse because you just put a giant target on your back as far as the COs are concerned, what would convince you to surrender?"

"If we're lucky, hunger will start to work on them."

"Or simply push that rage higher. It's a fine line to walk. Abused inmates, some who have impulse control issues, many of who are struggling with mental illness and are now officially off their meds. Their first impulse may be to make the hostages pay for any mistreatment they've ever experienced. We have to find a way to keep that from happening."

The door to the hallway opened and Williams slipped silently into the room. Once he saw Gemma's headphones hanging around her neck, he let go of the door, letting it close on its own. His mouth was a grim line. "We have a problem."

The urgency in Williams's voice sent a bolt of alarm through Gemma. "What?"

"Davis came in wanting an update. While I walked to his office with him, I made it clear that this room is off-limits unless one of us brings him in here because we can't afford interruptions when negotiating unless it's an emergency. But while I was talking to him, Cartwright called."

"Is there movement in there?"

"You could say that. They just tossed a CO into the hallway." Williams scanned each face in turn. "He's dead."

CHAPTER 8

*W*ith Davis and Coleman, Gemma jogged down the corridor, past a spacious outdoor recreation yard, deserted during lockdown, and into a hallway leading to the tower that housed the Emergency Segregation Housing units. The taller of the OBCC's two towers housed the Central Punitive Segregation Unit—solitary confinement, better known on the Island as "the Bing"—but this tower contained some of the slightly less restrictive security areas, including the two ESHs.

The drab, gray hallway could have been any of those Gemma had just traveled, except for the cluster of A-Team officers to her left. Two officers stood with their backs to the crowd, their rifles raised and pointed toward the large steel-and-glass door sealing off the ESH. But inside the circle of officers, a lone figure lay prone on the floor with Cartwright crouched over him.

Gemma had to come. She hadn't wanted to leave the phone in case Rivas attempted contact, but at the same time, she had to see what he or his fellow inmates had done. She didn't want to rely on anyone else's eyes to describe whatever horrors had taken place behind that locked door. To be able to deal with Rivas at the basest level, she needed to know exactly who had died, and how, because it would shape everything from here on out. It would be bad enough if a CO died in the initial riot, but if the inmates killed a CO in cold blood after calm was restored and after Gemma had warned Rivas to stay away from the hostages, it could only have been done to make a point to the authorities outside the facility.

It would change everything. If any of the inmates had hoped for amnesty, it wouldn't come. Someone was responsible; someone had to pay.

She'd barely started; how could it have fallen apart so quickly? She'd honestly felt like she was making progress, making a germinal connection with Rivas.

Guess not.

Deciding how to proceed in this moment would affect everything else. Cartwright would want to take his men in before anyone else died, and where she would normally argue to the ends of the earth for calm to continue the negotiation, she knew she'd be in the minority. The negotiation team would try to end the standoff peacefully, but when it came down to the wire, it was the A-Team commander who got to make the final call on a tactical resolution.

By and large, tactical officers considered a tactical resolution the most effective way to end a standoff. It was simply in their nature and training.

She'd left Williams at the phone and everyone else in their assigned positions before following Davis and Coleman down the hallway to retrieve their lost officer. She'd texted Garcia as she rushed through the hallway. His one-word answer—**Coming**—said it all.

This death changes everything.

Davis and Coleman pushed through the A-Team officers, Davis snarling a curse when one officer didn't get out of his way fast enough. Then they were both on their knees by the body as Cartwright stood to give them room. Gemma circled around to the far side and slid into a gap between officers.

"We got him away from the door so no one could come through at us." Cartwright threw a glance back to the facility. "Then we checked for a pulse, but he was already gone."

The officer was younger than Gemma anticipated, his dark hair shorn close and his slack face tipped to the side where blood trickled from the corner of his mouth and down over his jawline. He wore the navy short-sleeved shirt and pants of the correction officers, with twin silver "OBCC" collar insignias and a silver DOC badge with his badge number and his name engraved underneath pinned over his left breast pocket.

Except for the blood on his face, she couldn't see any sign of the fatal injury.

Davis bent forward to study him more carefully. "I don't know him," was his perfunctory judgment. He swiveled toward Coleman. "You?"

Coleman didn't reply right away, but sat back on her heels, her eyes fixed on his face. "I . . . no." Guilt and anguish twisted her features. "I thought I knew everyone we had here." Stiffening her spine, she leaned forward and rested one hand against his unblemished cheek.

With a gasp, she yanked her hand away.

"What's wrong?" Davis demanded. "You *do* know him?"

Coleman's whole attitude changed, grief falling away and determination setting her features in stone as she narrowed her eyes on the man, scanning his face and uniform. She repeated the action, then slid her hand over his shoulder and down his arm to his hand to take his hand in hers.

The dead man's hand didn't move easily.

Realization coalesced and Gemma suddenly saw what Coleman was doing. She hadn't been shocked because of the fresh death of an officer. She'd been shocked because she'd touched a body already cooled with death. A body dead long enough that rigor mortis has already set in.

He'd died hours ago. Maybe yesterday during the initial riot. This wasn't a sign of rebellion from Rivas.

All was not *lost.*

Coleman pushed to her feet to tower over the body. "This isn't a CO."

Davis staggered upright with considerably less grace. "What do you mean?"

"I was so fixated on his face I didn't pay attention to the details. His badge says 'Hoffstatler' but that's not Hoffstatler. And this isn't this man's uniform. See how it's too big for him? How they've cinched in the belt so the pants stay on? This is one of the inmates."

Gemma stepped forward to study the badge. "Hoffstatler isn't one of the names on the hostage list."

"They had to figure we'd know exactly who's in

there," Cartwright said. "If that's not Hoffstatler, how did he get that badge?"

"Hoffstatler was one of the COs who got out of the ESH when the ERSU arrived," said Coleman. "He was involved in the initial efforts to contain the riot. His badge must have gotten ripped off in the struggle."

"So they took a uniform off one of the COs in there and put this badge on it to confuse us?"

Gemma looked from the fury radiating from Davis at being tricked to the relief on Coleman's face that this wasn't one of her officers. "They had to know it wouldn't work for long. It's a high-security prison. All employees check in and out daily. No one is a nameless face."

"What was the goddamned point, then?" Davis nudged the body with the toe of his boot. "And who's this?"

"The point was to twist the knife, which they succeeded in doing. They had us convinced they'd killed a hostage."

"Then they've got a death wish," Cartwright stated. "This could've been enough for us to go in and end this."

"I agree it wasn't thought out. And, trust me, this will be the first thing I discuss with the inmates when I get them on the phone. For now, we need to call the Office of the Chief Medical Examiner, but this man has been dead for a while. It takes hours for rigor to set in, then hours to ease off. I bet this man was killed yesterday and he was just a handy way of ratcheting up the tension. Of showing us that they still have ultimate control of the situation."

"Well, mission accomplished," Davis spat out. "And now whoever is responsible for this man's death will have charges coming his way."

Gemma studied the inmate's face, completely devoid of life and spirit. "I need to know who this is. I can work this into the negotiations, but I need to know his name and gang affiliation. There's a good chance he was killed yesterday when the riot took place, or immediately afterward. If there were any long-standing grudges or gang disagreements, yesterday's riot was the perfect time to take advantage of the chaos to quietly settle a score."

"Or two. Or three," said Cartwright. "Who knows how many are dead in there."

"I can get you all the information you need." Coleman pulled her radio off her belt. "Let me contact a couple of the unit COs. They'll recognize this man and we can go from there." She pushed her way through the ring of officers.

"I'm going to call this in." Gemma didn't want to overstep the authority of the jail, but this was now a crime scene and whatever evidence was left needed to be preserved. "He was moved because you needed to get him away from the unit when you thought there was still a chance to save his life. But now we need to look at who's responsible for his death." She turned to where Cartwright stood on the opposite side of the body. "We need to step back and not touch him. You and your officers will be able to preserve the scene while still maintaining surveillance on the ESH?"

Cartwright gave her a sharp nod. "Affirmative."

"Thank you. I need to get back in case they call through." She spun to weave through the officers and found herself standing chest to chest with Logan.

"Excuse me." Without making eye contact, she slid

past him and through the men to stride toward the corridor leading to the negotiating room. She'd just made it to the main hallway when her phone buzzed. She pulled it out to find a text from Joe.

Here. Just about to go through security.

She quickly typed a response.

Wait once you get through security. I'm on my way.

Williams would have to hold the fort a little longer. She'd go meet her brother and find out what was so bad he needed to come to the most godforsaken spot in New York City.

CHAPTER 9

Gemma found Joe waiting in the hallway past security, his back against a wall, his ankles crossed, and his head bent over his phone. Tall and thin, he had the Capello olive skin tone, but unlike their youngest brother, Alex, who left his hair long enough to curl like Gemma's, Joe kept his cropped short. He was off duty, so he was in jeans, a three-button Henley, and his brown leather jacket. His shield was clipped to his waistband and visible through his open jacket, so there was no mistaking his affiliation.

The oldest of the Capello siblings, Joe was part of the Organized Crime Control Bureau, and more specifically was a lieutenant in the Manhattan Gang Squad. His knowledge of the players could make or break how she played this case.

She waved her hand in greeting when he looked up

from his phone. "Thanks for coming all the way out here."

"No problem."

"I have to admit, you caught me off guard when you didn't want to discuss this on the phone."

"We could have, but I think I'll do more for you coming in, especially since I took the time to quickly review their files before I left this morning. The two you discussed are bad enough on the surface, but knowing the personalities and how many other inmates have to be involved, you have a very sensitive situation in there."

"If I didn't know that before, I do now. Follow me." She led him down the hallway.

He cast her a sideways glance. "Why do you know that now?"

"Because they just tossed a body out of the ESH, dressed in a correction officer's uniform. But the deputy warden figured out quickly that the name on the badge didn't match the face. It's one of the inmates. And from the state of the body, we think he was killed yesterday."

"Got an ID on the body?"

"Not yet. But I have a full roster of the inmates involved, including what we know about their gang affiliation. He has to be one of them."

"How many are in the ESH?"

"Forty-two inmates, but they also have eight COs."

Joe whistled. "I knew there were hostages, but I didn't know how many."

"We're trying to keep a lid on that for the media, but those numbers are going to get out. Any time, I suspect."

"And if you're looking at a bunch of gang members in there, you need to remember that they have one obvious go-to when it comes to solving problems."

"Violence."

"Got it in one. They're not inventive—they don't need to be. It's the method that works for them, and most of them have been at this for so long that they aren't bothered by cumbersome things like ethics. It's a means to an end."

"Someone's end is the means to an end, you mean."

"Pretty much."

"Capello!"

The siblings stopped and turned in unison at the sound of their name.

Garcia was half jogging down the hallway toward them. "Status?"

They waited for Garcia to catch up. "The dead man outside the ESH isn't a CO. He's an inmate, and we think he died yesterday during the riot. They tossed him out today to make a point."

"To get the A-Team to storm the place?" Joe asked dryly.

"If Cartwright had made a call on the situation before we'd figured out what was going on, that's exactly what would have happened. Fortunately, he didn't jump the gun. I think the inmates were trying to tell us they're in charge and this could happen to any of the COs at any moment. But it nearly blew up in their faces. I'll be sure to let Rivas know the next time I talk to him."

"He's the one you're talking to?"

"So far." She looked between her brother and her lieutenant. "Sir, I don't know if you've met my brother, Lieutenant Joe Capello, out of the Manhattan Gang Squad. Joe, this is Lieutenant Tomás Garcia, head of the HNT."

The two men shook hands.

"I asked Joe to come down to share his insight into the

personalities involved in the ESH." Gemma caught her brother's sidelong glance at her slight alteration as to whose decision it was to come to Rikers in case of negative fallout, but he didn't say anything.

"That's a good idea. Were you going to call the ESH?"

Gemma started down the hallway and the two men fell into step with her. "Not yet. I think the best way to handle this is to give them some time. They think they showed us their position of superiority. I don't want to contact them right away to confirm that. I'd prefer for them to think on it for a while, and for that to shake their foundation. In a vacuum, they're going to doubt the impact of revealing that death to us, and that doubt will make them unsure. That gives us leverage. I want to push for medical to go in there, but they're resisting."

"That body is probably why," Joe said.

"One dead inmate makes you wonder how many other dead inmates there are," Garcia agreed. "But if they're smart, they left the COs alone."

"We don't know their status, so finding out is top of my list. But the inmates may be concerned that if we send someone into the facility, they'll want to do a head count, and if anyone else is dead, it will become apparent. They're going to have another issue, though, if that question drags on. This is day two. This could easily go on for three or four days, or even a week. And that's going to be a problem for any dead body."

Joe's lip curled. "Valid point. They could close up the dead in a cell, but while the cells are secure with solid doors from the photos I've seen of the facility, they're not airtight. The smell of decomposition will become overpowering. Trust me, I had a few overcooked DBs in my patrol days. It's not a smell you forget. That alone could drive them out of the ESH."

"I think we'd all like to have this settled before we get to that point. And hopefully, there aren't any more bodies in there to put them in that position." Garcia moved to open the conference room door. "This is us." He opened the door a few more inches, peeked in to ensure there was no active communication ongoing, and then pushed the door wide, gesturing for Gemma and Joe to precede him.

After giving an update on the situation at the ESH, Gemma made introductions around the table—Williams was the only officer Joe was already acquainted with— and then they pulled up chairs, packing in tight around the skinny table.

Gemma pushed the inmate binder across to her brother who sat at the end between McFarland and Williams. "Start with this. These are the records of every inmate inside, including ID and gang affiliation."

Joe opened the binder. "Current gang affiliation, you mean."

"Don't most just have one?" McFarland asked.

"Actually, there's a lot more movement between gangs than you'd think. That can lead to some resentment and hatred. That could also be part of what's at play inside." He took a moment to flip through the binder, sometimes nodding or frowning, occasionally stopping to read further before moving to the next page.

"Coffee?" McFarland offered. "We bring in our own because the stuff here is undrinkable."

"Appreciate that, thanks. Black for me."

Joe took another few minutes to leaf through the binder, sipping his coffee.

A soft rap came at the doorframe and Coleman stuck her head cautiously through the gap.

"Nya, come on in," said Gemma, rising to her feet. "Is everything okay?"

Coleman pushed open the door and stepped in. "As okay as it can be. We've identified that inmate. His name was Tyrell Rush. He was twenty-three and here on a nine-month petit larceny sentence."

"Gang affiliation?" Chen asked.

"He didn't have one outside. Inside he was loosely affiliated with the Gutta Boys. But he had a rep on the block as a snitch."

"And someone took advantage of the riot for retribution?" McFarland suggested.

"If you're asking my opinion, I'd say yes. Inmate loyalty is highly valued. Getting another inmate into trouble with the COs is considered a serious infraction. If anyone figures out who snitched on them, there could be serious repercussions." Coleman looked down at Joe's bent head as he flipped through the book. "Sorry, I didn't mean to interrupt, but I wanted to make sure you knew this immediately."

"Thanks, Nya. We appreciate it."

With a smile, Coleman slipped out of the room, leaving the door slightly ajar behind her.

When Joe got to the end of the binder, he put down his cup, and flipped back to Rivas's page. He paused for a moment, staring at the picture.

Tension crawled up Gemma's spine at the continued silence. "So . . . ? What's your take on the situation?"

"The combination of gangs and personalities could be extremely volatile for the inmates, but more so for the COs. Assuming not everyone is as immersed in gang culture as me, let's get on the same page. Across the five boroughs, the old days of the big national gangs are gone. Smaller neighborhood gangs are the norm, which is why you have groups like the Filero Kings and Gutta Boys at play, as opposed to the Bloods and Crips. Now, the exception to that is inside jails and prisons, where since the early nineties the Bloods have been the gang in power here at Rikers. But it looks like the smaller gangs still rule this particular cell block."

"You said there's movement between gangs," Chen said. "Do members change affiliation when they get to Rikers? Do they maintain that new affiliation once they leave?"

"There's certainly pressure inside the facility to change gang affiliation. That's part of the inmate-on-inmate violence inside. But it doesn't last. When guys are released, they go back to their original gangs. And that's where we're different. This isn't L.A. or Chicago where large, sprawling gangs of a certain race rule. Many of our gangs are hybrids, with members crossing the racial divide with geography playing the main role in inclusion. Being black or Latinx isn't what decides what gang you belong to. It's your turf. The neighborhood, street, or hell, even the housing project you belong to. Larger national gangs still exist in the city, but compared to the hybrid gangs, those members are actually in the minority now. We have hundreds of smaller gangs in the city, and the NYPD database has nearly twenty thousand people listed. Most of the gang members are older teens and young men, though the database lists members as young as thirteen.

"As in the bigger gangs, drugs and guns are the driving factors. A lot of gang members use themselves, but many tend to keep it to lighter drugs like pot because they need to be able to protect themselves and their fellows. But they'll peddle the hard stuff."

"Any cross-turf dealing?" McFarland asked.

"You bet, and that's when things go sideways. Turf boundaries aren't clear-cut and lots of gangs overlap. That's where the trouble starts. Shootings, stabbings, retributions then follow. Those bad feelings can follow gang members into incarceration."

"The Filero Kings and the Gutta Boys?" Gemma asked.

"In spades. But when you're talking about Rivas and Burk, there's gang retribution and then there's personal vengeance." He picked up his coffee cup and took a sip. "And this is all about personal vengeance."

"What did Burk do to Rivas?"

"It's not about what Burk did to Rivas, it's about what he did to Rivas's sister." Joe met Gemma's gaze with a raised eyebrow. "Allegedly."

McFarland whistled. "Never mess with a guy's sister."

"Or his mother. Especially when there's no father in the picture, like there isn't with Rivas."

"What happened?"

"There never was a father in the picture. Three kids by three different men, two boys and a girl. Rivas is the middle kid. The older brother was killed in a gang hit when he was fifteen and Rivas was ten. That made a pretty big impression on him. His mother managed to keep him out of the gang life until he was fourteen, but it gets to a point with a kid like that when a parent can't hold on to them. Rivas never looked back. The sister though, she never joined a gang. Whether that was Rivas's influence, or the mother's, I'm not sure, but she stayed clean. The story on the street, though, is that Burk sexually assaulted

Sofia Rivas earlier this year. If that's true, and those two are together in the ESH, the brutality of the initial attack doesn't surprise me."

"It may not even need to be true," interjected Garcia. "He only needs to think it's true. Was there a baby?"

"No, but Sofia came home bruised and bleeding and fingered Burk for it. She never filed a police report because, in the gang world, you take care of a problem like that yourself. I only know about this because we have CIs embedded in various gangs and it was a big enough event that we heard rumors of it from them. Afterward, there were a number of retaliatory attacks on the Gutta Boys and on Burk specifically. Burk was only a lieutenant in the gang then, so the attention on him seemed a little out of place until you parse this backstory into it. Then, coincidentally, the attacks against the Gutta Boys stopped when Burk was nailed for dealing and possession of a deadly."

"Because Burk was the target and was then out of reach." Williams tapped an index finger on the open binder. "Didn't I see a bunch of attacks on Burk in his file?"

"You did," Chen confirmed. "Was that the long reach of Rivas into Rikers?"

"That would be my guess. Then Rivas got sent inside." Joe ran an index finger down the record. "He was first at the George R. Vierno Center, but then was transferred here to Otis Bantum."

"Then ended up in the ESH with Burk." Gemma sat back in her chair and studied Rivas's picture thoughtfully. "How does that work timewise?"

Joe marked Rivas's page with a pen and flipped to Burk's records. "Well, fancy that. Rivas made the move within six weeks of coming to Rikers and that's the same time Burk's attacks stopped. That was two weeks ago."

"Because he worked it to get them together so he could take care of everything himself?"

"And yesterday may have been his first chance to make the hit." Williams looked over at the list of inmates on the wall. "We have no idea if Burk is alive or dead. All we know is the dead inmate sent out isn't him. We don't know who else might be dead. Or close to it."

"I want to know how that transfer occurred. There's zero chance it was a coincidence. From another jail on the island to this one and then into the same closed facility?"

"Coincidences don't exist in our line of work." Joe flipped back to Rivas. "Someone in the DOC, from the wardens to the administration, has to have approved this request. I'd put money on a bribe coming into play. Rivas may be inside, but his Filero Kings brothers are outside."

"If that's true, and what you say holds about violence being their go-to pressure, then maybe they threatened some poor administrative shmuck or his family," McFarland suggested. "That sounds like something they'd do?"

"Sure does." Joe turned to Garcia. "You should pass this on to the DOC to investigate. Doesn't have anything to do with your current scenario—who's in there is all that matters, not how they got there—but there may be a leak they need to plug in their own administration. What's clear here is that outside or inside, Rivas is the shot caller, and his guys will fall in line behind him to do whatever he orders."

"The shot caller? Meaning the guy in charge?"

"Essentially. In gang life, it's the guy at the top who

makes the decisions but never gets his hands dirty. He lets other people do that for him. Though apparently that line is blurred when it comes to Burk and Rivas. For Burk, Rivas is willing to get his hands not only dirty, but bloody."

"As you said, it's the line between gang retribution and personal vengeance," Gemma said. "Burk and Rivas aside, what other problems are we going to have considering who's in the ESH? Will there be conflicts simply because of gang affiliation?"

"Without a doubt. Going back to the concept of neighborhood turf, this can cause some real overlap problems. And I see one very large red flag in your mix."

"Besides the Filero Kings and the Gutta Boys?"

"Yes. Those two gangs overlap territories and that turf war could have led to Sofia Rivas's sexual assault. But that would be an escalation in hostilities. There's already been bloodshed, a stabbing, and a fatal shooting."

"A sexual assault doesn't seem like much of an escalation compared to those," William stated.

Joe shook his head. "It does if you run that gang. If a rival gang goes after your sister, that means war. If Burk hadn't been arrested, he could easily have been the next one killed. But beyond that, you're got Precinct Seventy-Three's big problem transplanted in there. Brooklyn has a lot of gangs, but these ones are all in a seven-block range: the HS-Hoodstars, the BFG/ZAE Gang, the 823 Crips, the Money Gang, and the 816 Crew. And with the exception of the Money Gang, there's one guy from every gang and two from the 823 Crips."

"Anything else you can add?" Gemma asked.

"Definitely. You got time to flip through them one at a time? I can run that with you."

"I want them to cool their heels for now so they don't feel quite so confident about trying to put one over on us. We have time."

"Great." Joe flipped pages in the binder to the beginning of the inmate section and angled it toward Gemma. "You may want to make notes." His eyes were deadly serious. "You may want to make a *lot* of notes. To successfully negotiate this powder keg, you're going to need to know how to deal with the players. Let's get started."

CHAPTER 10

*I*t took several rounds of calling to get through. Even though they now had a number to call her, the inmates hadn't tried to make contact. The negotiating team had given the inmates the whole afternoon to stew and it was now approaching the end of Gemma's shift, but she wanted to make contact before turning control over to Taylor.

She wanted to be there for the transfer, to make the introduction, and to ease the way. Taylor was entirely capable of managing both the inmates and the situation, but up to the end of the previous phone call, Gemma thought she'd been making progress. Not in leaps and bounds, but initial progress never moved like that. Trust had to be built and connections formed; that's when progress inched ahead.

She wanted to have a hand in smoothing that progress, but that wasn't going to happen if no one answered the phone.

She summoned her patience and called at five-minute intervals, hoping they'd catch on to the pattern and would be available during one of her calls.

Finally, her persistence paid off and someone picked up the phone. "Yeah."

"Rivas?" Gemma opted not to use his birth name. She'd save that for moments when getting through to him on a particular point was crucial, perhaps making the difference between life and death.

"Yeah."

"You surprised us earlier today."

A grunt was his only response. At least he'd answered, even if it was clear he was in no mood to be chatty.

"I'd like to talk to you about that. Do you know that nearly brought the A-Team through your door? If it hadn't been for Warden Davis and Deputy Warden Coleman realizing the deceased wasn't actually a CO, things could have gone south quickly."

Rivas let out a sharp crack of laughter. "Warden Dipshit wouldn't know one of his COs if they walked by him with a marching band. Coleman made that call."

Gemma caught Chen's arched eyebrows and nodded her agreement. *That's a surprising amount of insight for someone who's locked away for seventeen hours a day.* "She did. She seems to know all the COs."

"Yeah."

"Do you have to deal much with either the warden or deputy warden?"

"No one deals with Dipshit."

Davis isn't anyone's favorite, from inmate, to CO, to

deputy. "Because he isn't involved in the day-to-day life of the facility?"

"Dunno. But if we see anyone, it's Coleman."

"From what I've seen, she's genuinely interested in the people of OBCC. *All* the people, employees and inmates alike."

"She's okay."

Gemma made a note on her pad and underlined it for emphasis. This sounded like faint praise, but in this facility and from this inmate, that was a ringing endorsement and a valuable piece of intel. Using third-party intermediaries was a risky proposition at the best of times—it certainly hadn't been overly successful when the hostage taker in the City Hall situation had insisted on talking to the mayor—but she would keep the concept of bringing in Coleman for a personal connection in her back pocket because it might come in handy. She'd seen genuine concern for the people involved in the ESH from Coleman; from Davis, she'd seen fury and outrage that this had happened on his watch, and a general lack of interest for the men in his care.

"If you wanted our attention from that stunt, you succeeded. But you had it before that. Now I need something from you in good faith."

"Oh yeah?"

"Yes. That inmate, Tyrell Rush, he was someone. He had a mother who taught in an elementary school. He had a girlfriend and they had a three-year-old daughter together. And now he's gone."

"I dunno nothin' 'bout what happened to him."

Gemma had a hard time believing that. If there was a power struggle going on inside the ESH, Rivas would be sure to know exactly what was going on below him in the hierarchy. Perhaps he wasn't responsible for the death, but either the power structure was incredibly unstable in there—which was entirely possible—or he was flat-out lying. Based on his confidence, and the fact that no one else ever talked to her so all contact bottlenecked behind one person, she was sure Rivas was lying.

"I was hoping we'd be able to talk about him. I thought you'd know what happened." Feeling like she was bumping up against a wall, Gemma pushed a bit. "Assuming you're in control, I mean."

"I'm in control." His words whipped out like the lash of a whip.

"But you don't know what happened to Rush."

"I can't see everything all the time."

"We agreed I'd be honest with you. That I won't lie to you no matter what."

"Uh-huh."

"Then let's be straight. Someone is responsible for that death, and someone will be held accountable. Before the riot yesterday, Rush was fine. Now he's dead. And whether it happened in the heat of the moment or as a calculated slaying later on, all that will change is the degree of charges. But there will be charges. So from our perspective, we had an agreement that no one was to be harmed."

"From now on."

"Pardon me?"

"You said 'from now on.' That's what I agreed to this morning."

Gemma closed her eyes, kicking herself for her own stupidity as she thought back to their arrangement.

"Everyone stays safe from now on."

"From now on . . . gotcha."

The body must have already been in the CO's uniform

before they talked. There was no way they could have tossed him out like that so quickly otherwise. But thinking back, she realized he'd made a decision during that pause. If they'd been holding on to Rush to use him as a threat for leverage, as soon as she and Rivas had made that deal to keep Cartwright and his men at bay, Rush's body inside the ESH was a liability. His way to deal with that liability had been to dump Rush while she'd given him immunity in their negotiations.

Rivas - 1, Capello - 0. He was making a point that he could play by the rules and still show who was in charge. Smart.

But it also gave her hope no one else inside was dead, or they might have all been ejected into the hallway.

"That is what you agreed to," she admitted.

"So you ain't got nothing to dish."

"Not when it comes to holding you to a promise of no harm before our agreement this morning. You have a handle on things since then?"

"They know better."

"Than to cross you?"

"Yeah."

"Good. But back to the good faith aspect. Because of Rush, I need proof of life on the hostages."

"They're alive." Rivas's tone was rock-hard.

Gemma winced—clearly he saw this as an insult to his control of the situation that he thought he'd established—but she pressed harder. "You understand I can't just take your word for that after this morning."

"No way am I bringing them in here for you."

Williams tapped the end of his pen on the radio that still sat in the middle of the table.

Gemma gave him a nod of approval. "Let's use radios

then. You have the CO radios. You can take one to them. But I need to hear each one of them speak."

"You talk 'bout trust." He nearly spit the words at her.

"This isn't me, Rivas. After this morning, tactical discussed storming the ESH. You and I both want to keep them out. We can find a better way. But to do it, I have to assure everyone that your hostages are alive and well. This is nonnegotiable. But if you agree, we can move forward."

Gemma let the silence hang heavily between them, not willing to break it as long as the phone line was open. It was crucial that he make an effort to compromise, crucial for him to see that for her to give something, he had to as well.

Gemma's gaze flicked toward the clock, tracking the second hand as it shuddered then jerked to its next stop, then quaked again and continued its journey.

Come on, come on . . .

She scanned the worried expressions around the table, reading the same thought in their eyes: *We're going to hit a wall if he doesn't agree to this*.

McFarland grabbed his pad and pen and started to scrawl a suggestion. *If he won't budge, offer—*

"Fine." The single word was nearly a snarl.

McFarland's pen froze where it dug into the paper, and Gemma sagged back in relief. But when she spoke, she made sure her tone of voice didn't convey the doubt she felt. "Thank you. Let's do it now. Are the radios near you?"

"Yeah."

"Turn one of them on." She picked up the radio, keyed open the mic, and counted to ten before talking into it. "Can you hear me?"

"Yeah. Give me five." Rivas's voice crackled with light static, but his words were clear.

In their headsets, the team heard the click of the line being disconnected.

"If we don't hear from eight COs, you're not going to keep Cartwright out of there," said McFarland.

"And you need to make sure he's not putting one over on you," Williams said. "Like having inmates stand in for COs."

"They could pull a stunt like that because we aren't going to have any visuals." Gemma reached out a hand toward McFarland. "Pass me the binder?" When he handed it to her, she flipped to the info on the COs. "Last name isn't going to cut it because it's on their badges."

"Ditto their badge numbers." McFarland leaned in to scan the pages with her.

"Even first name might not be a good test," Chen said. "Depending on how long the COs have been assigned to that unit, some of the inmates might know them well enough to know some personal details. First names, family members, that kind of thing. We need to find something the CO will know from their records that the inmates won't."

"Anything general, like birthday or the neighborhoods they live in won't do. That could be something that's come up in conversation."

McFarland ran his finger down the information of one of the officers. "Could go with something as basic as when they started working at Rikers. Not something vague like the year, but something specific, like the exact day."

Williams shook his head. "Do you remember the exact day you started? I don't. The year, sure, even the month, but not the exact day. And if some of these COs have been at it for a while, they likely won't remember either and then we might not believe someone in error. We need something more foolproof."

Gemma scanned down the information. A lot of it was standard employment data—social security number, home address, license plate for their parking permit at Rikers, commendations and disciplinary action, history on the island, where many of them had moved from building to building over the years—

Gemma's gaze ran back a few lines. Then she moved to the next CO, then the next. "Here's something they should know offhand. Their license plates. Six of the eight COs drive to work and park on the island so their plate numbers and vehicles are listed on their records. Two of them don't drive, but that in itself is valuable information. And because they won't know what question we're asking, they won't know to have primed someone on how to answer it. Better still, one of the two COs who use public transit or are dropped off is Officer Andrea Montgomery. They won't be able to fake that replacement."

"I like it," said Williams. "Unless it's a new plate, chances are good the COs will know it."

"Then that's what we'll ask them. The two who don't have cars will say so, and that will line up as well." Resting her chin on her hand, Gemma contemplated the phone system. "We've been using this to record the calls, but we won't be using the phone this time."

"We can fix that." McFarland picked up his phone, typed in his password, flipped through several screens, and opened his voice recorder app. "I'll start this when the radio call goes through. We'll capture the whole thing."

He was silent for a moment, then he nudged Gemma with his elbow. "What are you looking at?"

She looked up from the correction officer record she was studying. "The infractions. The disciplinary actions. The complaints. Look at the length of some of them." She turned the book toward him and ran her finger down the list. "Evans." She flipped a page. "Garvey." Another page, then another. "Rogers."

"What I see is a lot more complaints than disciplinary action in response to them."

"Exactly. Put that together with Davis's attitude concerning the inmates needing a heavy hand to stay in line and none of it surprises me. If there's no enforcement of the rules around use-of-force by COs against inmates, why pay any attention to them?"

Seven minutes later, they were still waiting for contact. Gemma ate the last donut from the box in the middle of the table out of sheer nerves, Chen doodled a complex design in the corner of his pad of paper, Williams was out of his chair, standing with his back to the table as he studied the blueprints, and McFarland drained the last of the coffee from his monster thermos into his cup.

Gemma pointed at his cup with her donut. "I can't believe you emptied that thing."

"Hey, everyone helped. I didn't drink all sixteen cups on my own." He gave what she'd previously considered a large thermos a pointed stare. "Yours didn't make it out of the morning."

"Yeah, I need to be prepared differently for tomorrow. Like bring food."

McFarland chuckled. "Didn't appreciate the cafeteria food?"

"It was god-awful and you know it. I've never seen you not finish a burger and fries . . . until today. Maybe I'll go home tonight and bake."

That wiped the smirk off McFarland's face and replaced it with longing. "And you're going to bring something in for your starving coworkers, right?"

Even through the stress of waiting, the hope in McFarland's eyes lightened her mood. Cooking was her go-to when she wanted to de-stress at the end of a busy day. She'd learned all the traditional Sicilian family dishes at her grandmother's elbow after her mother died, and there was nothing her father and four brothers liked more than any dish that came out of her kitchen. Considering where she lived—in a tiny apartment in the East Village—they were always impressed at how she turned out so many delectable meals. And desserts. *Especially* desserts with her family.

"What about those cookies?" McFarland wheedled.

"Which ones?"

"The almond ones that look like little swirls with sugar on top."

"Ah. *Biscotti con mandorla*. I could do that."

"I'll bring the coffee. You bring those." Joy sparkled in his eyes. "We'll all be happy."

"I'm not sure that's a completely balanced diet—" Gemma cut off as the radio gave a static buzz.

"You there?" Rivas's tinny voice burst through the radio speaker.

Gemma raised her radio to her lips. "I'm here. One at a time, please. I need to hear each name and I will ask each of them an identifying question."

"You didn't say you were gonna do that." Anger flowed through the speaker.

Doesn't take much to set Rivas off. "This is proof of life, but also proof of identity. Otherwise, you could just pass the radio around to your guys. Now, let me talk to the first CO."

There was a pause and then a new voice came on the line. "Officer Vic Keen." The voice was deep and steady, reminding Gemma they were dealing with officers, not their usual citizen hostages. Officers were used to dealing with crises, so they would be harder to shake than most people. Especially correctional officers, used to dealing day in and day out with inmates.

Gemma looked at the alphabetical list of officer names posted on the wall. Keen was a third of the way down from the top. She flipped to his record in the binder. "We need to confirm your identity. Can you tell me your car's license plate number?"

"My . . . my car?"

"Yes, sir."

Keen rattled off the correct plate number so quickly that Gemma was satisfied she had the real Officer Keen.

"Thank you. Officer Keen, are you all right?"

Keen paused long enough that Gemma knew the answer was "no."

"I'm all right."

"The truth, please. We're attempting to assess medical needs. I've been assured you won't be harmed."

His rough laugh told her more than any words. *These men are brutal. They're untrustworthy and dishonest.*

She had to hope Rivas realized he needed to be a man of his word. More than that, she hoped he knew he needed to make sure his men understood their agreement as well.

"Officer Keen?"

"They beat me half to death. Is that what you want to hear?" Stress broke through to shimmer behind his words.

Cracks starting to form.

"Do you need medical assistance?"

"Probably."

"Are any of your injuries life-threatening?"

"No."

"Thank you. I'll do what I can to get you medical care as soon as possible. Please pass the radio to the next officer."

There was a pause, and then the next voice came on the line. Another man, but quieter and higher in pitch with a quaver that spoke to Gemma of youth and courage pushed to the limit. "Officer Nico Duran."

She flipped to his page in the binder, skimming down his data until she found the information she was looking for. "Officer Duran, I'll ask you the same question. Can you tell me your license plate number?"

After Duran confirmed his identity, she asked, "Are you hurt?"

"No."

"I need you to be honest, Officer Duran. I can't get you help unless you are."

"No, no, I'm okay. They've . . . threatened. But nothing so far."

"I'm glad to hear that."

She moved on through the COs, each confirming their name, health status, and plate number without her needing to ask.

The fifth officer was the sole woman in the group. Gemma could hear her unspoken nerves in both her tone and her hesitation. "This is . . . this is Andrea Montgomery. I . . . I . . . I'm okay. No one's . . ." A longer pause this time.

Gemma's eyes narrowed in suspicion at the photo on the page in front of her. As the only female in the group, Montgomery would be under more pressure and under more threat than the men. The specter of sexual assault had to be a constant terror. Did Montgomery take care with her words for fear of retribution? Gemma was about to speak, to ask her about her physical well-being, when the woman spoke again.

"I'm all right. Not injured. But . . . but I don't have a car." The end of the sentence came out as a rush.

Bingo.

"That's okay, Officer Montgomery. How do you get to work?"

"I take the Q100 bus."

"Thank you, Officer. Please pass the radio along."

They got through the next two officers quickly, then the radio was handed to the last officer.

There was so long a pause between the seventh and eighth officers that Gemma prompted a response. "Rivas, are you there?"

"Yeah."

"Is there a problem?"

"Nah. The last guy, he just stepped out. You know, for a private moment."

You let a hostage step out? Do you think I'm an idiot? Our reports had them in multiple cells, but you've obviously brought them together to pass the radio around quickly. There's no way he stepped out.

A glance around the table told her the rest of the team shared her disbelief.

The moment when a negotiation team was looking for proof of life was simply not the moment you let one of the hostages go to the bathroom. Besides, they probably locked them in the cells and made them use the toilet publicly.

Gemma turned to the record of the only officer she'd not talked to—Jermaine Evans. "I need to speak with the last officer." She studied the photo. Evans was a big man, the kind of man who could have easily played offensive lineman. In his badly lit ID shot, his sunken brown eyes recessed into his dark face, and his lips were a thin, almost sullen line. She flipped the page, studying the length of the list of complaints and disciplinary actions on his record. The list told the tale of a tough, angry CO, who had no trouble using force to bend an inmate to his will.

This was the kind of CO the men would exact their revenge on. Now the question was simple: Was Evans already dead, or was he so badly injured he couldn't talk?

"Rivas." Gemma's tone bordered on steel. "I need to talk to him now."

"Yeah. One second."

Gemma leaned over to peer at McFarland's cell phone to make sure it was still capturing the exchange. He tipped it in her direction so she could see the clock counting up over the large red recording button. She wanted to make sure Coleman heard the recording. If anything was off, she'd be able to help identify the issue.

"'Lo?" The voice was low, the single syllable wavering slightly.

"I need your name, please, sir."

"Jer . . ." He paused to draw in a noisy breath. "Jermaine Evans." The words were so slurred Gemma wasn't sure she'd have understood if she hadn't had his data in front of her.

McFarland scribbled the word "beaten?" on his yellow pad. Gemma returned a single word—"concussion?"

She raised the radio to her lips again. "Officer Evans, are you injured?"

"Need help."

The words were quiet, so quiet and indistinct, Gemma nearly missed them. "Officer Evans, can you repeat that?"

"You got your proof of life." It was Rivas's voice again. Sharp. Clipped with anger.

"You have multiple injured in there, Rivas. I need to get them medical assistance."

"No."

"This is what negotiation is about. You help me, I help you. You let me send in medical to evaluate the hostages and inmates and I'll give you something in return."

"What if we don't want nothin'?"

"There has to be something. Rivas, you know that if anyone dies, especially if it's one of the hostages, it will all hit the fan. I won't be able to do anything to keep tactical out."

"No one's gonna die."

"I don't know." Gemma let every ounce of skepticism fill her tone as she circled the word "concussion" on her page. "Officer Evans doesn't sound good."

"He may have taken a shot to the head during the scuffle. Ain't nothing a little time won't fix. Besides, you said proof of life would keep tactical out. You said you wouldn't lie to me."

"I didn't lie to you, but a badly injured hostage changes the game."

"You got your proof of life. Stay out."

"It's not that simple, Rivas. We need to find a middle ground here."

Silence.

"Rivas? Rivas, come in."

Silence continued to stretch.

"I think he turned off the radio," Chen said. "He just gave you his last word."

That last word better not be the death knell of a hostage or there would be serious hell to pay.

CHAPTER 11

Gemma's temper was high from the moment she walked into the negotiation room the next morning. "Tell me you got them to talk overnight. Better yet, tell me you got medical in there to see to our hostages." Just inside the doorway, she stopped dead at Taylor's grim expression.

"I'd love to tell you that. I'd be lying though." Taylor ran a hand over his hair and slouched in his chair.

"I don't know what magic you spun, but no one else can get them to talk." Shelby stood and, bracing her hands behind her hips, arched backward, her head tipped up and her eyes closed for a moment. She straightened and threw a sour glance at her chair conveying her disgust at the flimsy support over long shifts. "They wouldn't pick up the phone. We even tried contacting them through the radios. They never responded. We think they turned them off, so they don't know anyone was trying to contact them."

"*Dannazione*." Gemma stepped into the room. "I'm extremely concerned about Officer Evans. That has to be priority one—getting him out."

"You sound mad and you haven't even started yet." Shelby bent down and grabbed her bag before stepping away from the table to make room for Williams who had appeared behind Gemma.

"I woke up mad." The lack of concern for someone so grievously injured had been gnawing at her like a rotten toothache since end of shift the previous night. "Leaving Evans in there, not attending to what could be a serious medical issue, isn't right." Gemma circled the room to her chair as Taylor vacated it, setting her thermos down on the table.

"You saw his list of disciplinary actions. Evans has been a problem for these inmates for likely as long as they've been incarcerated," said Williams.

Gemma stared at him, openmouthed. "You're justifying their actions?"

"Not at all." Williams took Shelby's empty seat. "I'm explaining how they likely see the situation. You know you can't let this color your view of those inmates. No matter how distasteful they are, no matter what they've done, we have to see past that. Or there's no chance of making a connection."

"And since no one but you seems to be able to get through to them, you know that's crucial," Taylor pointed out.

"I'm pretty sure it's not me." Gemma flopped down into her chair. "I don't think they'd talk to any of us after yesterday. But I need to get the conversation going again. I need to work the mad off now so there isn't a trace of it leaking through."

"You have to be the calm voice of reason," said Taylor. "You might remind him he can talk to others. It might expedite things for them to not keep communication to a twelve-hour window."

McFarland came in with a hand raised in greeting, Chen following.

"If I can get him to talk to me, I'll definitely make that point. And if you can't get your point through to him tonight, let Shelby give it a go. Maybe Rivas won't talk to her either, but it's worth a shot."

Taylor nodded in agreement. "The worst we're going to get is exactly what we're getting now. Shelby? You up for it?"

Shelby sent him a look that clearly said, *Are you kidding me?* "Yeah, I'm up for it. But for now, I'm up for breakfast and a solid eight on the rack. Oh, before we go, we did learn something after you left last night. I called in a favor from a contact in the ME's office to get some preliminary information on Rush."

"They've done the autopsy already?" Gemma asked.

"No, but they prepped the body for storage and collected evidence," said Shelby. "He wasn't killed in that uniform, so there was no obvious cause of death externally. But under the uniform, COD was obvious. He'd been stabbed multiple times in the chest and abdomen. Probably bled out. My contact said it was brutal. Someone really went to town on him."

"Rage killing. Just what we need. Thanks for the intel."

"No problem. Have a good shift." With a wave, she

slipped through the doorway, the rest of her team following her, the men arguing over eggs versus pancakes for breakfast.

McFarland set down his massive thermos, pulled out his chair, and sat down. "Another day, another dollar. Let's do this!"

Gemma gave him the side-eye. "How much coffee have you had already?"

McFarland dropped a hand onto the thermos, actually petted it. "This baby, nothing so far. Two cups at home."

"That explains it."

The team took a moment to organize their notes and put on their headsets.

"Ready?" Gemma asked.

"Ready," Williams replied. "You're going to push for medical care, I assume?"

"Yes. That's job number one. Really, it's the only job for now. I want a med team in there. Barring that, I'll negotiate for them to release Evans. We're on day three. They have to be hungry. So that puts food in our corner."

"Excellent trade-off," Chen said. "Also, they may be more inclined to losing a single hostage than letting a doc or the A-Team in there."

Williams looked over at the lists of names, inmates and COs alike. "Especially if there are more dead in there than they've let on."

McFarland winced. "Hating to be indelicate, but we're on day three. If there's another DB in there, the moment the door opens, we'll know it."

"Yet another reason to get them to open the door," Gemma said. "Though if someone's died more recently from their injuries, there may not be any smell yet to give it away."

She dialed the phone and they sat as it rang a full dozen times before she cut the line, waited a few minutes for someone to react to the ringing phone, and then dialed again.

She was pleasantly surprised when the call was picked up on the second ring. "Yeah."

"Good morning, Rivas."

"Uh-huh."

"I'd like to talk to you about making a deal. You know how this goes. You give something to me. I give something to you. So let's talk about—"

"No medical."

Gemma smoothly switched to Plan B. "Fine. If you don't want anyone coming in, you need to let Evans come out."

"Why would I give up a hostage?"

"How about to save a life?"

The cynical sound that came across the line said it all.

"Then how about in exchange for food?" The silence that followed brought a smile to Gemma's lips. "You guys have been a few days without fresh food. How about some breakfast? For everyone, including the hostages, in exchange for Evans."

"What if we want something else?"

"I'd be happy to negotiate. What do you want?"

"There are a few things."

Something to trade. Real progress, finally. But trying to negotiate with inmates who were stressed, exhausted, and hungry was a recipe for disaster, and she needed to stack the deck toward a reasonable discussion. "I'd be happy to discuss those with you. But let me suggest this. I'll have the team of officers outside your door deliver food for everyone there. We'll trade the food for Evans.

That's a fair exchange. We'll give you guys an hour to get the food out to everyone—and I mean everyone, Rivas. No starving the hostages or the deal's off. Then you and I can talk again. Evans will be out, and I'll feel better. You'll have eaten and you'll feel better. I think we'll deal fairly with each other at that point. Let's set ourselves up for success."

Rivas took a few seconds to weigh his options, but it was a short enough time that Gemma wondered if the men inside were getting harder to handle because of hunger.

"No Ninja Turtles. I see one of those bastards, it's off."

"They'll all be my men. Let me make arrangements, and then I'll get back to you in a couple of minutes. I'll make sure you know exactly how the transfer will work and at what time so there are no surprises." She ended the call and met McFarland's grin with one of her own. "Finally."

"Definitely about time."

Williams pushed away from the table. "I'll go find Coleman. She'll be the one to get this going quickly."

"Tell her not to skimp on breakfast. We need something for everyone in there, and it needs to be decent food."

"Decent food?" Williams's tone was skeptical. "That may be a challenge based on the small amount we've had."

"Agreed. Tell her she needs to try. Breads, fruit, juice, coffee." At McFarland's hum of displeasure, Gemma backtracked. "You may be right. Skip the coffee. Unless they're used to it and actually enjoy it. Eggs, if they're not powdered. Bacon or sausage is likely asking for the moon on short notice. But it needs to be as good and as plentiful as they can make it. We're about to start negotiations for real now, so we need them well fed and content. Then they'll be more reasonable."

"Agreed. Let me see what I can do." Williams disappeared into the hallway.

Gemma hoped Williams would be convincing because it could mean the difference between success and failure. And when failure meant death, the stakes couldn't be higher.

CHAPTER 12

*C*artwright studied the blueprints in the negotiation office. "How long until Coleman is bringing the food to the ESH?"

Gemma rose from her chair to join him. "Within the next ten or fifteen minutes."

"We're ready for it. I left Logan in command, so if it arrives early, he'll hold position until I get there."

"How do you want to play this?"

Holding his rifle steady with one hand on the grip, Cartwright's gaze roamed over the blueprints. "Fast. Evans will come out first. Then they can have the food. After that we'll pull out and seal the place up again." He jabbed an index finger at the two cells marked for the hostages. "As far as we know, this is still where the hostages are kept. I'll try to confirm that while the door is open. I'll also check the emergency exits haven't been blocked and they haven't made any kind of basic structural changes."

"You don't think you would have heard that?" Chen asked.

"That first day was loud. Yelling and screaming and crashing. They were trashing the place. And we've been staying away from the main entrance to ensure the safety of the hostages. We haven't been able to study what they're doing in there."

"This will give us our first really good look at the place. Try to capture as much footage as you can with your helmet cam, and we can break it down later."

"Affirmative." He turned away from the blueprints to look down at McFarland. "You have everything you need?" He tapped his helmet next to the camera mount over the center of his forehead.

"Sure do. Thanks."

With a curt nod, Cartwright left the office to return to the ESH.

Gemma slid back into her seat. "He's all set for livestreaming?"

"That and recording. He'll be front and center when they retrieve Evans and deliver the food, so this will give us our first view into the facility and of the people involved. Give me a minute and I can show you."

McFarland pulled a laptop out of his bag and set it up at his end of the table so they could watch the operation. He worked some geek magic, and then they were looking at a view of the hallway from inside the A-Team. Black helmets crowded in, and, over their heads, the gray steel sliding door to the ESH was visible.

Williams studied the screen. "Nice. That's better clarity than I expected."

"Some of these newer units are really compact but capture a lot of data."

On screen, Cartwright suddenly swung around at a rattling sound—Nya Coleman and a uniformed CO wheeled two carts with stacked towers of covered trays down the hallway.

"Deputy Warden." Cartwright's voice was tinny but clear through the helmet cam.

"Lieutenant." Coleman stopped a full twenty feet from the ESH entrance, her assistant rolling the second cart into place beside hers. Then they both stepped away. "These are ready to go. Do you need anything else from us?"

"Negative. If you could clear the hallway, we'll proceed."

"We'll pull back and wait for Officer Evans. We have EMTs already on site for him down the hall."

"Good."

Cartwright turned to his men, standing far enough away that they could see most of the six-man team. The officers were ready for the op, with helmets, safety glasses, and rifles already in place. "Johnson and Hill, you take the carts and wait for my instruction. Logan and Mulgrew, you're with me at the door and will escort Officer Evans out to meet the EMTs. Sims and Peterson, fall back and take up a defensive position. Be prepared to take action if anyone rushes the door, but wait for my command."

There was a chorus of "Yes, sir" and the group quickly fell into position in front of the main entrance. Raising a fist, Cartwright pounded three times on the door. For a good thirty seconds, there was no visible movement, but then a dark shape stepped in front of the far side of the sliding steel door. From the angle of the helmet camera, his face wasn't clearly defined through the strips of glass that broke the steel door into segments.

The door slowly slid open with an ominous scraping sound to reveal the space beyond.

Gemma only allowed herself a brief scan of the background—toppled tables, garbage and belongings strewn everywhere, men in various stripped-down versions of the classic prison uniform—and then focused on the man standing in front of Cartwright.

Rivas.

He was big, bigger than either Cartwright or Logan, his ragged white T-shirt stretched taut over a wide chest and muscled arms to fall over the orange pants of his prison uniform. His hair was buzzed short, a skim of dark shadow over his skull. Thick black brows over wide-set eyes paired with a pencil-thin mustache and dark soul patch set into several days of scruff. His lips were unsmiling. But it was his dark eyes that drew Gemma.

Cold. Dead.

This is a man who'd kill without a second thought.

"We have your food." Cartwright's body twisted slightly toward the cart as he must have gestured in that direction.

"Push it in. But not you or your men." Rivas's dark gaze ran quickly over the team of officers.

"Evans first." Cartwright's tone brooked no argument. "Then the food is yours."

For a moment, Rivas's eyes stayed fixed just below the level of the camera, and from the way he didn't avert his gaze, Gemma was sure the two men were both sizing each other up and staring each other down. The silence extended almost painfully, but Gemma knew Cartwright and knew he wouldn't step back.

Finally, Rivas gave a shrug and half turned into the facility. "Hernandez," he shouted. "Bring him."

Cartwright used the brief moment of divided attention to turn his head through a subtle pan across the breadth of the cell block.

Cartwright's description that they'd trashed the place was absolutely accurate. Several tables originally bolted to the floor in the main area had been ripped from their moorings and hurled onto the entranceway floor, four feet below. Shattered TV screens dangled drunkenly from the mezzanine support posts or lay in pieces on the floor below. Inmate belongings and garbage were strewn over every open surface and clothes and bedding draped off railings. Someone had fashioned a noose from a bedsheet and it dangled from the second-floor walkway near the main door. Men stood in the background in groups, some with the posture of the victors and some with considerably more caution as they eyed both the other inmates and the officers in the doorway.

Cartwright jerked toward the far side of the facility where, over the mezzanine railing, the head and shoulders of a tall, black man was visible from the vicinity of the hostage holding cells.

Gemma knew what Evans looked like from his Rikers ID photo, but the man staggering toward Cartwright barely resembled that CO. His right eye was swollen shut; the purple upper lid so distended it appeared his entire eye socket had shifted south. A gash rode his hairline over his left eye, and smudged blood trails meandered down his cheek and under his ear. The left side of his jaw was reddish-black, the puffy skin stretched taught over a weeping abrasion.

Someone had really worked him over.

Suddenly Evans staggered, falling forward and nearly going down, only saving himself with one meaty fist wrapped around a cross bar of the mezzanine railing. The scruffily bearded, dark-haired man behind him gave him another shove and Evans hung on.

"Tell your man to get his hands off Evans, or this trade is done," Cartwright ordered.

Rivas's face darkened—even though he had to be used to taking orders inside the ESH, he clearly considered himself back in charge—but he turned and snapped at his men. "*Quita tus jodidas manos de él.*"

Gemma's high school Spanish was extremely rusty but her Italian was not, and Spanish was similar enough to Italian that she understood the vulgar hands-off order.

Radiating rage, Hernandez stepped away from Evans, his hands in the air. But he followed his captain's orders.

Rivas is *the shot caller, and his guys will fall in line behind him to do whatever he orders.*

Joe had nailed it.

Evans pulled himself upright, pausing for a moment to stare at the entrance to the ESH.

"I don't like the way he's squinting," Williams said. "He can't focus on Cartwright. Or maybe even on the doorway itself."

Gemma cataloged the CO's unsteady stance and the

desperation carved into his expression. "I'm glad we're getting him out. He needs medical attention ASAP."

"Evans!" Cartwright called out. "This way!"

Keeping his hand on the edge of the mezzanine floor, Evans took a stumbling step forward, and then another. The concentration on his face said everything about the effort required to stay upright, let alone move forward. At the edge of the mezzanine, he tottered toward the far wall, briefly disappearing from the camera's view, but then appeared ten seconds later, holding on to the wall. He staggered around the corner as he picked up speed, determination and hope lighting his open left eye at the sight of the officers there to take him out. A few more steps and Logan and Mulgrew grabbed him, each of them swinging one of the CO's massive arms over their shoulders to walk him down the hallway. They disappeared around the corner as Cartwright turned to Rivas.

"Johnson. Hill. Now."

Two carts rolled into the peripheral view of the camera lens. Without looking away from Cartwright, Rivas grabbed one cart, pulled it past him, then sidestepped and did the same for the second. Still holding Cartwright's gaze, he ordered, "Close it!" to someone out of sight, and the door slowly slid shut to close with a metallic *bang*.

Through the strips of the glass, they watched men converge on the carts, only to abruptly freeze in place.

Gemma leaned in, mesmerized by the small amount of action she could see. "Do you see that?"

"The absolute control he has?" McFarland asked. "Oh yeah. He's running that place. Just like Joe said."

"More so than I even thought. That could play to our advantage."

"For sure. You keep him onside, you may be able to bring the entire group with him."

"That's the goal."

"I've never worked a hostage situation like this," Chen said. "Only with single hostage takers."

"Trust me, this isn't typical." Williams's tone carried the weight of decades of experience. "All these years, I've only worked a handful of cases that might compare to this one, but hands down, none of them were this complicated and with this many potentially conflicting personalities." He met Gemma's gaze. "I agree that keeping the man in charge onside is a huge advantage. It doesn't guarantee there won't be a mutiny, but while he runs the show, that connection is crucial."

Gemma marked the time on the clock on the wall. "They're going to be tied up with the food for a while." She pushed back her chair. "I'm going out to see how Evans is doing. Williams, can you watch the phone line?"

"Absolutely."

"Thanks. McFarland, tag along. If he's as unclear in his speech as he was yesterday, I want a second set of ears when we talk to him."

McFarland grabbed his phone and stood. "I'm not sure we'll get anything out of him, but I'm game."

They jogged down the hallway and past the courtyard where they found a group of A-Team officers, COs, and paramedics surrounding a gurney.

"How is he?" Gemma asked.

"Fading in and out," said Logan. "We basically had to carry him out of there."

Gemma slipped into the group, McFarland squeezing in after her. She stepped up to the foot of the gurney, keeping out of the way of the two paramedics who checked his vitals and physical status.

Nya Coleman stood on the other side of the gurney, holding Evans's hand. "Jermaine? Jermaine, stay with me. Who can I call for you?"

"Wife . . . Melissa . . ." Evans's slurred words made him sound half-drunk.

"I'll call her." Coleman turned to the paramedic at her side. "Where are you taking him?"

"Elmhurst." The young woman looked up at her partner. "Left pupil only is dilated."

"Breath sounds are clear on both sides. BP is 147 over 113."

"We need to take him now. It's already been too long."

The paramedics quickly tucked their equipment away, tossed their bags onto the gurney between Evans's sprawled legs, and cleared a path before trotting down the hallway, the gurney between them. Through the front doors, past security, flashing red and white strobe lights from the ambulance awaited them.

McFarland loosed a disgruntled breath. "So much for getting any information out of him."

"We can't stall them getting him the care he needs."

"No, but it might have been useful."

"He could still be useful later. Let them get him to the hospital and stabilized. Maybe, if we're lucky, he might be up to talking to someone tomorrow, although there's a chance his head injury may be severe enough he doesn't remember anything." Gemma turned to the A-Team officers, her gaze skimming past Logan to settle on Mulgrew. "Thank you. Getting Evans out will not only save his life, but may give us crucial information about what's going on inside the ESH. It certainly got us our first real visual of the state of the facility." She glanced at McFarland. "We can review the footage?"

McFarland nodded. "You bet. Let's do that now and see if we can find out anything new before you get in touch again."

Knowing Evans was in good hands, they slipped out of the group and made their way back down the hallway.

Finally, it was time to get down to real negotiations.

CHAPTER 13

*T*he team gave the inmates two full hours to eat and settle in after their meal. During that time, they poured over the footage, orienting themselves around the ESH, making notes on the blueprint on the wall and on the players involved. Gemma had already jotted down her impressions about Rivas, but grabbing a fresh pad of paper, she crafted a new composite list of characteristics that would help her understand the way he ticked.

Garcia came in a half hour after the exchange and joined in the brainstorming following a full update.

Finally, marking the time, Gemma set down her pen. "It's just past eleven. I think that's enough time. Agreed?"

"I think this is as close to a sweet spot as we're going to manage." McFarland poured himself more coffee. "Time to power up and get to it."

Gemma's first call went unanswered, but she expected that. Surely, no one was hanging over the phone after enjoying their meal, but hopefully someone heard the call go through. She waited for a count of sixty before calling again.

The call was picked up almost immediately. "Yeah."

"How was breakfast?"

"Good." Rivas's tone was neutral, lacking its usual razor's edge of hostility. "Well . . . as good as you can expect."

"I learned that one the hard way." Gemma jumped on the thread of connection. "I tried the coffee. It nearly killed me."

Rivas was silent, which Gemma read as caution in the face of her casual conversation.

The connection between negotiator and hostage taker was paramount to the success of any hostage situation. Negotiators faced with aggressive hostage takers who wouldn't deal with them often knew ahead of time they were headed for disaster. It was only through a negotiator-suspect connection that compromise could be reached. However, the savviest of hostage takers would question any attempts at friendliness as strategy.

So far, Rivas seemed anything but stupid.

The bottom line was that negotiators could despise what the hostage taker had done but they had to deal fairly and respectfully with them. Failure to do so would simply result in any aggression reflecting back on the hostages, often ending in injury and sometimes death.

Respect above all else was the golden rule.

When Rivas stayed quiet, Gemma forged ahead.

"Now, what about you and your men? There was a riot, a fight. Even if you won it and gained control, those COs wouldn't have laid down and taken it. Do any of you need medical attention? As I said, I can bring in someone from outside the OBCC who—"

"What is this bullshit? You don't give a damn about us." The sneer rolled through his words. "You said you weren't going to lie. Guess you lied about that too."

The vehemence of his response, the speed of it coming out of the blue, caught her off guard. *So much rage simmering on the back burner, just waiting for a chance to explode.* "Wrong. You think I don't see who you are? *Cazzate.* I'm a cop. Of course, I do. More than that, I'm from a family of them. Three of my brothers are cops. My father is a cop. I was raised understanding the streets. I know exactly who you are." Gemma forced herself to stop and take a breath. Meeting his anger with her frustration was not a successful strategy. "I know your charges are not who you are. They're partly a product of circumstance and desperation. I'm also not so naive that I don't know policing practices have to be responsible for some of your early charges." A harsh laugh came across the line, confirming her suspicions. "Let's put all that aside. I'm talking to you, Eduardo. Not your past. Not your charges or convictions. You. Lives are on the line. The COs you're holding. You and your fellow inmates. I'm what stands between you and the A-Team outside your door. You've shown yourself to be a leader, so lead. You and I can work through this, but you need to meet me halfway. What can I do to allow you to save face with your men while you release the hostages?"

"It's not about saving face."

"Then what's it about?"

"Do you know the hell we go through in here?"

She suspected she only knew the barest fraction of the truth. "Some of it. But not enough. Is that where your 'few things' comes in?"

"Yeah. We want better, so we made a list of what we want."

Gemma sat bolt upright in her chair. Based on how hard it was to get him to talk in the past, she thought he'd have a few vague suggestions. An actual list of demands was better than she anticipated. "And if we meet some of those demands, you'll release the hostages?"

"Maybe."

Gemma met Garcia's gaze and he gave her a single nod of approval. Seeing that all eyes were on her, she pointed at Chen, who looked up from his pad of paper where he was transcribing the conversation, and then pointed at Williams and McFarland and then at their own pads of paper. They both nodded, the message received—*everyone makes notes, we need to make sure we get every detail of this list.*

"So give me your list then. Do you have it with you?"

"Not really."

"It's in your head? You and the guys have discussed it?"

"Yeah."

"Then take some time and write it down. Let's do this once and do it right. We can wait for you." Gemma glanced at the clock—11:11. "I'll call you at twelve-thirty. I'll hold them off that long, Rivas, because we're moving forward, but then we need to make progress. That's the only thing that will keep them out."

"Got it."

The line went dead.

Gemma took off her headset and tossed it on the table. "Finally." She turned to Garcia. "We need to have someone from the DOC here. Someone who can make snap decisions in case we can offer them something right away. *But not* the warden."

"Yeah, we're going to need to go over his head," Garcia agreed. "Davis isn't going to want to do anything for these inmates. To him, punishment is the only option. And that would get every CO in there killed." He pushed away from the table and stood. "Let me contact the DOC. It's going to be pushing it, but I want someone over here by no later than twelve-fifteen. We may be wasting their time, but I'd rather do that than lose someone in the ESH if things go wrong."

"What about the city administration?" Gemma winced. "I hate to even suggest it, but . . ."

"Rowland." The twist of Garcia's lips conveyed his reluctance. "Yeah, we're going to need to keep him in the loop. But I don't want him here. I'll contact him and tell him we'll keep him informed, but we know from past experience how impatient he can be with a hostage situation."

The team spent the next hour preparing for discussions. Garcia dealt with the officials. McFarland went to the ESH and updated Cartwright and his men. Williams met with Davis and Coleman. And Gemma and Chen brainstormed tactics.

At twenty minutes past noon, the team met again in the negotiating room.

"We're ready?" Gemma asked.

"Darren Greene, DOC First Deputy Commissioner, is here in place of Commissioner Frye, who is off-site and couldn't get here in time. He's in with Davis in Davis's office."

"Coleman is in her office and says she's here for us whenever we need her," Williams said.

"I think we need her now." Gemma looked over at the wall and the lists of names. "No one knows better than Coleman the personalities involved. I think she'd be an asset as a consultant. Thoughts?"

"Makes sense," Garcia said.

"Yeah," McFarland agreed. "We might get her on the line if things stall. The men seem to like her and genuinely respect her, which is rare in this group. Let's take advantage of that. Want me to go get her?" He glanced at the clock. "We've only got five minutes."

"Yes, thanks." Gemma looped her headset around her neck. "We want to start on time."

They called through at exactly 12:30 as promised, and the phone was picked up on the second ring. They were ready and waiting.

"Did we give you enough time?" Gemma asked.

"Yeah."

"This is your list, or you've discussed this with your guys?"

"It's for all of us."

"Good. Now, so we're on the same page, I want you to understand that these aren't necessarily concessions that I can give you, but we have the First Deputy Commissioner from the DOC in the building and Mayor Rowland in his office waiting for our call. Also in the room with us is Deputy Warden Coleman." Gemma nodded at Coleman who sat at the end of the table beside Garcia wearing a second mic'd headset.

As previously agreed, Coleman said, "Good afternoon, Eduardo. I'm here to help if I can. Please tell Detective Capello and me what you need in exchange for the hostages." She nodded at Gemma, passing the conversation back to her.

"Go ahead, Rivas. Give us your list."

"No."

Gemma simply stared at Coleman, slack-jawed, reflecting the deputy warden's shocked expression. "What do you mean, 'no'? I thought we had a deal? We brought people in to discuss your list."

"We talked about it. We don' want our demands going just to you. You guys already know what it's like here. You'd be happy to keep that information here. We need the world to know 'bout Rikers."

Gemma's gaze snapped up to find Garcia's eyes locked on her as he leaned forward, both hands curled into white-knuckled fists.

She closed her eyes. She knew exactly where this was going. So did Garcia.

"We wanna tell it to the media."

Gemma's eyes opened in time to see Garcia's vicious, silent curse.

She wanted to mirror his reaction, but when she spoke, she kept her voice calm and neutral. "And what if we don't want to include the media? This isn't between you and them. This is between you and us."

"Then we done talkin'. You said you won't lie to me,

but you don't give me no guarantees that we'll get anything we ask for."

"I never said you wouldn't either."

"True that. But you just one lady cop, not the whole DOC. As we see it, our only chance of success is to hold you 'ccountable."

"And the media will hold us accountable?"

"Sure will."

Time to stall. "This is going to take some time, Rivas. This isn't my call to make. You just went above my pay grade."

"You ain't going to put us off forever, either. Three o'clock. I want him here by three o'clock."

"Him?"

"Only one reporter we agree on. We want Greg Coulter."

Gemma stiffened in her chair, her eyes going wide at the mention of ABC7's hotshot investigative reporter.

Greg Coulter. The reporter who had chased her and John Boyle as they'd desperately tried to escape through the streets of the Lower East Side. Coulter, the arrogant son of a bitch, who'd happily put the good people of New York City at risk in his drive for a hard-hitting story. The man who'd nearly died in his pursuit for glory.

But she wasn't the only one who hated Coulter.

Garcia's face was flushed crimson, and Gemma was tempted to put her line on mute just to remind Garcia to breathe. It made her feel the tiniest bit better to see Garcia suffused with the fury she felt.

"What if we can't get ahold of Coulter?" A combination of relief and satisfaction filled Gemma that her words didn't reflect any of her inner turmoil.

"Dude has his own hotline. Call it."

Everyone who lived in New York City had seen Coulter's giant billboards. On them, Coulter was splashed, large-as-life, the station's signature bright blue polo shirt setting off his bleached teeth and salon-bright blond hair. Stretched across the top of the billboard was his phone number: 1-800-TIPSTER and his slogan DO YOUR PART TO BALANCE THE SCALES layered over a depiction of the scales of justice. The message was implicit: You snitch, I'll expose some poor schmuck you don't like.

Despicable man.

"Coulter may not be at the station to contact so quickly. He may be already out running down some other tip. You're giving us a deadline, but it needs to be realistic. How about a secondary list? What about Reynolds from the *New York Times*? Or Schneider from the *New York Post*?"

"No newspapers. We want TV. We want Coulter."

"And if we can't get him?"

"You have almost three hours. Try hard. Or maybe I'll take a harder look at those hostages."

The line went dead.

"Goddammit!" Finally free to let out his frustration, Garcia exploded. "Coulter?" He sat back and stared up at the ceiling as if praying for patience. "Why does it have to be him?"

Gemma sagged in her chair. "Because we're cursed." She rolled her head to the right, found Coleman looking nervously between Garcia and herself. "I'm sorry. That caught me off guard. There'd been no indication he wanted to speak to the media."

"It sounds like you're familiar with the man," said Coleman.

Garcia merely growled.

Gemma shrugged. "We've run up against him a few times. Most of the time it doesn't work well for us. Last time it didn't work well for him."

"But you're okay with a list of inmate demands being aired for the general public?" Coleman asked.

"Absolutely not." Garcia took a deep breath and straightened in his chair. "This is an unexpected challenge, but despite it, this isn't going to air for the general public. That isn't a precedent we're going to set."

"No reason not to let them think it's live to air," McFarland said reasonably. "That will make them more receptive to talk. And it's a way to get us something in return. Maybe another hostage."

"Or maybe a medical visit." Williams swiveled in his chair to study the list of hostages. "An attendant media person is a big ask. There will have to be something in return for that. If you negotiate for a doctor to visit the facility, he'll be able to check out hostages and inmates alike. We'll get a feel for what's going on in there, and we'll get confirmation of any more injuries."

"Or deaths," Chen interjected. "Because we don't know who else may have been killed behind the scenes."

Gemma sat, staring at the table, the ring finger of her right hand *tap-tap-tapping* a rapid-fire staccato on the tabletop.

McFarland studied her through slitted, suspicious eyes. "I've seen that look before. What are you thinking?"

Tap-tap-tap-tap-tap.

She exhaled heavily and pinned her gaze directly on Garcia. "I want to make an exception for this."

"What do you mean?" Garcia braced his forearms on the table and leaned in.

"He's made an ask—media coverage of his demands. I should be insisting on something in return."

"And you don't want to?"

"Not this time. I'm getting a gut feel for Rivas. He refused to tell us his demands over the phone. Our only way forward is to work with them on their demands. If we tell him no media crew unless we tie a medical visit to it and he says no . . ."

"We just closed off the way forward," Chen finished.

"And, in doing so, may end the conversation and condemn the hostages to whatever fates the inmates decide for them. Worse would be if we then tried to backtrack on our need for something in exchange. We do that, and they'll know they have all the power and will never compromise with us. This isn't a strategy I'd normally recommend, but we're on day three of a standoff that could last for who knows how long, and only now are we getting to a place where we can actually make progress. Keeping food out because they won't agree to an exchange is one thing. Blocking our own progress would be shortsighted." She locked gazes with Garcia. "We need to let them have this one. Or else we may never have a chance of ending this peacefully."

Seconds ticked by as Garcia weighed the request. The silence stretched on long enough that Gemma braced for his refusal when he said, "Okay, let's play it like that. We need to get Coulter in here. I can contact him."

"No, sir." McFarland shot out a hand as if he was going to grab Garcia's arm, changed his mind and pulled back. "Let me contact him. He doesn't know me. We don't want him arriving already gunning for the NYPD."

"Good idea," Gemma agreed. "He doesn't like either of us, but I'm going to be the icing on the cake. Let's get him in here. Coulter's going to figure out he's working with me sooner or later. Might as well let him have his temper tantrum now."

CHAPTER 14

*G*emma waited while Coulter came through security. He was wearing a dark suit, a blindingly bright white shirt, and a tie in ABC blue. He walked with his back ramrod straight, his chin up, and his ice-blue eyes taking in everything around him. From his perfectly arranged hair to his calmly set features, he oozed superiority and confidence. He was *someone*.

He was someone, all right. A pain-in-the-ass someone who could stand to think a little less of himself.

But he didn't move like a man who'd nearly lost his life a couple months ago in a back alley in the Lower East Side.

Guilt crawled through Gemma as she remembered lunging for the gun before it went off, and the helplessness of knowing she was too late. Of seeing Coulter hit in the shoulder, sliding down the brick wall leaving a trail of blood behind. He'd survived, but it had been a near miss. A fraction of an inch difference in trajectory, and it would have been game over.

She'd never liked Coulter. His on-air persona had always struck her as overconfident and slightly condescending. But the first time she'd seen Garcia and Coulter go toe-to-toe at a hostage situation, she'd realized that under that persona lay an ugly arrogance and a significant level of aggression. She thoroughly disliked him from his perfectly styled, ready-for-my-closeup coiffure to his ox-blood Italian leather Oxfords so shiny he'd be able to fix his makeup in their reflective surface.

She'd tried to keep him out, but she'd lost that argument. *Rivas - 2, Capello - 0.*

Time to turn that trend around.

A cameraman and soundman were still caught in security as correction officers searched their heavy equipment bags. But Coulter wasn't about to wait for them. He strode out of security and then paused, as if waiting for an expected greeting, but none came. His lip curling slightly in distaste, he scanned dingy hallways teeming with bustling admin staff and COs who stared him down as if he were an exotic plant. His icy blue gaze traveled over and past Gemma . . . and then froze and darted back to her.

You.

She couldn't hear the word, but saw it fall from his lips accompanied by a glare that would have sliced right through her if he'd been able. She'd wondered if he'd recognize her on sight, or if it would take hearing her name for him to connect the dots.

Apparently her face was all the connection he needed. She pushed off the wall and covered the distance between them to offer her hand. It grated on her, trying to make nice with this man who clearly thought the public's right to know far outweighed anyone's right to privacy. He'd go to the end of the earth for a story—forget a dog with a bone; he was a terrier with a rat and wouldn't stop until his prey lay limp and lifeless in his jaws.

She only hoped she wasn't radiating her distaste. Rivas had boxed her into this scenario, and they had a job to do. She smiled, hoping what felt like bared teeth looked friendlier from the outside. "Mr. Coulter."

He glanced down at her hand, then back up to her face with a sneer. "They didn't tell me you were here."

She dropped her hand, refusing to let him make her feel small. "I'm primary negotiator for this case."

"Because you did such a great job last time. Anyone been sent to the hospital yet, or is it too early in your process for that?"

Anger simmered in the face of his hostility, but Gemma tamped it down. "It wasn't my idea to ask you here. Just like it wasn't my idea for you to get hurt in August. You were in the wrong place at the wrong time."

"And you were in league with the wrong man."

"I wasn't in league with him. I was trying to isolate him and take him into custody without anyone getting hurt."

His furious eyes narrowed on her. He didn't need to say anything; her memory of his shooting was still fresh months later.

"Anyway," she continued. "Thank you for coming in to help us mediate this situation. The inmates have demands, but they won't tell them to us without you specifically there to record it."

Coulter glanced back at his crew, who were now

through security and lugging equipment in their direction. He looked first one way, then the other, down the hallway before picking a direction and taking several steps. "Then let's get on with it. This way?"

"Wait." Gemma lunged for his arm. The muscles under her fingers clenched tight and then he yanked away from her. "We need to get a few things straight first."

"There's nothing to get straight. You need the inmates' demands recorded. We're ready to do that. Why are we wasting time? This is news. Every second counts."

"Because you need to understand there are more important things at play here than ratings. We told them we'd bring you in because we'd hit a wall." She wanted to grit her teeth into a snarl at his satisfied smirk, but she carefully schooled her features into utter calmness. "But it's not news. This footage can never air."

His gaze had been wandering off over her shoulder as if he was bored with her conversation, but he snapped back to her face abruptly. "What do you mean it can never air? That's why I'm here."

"You're here to record their demands. We never said anything about airing it."

"Is this some kind of sick joke? Of course, I'm going to air it. This is a scoop. The people of New York will want to know what's going on in their own tax-payer-funded facility. It's their right to know."

"If you air this footage, you'll change the face of hostage negotiations countrywide. If every suspect thinks he can become a worldwide media superstar, this will become the gold standard of negotiation. You'll put every hostage negotiation team in the country on the back foot in every situation. It's not a precedent we can afford to set."

"Then why am I here?"

"To make it *look* like you're going to make them worldwide media superstars. But that footage can never air."

Angry color was rising on Coulter's perfectly sculpted cheekbones. "So you think it's just fine to bring me and my guys down here and to waste our time as props in your game?" His voice rose until, by the end of the question, people around them stopped and turned to look with alarm at the commotion.

A CO across the corridor noticed Coulter towering over her, misconstrued she was in trouble, and marched toward her. She turned, drawing back one side of her blazer so he could see her NYPD shield clipped to her waistband, and held out a palm with a nod, gesturing that she was fine.

As tempting as it would be to take Coulter down in hand-to-hand—and she knew without a doubt she would win that contest—now was not the time to rub his nose in the dirt. She needed him onside. Maybe it was time to bring a little humility to her plea, to make him feel like he was needed, rather than strictly wanted.

"It's not a game. I need your help. You. They want you, so I do too."

"But you also need me to spend my time on something I'm never supposed to report on. Sorry, that's not how I do business." He turned to his men. "False alarm. We're heading back to the station."

"No, wait!" She didn't want to grab him again, so she moved quickly, putting herself directly into his path. "You can't give an hour of your time to keep seven men and women alive? I'm not sure what will happen to them if we don't move forward with this. It's just an hour. Maybe less. Then you can be on your way."

Coulter leaned down so they were eye to eye. It struck her that while he'd been blessed with perfectly symmetrical features most women would consider handsome, his arrogant, disdainful expression completely erased his good looks.

"Honey," he said so quietly she had to strain to hear him in the bustling hallway. "Contrary to you, my time is worth something. An hour of my time is valuable. The people of this city *need* me. They need my reporting. It's important. And you're wasting my precious time." He purposely stepped around her, waving his coworkers to follow him, and headed off down the hallway without a backward glance to see if they were following. Because he knew they would be.

Gemma gave herself a full second to revel in the fury whipping through her veins. *Pezzo di merda, fa schifo.*

She forced herself to stop and take a breath so her voice would be carelessly calm when she finally spoke. "I guess we'll have to get someone else then. Maybe Cynthia Naylor from WNBC would be a good choice. Not the inmates' first choice, but I know I could talk them into it. I'm sure the guys are dying to see a woman in a skirt and heels, and she'd be happy to do a story after the fact about her role in our success. Of course, your refusal to waste your precious time because there just wasn't enough glory in it for you will be one of the highlights of her story. I think it'll play well for her viewers. Though I'm not so sure yours will like it." She got a glimpse of the bright color suffusing his cheeks just before she turned her back and walked away from him.

The mumbled vicious curse behind her brought a wide smile to her lips and a pause to her step. She wiped her expression carefully clean before she spun around to face him. "Pardon me?"

"Fine. I'll do your interview. And I won't air the footage. But I'm going to record it and I want to be able to do a story on it afterward."

"I can't guarantee you'll be able to use any of that footage. That will be up to the Office of the Deputy Commissioner, Public Information."

Coulter bared his teeth in a growl.

"I can talk to Lieutenant Garcia about putting in a word for you. In good faith, you know, since you're helping us out."

Some of Coulter's color faded, but his gaze still drilled into her, his fury palpable.

You better hope you don't screw up around him someday or you're going to be the story he won't let die for weeks, just to humiliate you.

"If you're ready." Gemma extended a hand down the hallway. "It's this way."

Without another glance in her direction, Coulter strode past her, his expression set in granite, while his crew scrambled after him.

Suppressing a sigh, Gemma followed.

She'd made a deal with the devil. Whatever it took to get him to the ESH and to get Rivas talking.

Hopefully there wouldn't be any consequences, but if there were, she'd deal with them later. Right now, the only thing that mattered was getting the hostages out safely.

CHAPTER 15

Gemma slipped through the door of the negotiation room, closing it behind her with a click to stand with her back against it.

Garcia looked up from the briefing book. "You got him?"

"Oh, I got him. Though he nearly jumped ship when I told him he couldn't broadcast the footage. He was literally walking away when I stopped him."

"Little shit," Garcia muttered.

"He didn't give me any choice. I had to basically blackmail him. I told him if he wasn't going to do it, we'd get Cynthia Naylor from WNBC instead, and I'd make sure she knew he'd turned the gig down because there wasn't enough glory in it for him." She paused for Mc-Farland's hoot of appreciation before continuing. "*That* finally got him on board."

"It works for me." Garcia's smile was filled with a grim joy. "He must be pissed."

"Oh yeah. Someday this is going to bite me in the ass, but for now, we're getting what we want from him."

"We'll deal with the boy wonder later. Where is he, anyway?"

"Out in the hallway with his crew. I told him I needed to touch base with the team before we went to the ESH."

Garcia began to say something, stopped, and simply stared at Gemma, his expression calculating.

She could practically hear the wheels turning. "What?"

He paused for a few more seconds. "I want you to go with them."

"With Coulter and the A-Team?"

"Yes. We get reports about what it's like inside. We see footage. You talk to Rivas on the phone. But I think we need more here."

Gemma wondered what Garcia was driving at, considering the last time she'd proposed this exact concept to him, he'd barred her and then watched her hand in her shield and gun and walk away from the team . . . directly into the path of the hostage taker. "You want me to go meet with Rivas?" she asked cautiously.

"God, no. We're not doing that again."

That's more like it. "Then I'm not sure what you're proposing."

"I'm suggesting it would be a good idea for one of us to go over there and it makes sense it's you because you know Rivas best. Put you in an A-Team uniform with full body armor near the rear of the group with a good view. This may be one of the most important moments in this whole crisis. The door is going to be open so Rivas can talk to Coulter. Unless Coulter pulls something completely insane, he's safe because he's the conduit for Rivas's message. So Coulter's at the front. Cartwright will undoubtedly have him surrounded by his officers. Rivas will be totally focused on Coulter, so he likely won't really see the A-Team. We put you where you have a good view. We'll be watching through Cartwright's helmet cam, but you know how different being there in person can be."

Gemma could see exactly where Garcia was going now. "You lose a lot of nuance through remote negotiating."

"Exactly. And we need that nuance right now. We're three days in. The DOC is starting to apply pressure. The mayor is losing his patience. We need to figure out how to move this along. Are you willing to do it?"

"Of course."

"I'll go over with you, then, and explain what I need to Cartwright. Harder for him to say no directly to my face. Because you know he's going to say it. McFarland."

"Yes, sir?"

"I want you to stay here with Coulter until we signal we're ready. Then bring him over. Williams, take over the negotiator position in case Rivas calls before we set this up. Chen, if he calls, be both coach and scribe. Once I'm back, I'll fill the fourth chair while Capello is gone. McFarland, you go out now, move them away from the door and make them wait for a few minutes."

"Yes, sir." McFarland slipped out the door and they heard his bright "Mr. Coulter—" just before the door closed behind him.

When Gemma and Garcia left less than a minute later,

they spotted McFarland about twenty feet down the hall stalling Coulter who clearly felt he should be calling the shots.

They turned away from the reporter and his crew and strode up the hallway to prepare for the coming show-down.

CHAPTER 16

"Cartwright." Garcia called the lieutenant's name the moment they rounded the corner. "I need a moment."

Cartwright stepped away from his men as they stood in a group facing the steel entry door to the ESH. "Garcia."

"We're just about ready to bring in the reporter."

"Fantastic." Cartwright's sour tone echoed how they all felt about Coulter.

"Before we start, I want to make a change. I want Detective Capello to be there while Rivas reads the list of demands. But I don't want him to know that. I want her to borrow a uniform from one of your guys and hang near the rear of the group so she can observe."

Cartwright's expression closed in, his eyes behind his safety glasses going to slits and his lips folding into a flat line. "I don't need someone who's not part of the group in the mix during a high-stress moment. It's enough to have to deal with the reporter."

"You do remember I'm not a civilian?" As she met Cartwright's cold gaze, Gemma could feel the eyes of every A-Team officer fixed on her as she went toe-to-toe with their commander. "I'm also not a rookie. I'm a detective with fourteen years of service under my belt. And it's not like I haven't worked with the A-Team before. I'm familiar with your protocols."

"Being familiar with them doesn't mean you'll follow them like one of my guys."

Gemma was drawing in a breath to ask Cartwright if that was the issue—that she could never be one of his "guys"—when Garcia spoke up.

"You know she's a solid officer and won't be a detriment to you if things go to hell. She can follow orders as well as any of your '*guys.*'"

Garcia's stress on his final word told Gemma he was following her line of thinking. *Some dinosaurs will never think it's okay for women to be on the front lines.*

"I need her to be there for this," Garcia argued. "Remote interactions are always the safest for us, but we can lose a lot in translation. This is one of those times. I need one of my officers here, and this time I need it to be Capello. She knows Rivas better than any of my team. He's never seen her, so he wouldn't spot her even if she wasn't wearing the helmet and glasses."

"I don't have a spare uniform. That means I'd lose one of my men."

"This shouldn't be an offensive scenario, so that shouldn't be a problem. But this actually plays to your advantage."

Cartwright didn't say anything, but his skeptical expression questioned *Really? How?*

Garcia pointed toward the ESH security doors. "The guy in there running the show has connected to Capello. Whether it's her as an officer or because she's a woman and he finds her less threatening, I don't know. I just know it works. So if things go to hell, she might be able to talk Rivas down before anything happens that goes a step too far. She's an asset, not a liability."

The set of his jaw radiating his unwillingness, Cartwright turned to one of his men. "Hill, you're about the same size as Capello. She needs to borrow your gear."

"Yes, sir."

A man of medium build and only slightly taller than Gemma, Hill pulled off his sling, handed his rifle to the officer beside him, and stepped away from the group. He eyed Gemma dispassionately. "The pants aren't going to fit."

"I'm already wearing black. No one's going to be looking at my slacks and boots and noting they're not in true tactical style."

Stepping a few feet farther down the hallway, ensuring no one inside the facility could see her, she slipped out of her blazer and tossed it to Garcia. Hill stripped out of his body armor and then his black tactical shirt, leaving him in a black T-shirt. He handed her the shirt and she slipped into the warm fabric, layering it over her thin, body-hugging V-neck and quickly fastening it. Hill was about her height, but had considerably more girth, so she gamely tucked the shirt ends under her waistband and then accepted the body armor from him. Covered in pockets jammed with gear, the vest was heavy, hot, and stiff. But she'd worn body armor before and shrugged into it, settling it into place over her slightly smaller frame. She gathered her hair into a twist at her nape and tucked it under the helmet to simulate the short hair of the men Rivas would expect to fill the group, before she snapped and then snugged the strap tightly into place under her chin. And then, finally, the safety glasses.

Hill gave her a brief nod of approval. "I'll stay here out of sight so the inmates don't realize there's an extra man. But I'll be close by in case I'm needed."

"Noted. Thanks for the lend."

Gemma stepped into Hill's place in the men and accepted his rifle, slipping the sling on cross-body, the weight and shape of the M4 carbine familiar in her hands.

Garcia stepped back. "I'll leave you to it. Everyone be careful. You'd assume this will be a relatively safe situation because Rivas needs his demands met, but it's when you think everything is stable that it can all go to hell. McFarland is coming with Coulter and his crew in a few minutes. We'll watch the live feed via the helmet cam and will stay in touch via radio if needed." Turning, he strode down the hallways and disappeared around the corner.

Cartwright swung around to his men. "Johnson and Logan, you're with the reporter. You keep at least six feet of space between him and Rivas. If he tries to move forward, you pull him back."

Behind them, Coulter's voice carried down the hallway before he appeared in person. "Start filming now. We can edit part of this together at the station." Coulter strode around the corner, holding a wireless microphone in one fist, and tossed a look over his shoulder. "Don't miss the SWAT team."

Gemma could feel the men around her bristle at being considered little more than window dressing. The kind of window dressing that was here to make sure nothing happened to Coulter or his team.

Coulter strode toward them like he was leading an invading army, rather than two scruffy technicians in wrinkled casual wear. "I'm here. Let's get started."

Cartwright stepped into Coulter's path, making him draw up short. Out of the view of the camera's lens, Coulter shot a poisonous look at Cartwright.

Cartwright clearly couldn't care less. "First, some ground rules. I tell you where to stand. You don't move a fraction of an inch from that spot." Coulter opened his mouth to speak and Cartwright simply steamrolled over him. "You will not move. I don't care if the camera doesn't get your best side. You stay where I put you. And so will your men. They'll get the best shot they can from farther back."

"What's the point of my being here if me and my team can't capture the inmates' demands?"

"You and your team will capture it, but you'll need to stay alive to come out the other side. These inmates are armed, but only with weapons to be used in close quarters. You'll stay out of range."

"Even if they have weapons, they won't hurt me. They need me to broadcast their story."

"No, they need *them*." Cartwright pointed past Coulter to the cameraman and sound guy. "The inmates could kill you in cold blood for the whole world to see. As long as those guys did their job, there'd still be a story to tell."

The brutality of the statement finally penetrated Coulter's ego. His face washed several shades whiter in response as his jaw sagged, leaving him gaping like a fish out of water.

Cartwright cracked a smile. "I see you take my meaning. Good. Now, stand there." He pointed to a spot four feet away from the door. "Your crew will stand there." He pointed to another spot, easily fifteen feet away, across the corridor on a diagonal from the doorway.

"But that—"

Cartwright held up a hand. "Cold blood, remember?"

Coulter paused for a moment, thought better of arguing, and simply nodded.

"Good." He turned to his men. "Johnson and Logan, flanking positions. Capello in behind and slightly offside from Coulter. Sims and Peterson on either side of Capello, Mulgrew in the rear. I'll fall back to this side so the camera can capture everything. We have no idea if the inmates are going to use this opportunity to make a stand. Be ready." He waited as his men fell into position, Logan to Coulter's left and Johnson to his right.

Gemma moved to stand about two feet behind Coulter's right shoulder. Like the other A-Team officers, she held her carbine ready in case of attack.

Cartwright looked over his shoulder at the tech crew. "You boys ready?"

"We're good."

"Excellent. Let's go." Cartwright strode over to the door and pounded on it with his fist. "Rivas! Your media crew is here!" He stepped aside to stand to Logan's left and slightly behind.

Gemma eased slightly to her right to give her a straight line-of-sight through to the security door.

The space behind the door remained empty.

"Does he want his press conference or not?" Mulgrew muttered.

To her left, Sims shifted his weight impatiently from foot to foot, eager for the action to start. In front of him,

Logan held absolutely still, his eyes fixed unblinkingly on the door in front of him. To Logan's left, Cartwright was glaring through the strips of glass.

"Let's give him another thirty seconds," Cartwright said. "Garcia, stand by. We may need you to call to let them know we've arrived."

They stood in tense silence, ready and waiting. Just as Gemma was sure Cartwright was going to send more instructions to Garcia, Rivas appeared on the other side of the security door. Rivas leaned in close to the glass, studying the group on the other side, a satisfied smile curving his lips. He spoke briefly to someone out of sight to their left, and then faced them as the door slid open.

Rivas's gaze was fixed on Coulter, allowing Gemma the opportunity to study him freely. She'd seen his image on the live feed through Cartwright's camera, but somehow it hadn't been able to capture the man's vibrant energy.

He exuded both power and control. His time at Rikers hadn't beaten those characteristics out of him, and a few days back in the driver's seat had floated those traits to the top. She'd known he was big, but now she could see he was the kind of big that came from meticulously working his body to prime condition.

She couldn't blame him. He was trapped in a cell block with men who could be sworn enemies, with nothing but his fists and own force of will. He was the type of man who would never let himself be taken advantage of and would never allow himself to falter during a physical altercation. One moment of weakness could spell certain doom as someone lower on the chain attempted to use his downfall to springboard to the top.

"Mr. Rivas, thank you for thinking of me." Coulter was all smooth elegance and deference.

Gemma's hackles rose. *Leave it to Coulter to suck up to Rivas. Anything for a story.*

"Are we on?" Rivas shot a glance past the armed officers to the cameraman across the hallway.

"We're already recording, but I'd be happy to do an introduction."

"Sure. That'd be good." Rivas held out his left hand and someone out of sight handed him a pad of paper. He let his arm drop, holding the pad of paper against his thigh.

Coulter turned, bringing the microphone up to catch his every word as his face fell into serious lines, a dedicated professional at work. "This is Greg Coulter reporting for ABC7 from Rikers Island. I'm here at the Otis Bantum Correctional Center to meet with detainee Eduardo Rivas. Mr. Rivas is one of forty-two inmates who took control of this Enhanced Supervision Housing unit three days ago, but he has agreed to meet with me to discuss his list of demands. So far, efforts at negotiation between the inmates and the NYPD Hostage Negotiation Team have failed. Hopefully, I can help bridge the distance between the two sides in this standoff."

It took everything Gemma had to not move, to not make a sound, and most certainly not reveal her presence by objecting to Coulter's utterly disingenuous self-aggrandizing. He had no idea how the negotiation process was progressing or what went into a delicate negotiation like this. He just wanted to make himself look like the hero riding in on his white charger to save the day, even though it was likely none of this footage would ever be seen by the public. It was the tiny chance that he could use the footage later that inspired his bravado.

Brutto figlio di puttana bastardo.

Out of the corner of her eye, she caught the barest of movements from Logan, no more than a slight tilt of his head, accompanying a short flash of blue eyes as he glanced over his shoulder at her before his gaze shifted back to Rivas.

Logan knew the woman she'd been all those years ago and knew the nuances of a negotiation this complex. He knew exactly how infuriated she'd be. She could only imagine the swearing going on in the negotiating room where no one could hear them. She couldn't decide who'd be more furious, McFarland or Garcia.

No, it would definitely be Garcia.

"Mr. Rivas," Coulter continued, "I understand you have a list of demands you'd like to share. These are demands you need to see fulfilled for you to consider releasing the seven hostages you currently hold?"

She didn't dare speak because it would give away her presence, an ace-in-the-hole she needed to reserve in case this meet went sideways, but she dearly wanted to tell Coulter to stop offering negotiation tactics to Rivas. Granted, she suspected that Rivas was too smart to require strategy assistance from the likes of Greg Coulter, but still.

Coulter suddenly stiffened, his face freezing into a blank mask as he paused for several long seconds. Gemma's confusion lasted only long enough for her to notice the earpiece and coiled wire that ran over the curve of his ear to skim his neck and disappear under his collar. She was sure it hadn't been there before.

Which meant that McFarland had fitted him with a wire so the negotiation team could have some control of the situation. Garcia was likely reading him the riot act.

The fury faded slightly, dulled by the warm glow of satisfaction that her team—her pissed-off team—was checking Coulter.

Coulter turned on again like a toy soldier that had been wound up and set free to march down the hallway. He cleared his throat. "Would you share that list of demands with us, Mr. Rivas?"

"Yes." Rivas raised the list of demands, but he didn't look at it. "First of all, we want no retaliation against any inmates."

"Retaliation stemming from . . . ?" Coulter let the question hang, trying to draw out more information.

"Anything that happened from the riot to now."

"Like?"

"Anything."

Single-minded focus. Gemma noted how Rivas didn't take his eyes from Coulter. She might have thought a less secure inmate might have spared the armed officers opposite him a glance, but Rivas was laser focused on Coulter. *Didn't even look toward the cameraman.*

For Rivas, it was all about the one man he thought could help him.

Gemma relaxed slightly. Rivas wasn't going to be a threat, at least not right now. There was no aggression in his stance, or anger in his voice. She'd seen that side of him more than once, but that wasn't the face he showed Coulter or the world. Instead, he came across as reasonable. As the wronged party.

It was a performance, but an effective one.

It was also smart. Coulter was wheedling for information about what had happened over the past three days and Rivas wasn't about to provide details. Because to do so would showcase the violence of the riot and the beatings that followed. Would highlight the death.

"Two," Rivas continued. "We want an end to the brutality."

"Brutality?" Coulter leaned forward, radiating eagerness, reminding Gemma of the Romans enjoying the blood sport of the Colosseum. "Between the inmates or between the inmates and the correction officers?"

"Both. Correction officers can be brutal with no cause, and they encourage fighting between inmates. It needs to stop. They supposedly had training, and maybe it helped some, but the bad ones are still bad. We know they got body cameras, but they don't use 'em, so when we complain, there's no proof. Davis don't care, so they only get a slap on the wrist. We get stitches. Or worse.

"Three, we can't live like this no more. No air conditioning in the summer so the joint pushes a hundred degrees. Sewage backing up. Ceiling tiles growing mold, making us sick. We're not animals. Stop treating us like it."

"That sounds . . . inhumane," Coulter interjected. "Would you be able to show us these conditions? Show the world?"

"No." Cartwright cut off the request as soon as it was out of Coulter's mouth, and Gemma would have bet money one of the negotiators was conveying a similar message through Coulter's earpiece. It would simply be too dangerous to take Coulter and his crew into the ESH.

For the first time, Rivas seemed to notice the A-Team filling the hallway. His gaze shot first to Cartwright and then traveled over the whole group. Gemma didn't blink when his eyes tracked over her and then past. *Nothing to see here. Just another officer.*

Rivas turned his attention to Coulter and then, for the first time, he glanced at his piece of paper as if Cartwright's interjection had thrown him off stride. "Number four. Medical. We want actual medical care. Saying we're sick isn't an excuse to get out of the ESH. Most times the docs don't believe us so we get zero treatment. That ain't right. 'Specially when this place makes us sick. It shouldn't be the only time we get minimal care is when a CO messes us up."

Interesting. The only way to get medical care currently is to bring in someone. Going to be hard to hide bodies if there are any, so that's probably a good sign.

Coulter looked concerned but remained silent.

"Five. Fair pay for work. Ten cents an hour ain't fair. We're not allowed to work, but some of us came from other units and we'll go back there. We're not slaves, but we're paid like 'em. That's for all of us." Rivas looked directly at the camera as if speaking personally to the DOC commissioner. "All of Rikers." He turned to Coulter. "You can talk to other guys in here or guys on the outside. They'll tell you."

"I'll do that."

"Six. Searches."

"Searches?"

"Yeah. They do searches. Shakedowns. They say they need to make sure we're not hiding illegals. But they do it at three in the morning, scaring the shit out of us, pounding on the cell door and screaming at us. They make us strip naked and then five or six of them search our cells."

"And you feel that impinges on your rights?" Coulter

was trying to lead Rivas into what he must have seen as a juicier story.

Like all this isn't bad enough.

"We ain't got rights. No one in here has rights. They try to terrify us. They laugh while they do the searches. It's a fucking power trip."

"You'd like the searches to stop?"

The look Rivas threw at Coulter conveyed how little he thought Coulter knew about his world. "That ain't gonna happen. But only do them during the day. And not to just terrify and torture the inmates for kicks. Seven, food. It's inedible. It makes us sick too. We need better. Better tasting, more nutritious."

Gemma couldn't help but agree with Rivas. She'd tried the food. To call it swill was putting it nicely.

"Eight," Rivas continued. "We want better education programs. We keep hearing 'bout how they want us to leave the Rock and go find jobs, but no one wants to hire an ex-con with no skills. We want skills."

Rivas's list continued. Grievance procedures. Communication with staff and the administration. Telephone time. Mail and package deliveries. Commissary pricing and stock.

As Rivas talked, Gemma kept her attention on his words but took several seconds in rounds to quickly scan the facility behind him. She took in the inmates behind Rivas, grouped together in clumps around the ESH—battle lines drawn?—with a few standing on their own, scattered through the space, watching the other inmates as much as watching Rivas, as if afraid to take their eyes off them for too long. The quick glance she got at faces covered a range of emotions—fury, fear, triumph, dread. Around them, the ESH was a whirlwind of clothes, paper, furniture, and garbage, exactly as it had been through Cartwright's body cam.

Rivas came to his final point. "If we end this peaceful-like, we want cameras here when we open the door. We don't want no Attica."

Attica. The prison uprising held up to negotiators as the perfect example of how not to manage an incarceration crisis. The uprising that culminated in the New York State Police sending hundreds of armed troopers into the facility to tear-gas the inmates and then spend a full two minutes firing into the smoke. In the end, thirty-three inmates and ten correction officer hostages died in the invasion.

Attica was known to prisoner and negotiator alike. If this situation fell apart like that, it would mean countless lives lost, inmate and hostage alike.

A shiver ran down Gemma's spine. She simply wouldn't allow it to happen.

There had to be a better way.

She just needed to figure out what it was.

CHAPTER 17

"*G*arcia is meeting with them again now." Gemma entered the negotiation room with McFarland right behind her. "After we delivered the list of demands yesterday, the DOC met with city administration. Garcia took the list over himself to get them talking and was going to come back, but things didn't go well so he stayed. From how he described it, it was like watching two bull moose fight."

"Meaning two obstinate males butting heads over and over again and no one making any headway?" Shelby quipped, one eyebrow arched.

"I think I should be offended by that remark, except, in this case, I agree with it," McFarland said.

Taylor stood from his chair and stretched. "Especially with that group." He sent a pointed glance at McFarland. "And especially if Rowland is involved."

"No kidding." McFarland sidestepped around Corbitt as he rose and pulled his coat off his chair. "Rowland can be a hothead. The people love it, think he's a passionate fighter, but then you actually have to work with him, and you realize a lot of that passion is simply bullheadedness." He sat down in the chair and then looked up, grinning. "Hey, there's one of your two bull mooses."

"The plural of moose is moose, you cretin." Shelby rolled her eyes in Gemma's direction.

Gemma grinned back at her. "You're lucky you didn't get 'meese.' Either way, I don't have a good feeling about how the DOC is going to respond to the inmates. Garcia certainly didn't think he'd have to stay with them to mediate the discussion because they couldn't agree with each other. Hopefully he'll have more luck today because the clock is ticking." She sat down in Taylor's vacated chair. "So, where are we this morning?"

Taylor straightened and snugged his tie. "Rivas has been talking to us since last night."

"He finally picked up the phone when you called?"

"Not at all. He called us."

Gemma froze in the process of laying out the cord for her headset. "Really? Is that the first time he's voluntarily reached out to you?"

"Yes."

"And then he kept contacting you?"

"He is, apparently, quite invested in his demands."

"He should be, if he's smart," Williams said as he stepped in. "Even if for nothing other than his first demand of immunity for all of them. Their first act of disobedience may have been an impulse, but someone died and that's going to bring down the hammer."

"Rivas's original attack was anything but impulsive," Taylor said. "He brought in a weapon and attacked Burk with full intent."

"But because he's officially a detainee waiting for his day in court, he's not assured a life sentence yet. Did you note his wording on that first demand? He wants immunity for everyone from the start of the riot. That would include his initial assault on Burk."

"That would also explain why he's so eager to get an answer," Gemma said. "Did he call in this morning?"

"Last night," Taylor said. "He wasn't expecting a resolution, but hoped we'd have an update on discussions. I told him I'd find out, but I couldn't get a hold of anyone last night. I didn't know Garcia would be stuck in the middle of the discussion or I would have gone to him. I called Rivas last night and let him know we'd have more information to share with him today. He called again just past seven-thirty, hoping again for an update."

"Which you didn't have," Williams stated. "They probably aren't meeting until . . ." His gaze tracked to the clock. "Now at the earliest. If Garcia's smart, he'll start them at nine so they've had more time to get organized and he'll have coffee waiting for them. I think they better have some comments for them today though, even if it's not a finished draft of their counterproposal."

"I agree. Or things will get dicey." Gemma pulled her phone out of her blazer pocket and sent a text to Garcia. "I'll see if he can nail down a time for initial comments."

"Good idea," said Taylor.

"Anything else we need to know?" Gemma turned in her seat to check out the information on the far wall. Someone had changed out the piece of paper under the clock with a new one that read DAY 4, but otherwise the information appeared to be identical to what had been there when she left last night.

"Call times and details are in the briefing book," Graham said. "I made sure it was captured. Not much on the surface, but I second what Taylor said about him being invested in the demands. We haven't talked to him much, but it was all in his tone and cadence."

"It was Rivas? No one else is speaking for the group?"

"Just him."

"So he's still holding on to control in there."

"You think that will be an issue?" Shelby asked.

"It's day four. Either every guy in there is one hundred percent behind him, or cracks are starting to form."

"You think it's going to fall apart because of the gang component?" McFarland asked.

"Exactly because of that. Maybe I've heard Joe talk about too many cases, but gang members are devoted to their gangs and their leader. And while Burk may have only been a lieutenant out on the street, he was a captain here in the ESH until Rivas took control after trying to kill him. And bad blood between the two gangs means they'll only hold hands and sing 'Kumbaya' for so long against a common enemy before the tensions between them rise to the surface. Really, we have no idea what the dynamics are in there. Rivas tried to kill Burk once. He's still got the switchblade. Has he tried again? We don't know. He's certainly not going to tell us."

"Or has Burk or his guys gone after Rivas?" McFarland wondered. "After an attack like that, in the gang world, there would be retribution. If it hasn't happened, it's only because both leaders are surrounded by their guys making a sneak attack impossible."

"So far, as far as we know. But given time, one of them may break through."

"We may not have to worry about the list of demands if that happens," Williams said. "There may not be much left of them."

"This is part of the problem with only talking to Rivas. We're only getting from him what he wants us to know, and that's absolutely not an honest interpretation of what's going on. Well, let's call him. We know he's up. And they'll likely want food by now."

"I didn't offer any last night," Taylor said. "I thought it would be better to stretch them to this morning. Make them hungry in more ways than one."

"Excellent plan."

The day team gave the night crew time to gather their things and go, and then settled in for their workday.

Gemma reached Rivas easily, which made her think that he was nearby waiting for their shift change. "Good morning."

"Yeah." It was the same monosyllabic greeting, but Rivas's tone sounded a touch more upbeat.

"First of all, I wanted to give you an update. The DOC is continuing to meet with members of our negotiating team and city administration as they discuss your list of demands. They'll update us as soon as they can. Did Detective Taylor tell you what to expect at that time?"

"'Bout their answer? He said they'll have their own ideas. Is that gonna be soon?"

Gemma could hear his anticipation in both the cadence and speed of his speech. "They're working it. That's all I can tell you at this point. And coming back with their own ideas is quite likely. You've taken the first step, but they won't be able to give you carte blanche on each of your points. Normal procedure at this point is a counter-offer. A revised list, essentially, dealing with each of your demands separately, either agreeing with it, proposing an alternate arrangement, or turning down the demand."

"They could say no to the whole deal?" Caution now slowed his words.

"That's not going to happen. The DOC and the city will want this resolved as quickly as possible. Turning down the entire list of demands isn't the way to do that. Now, while they're discussing, how about some food? Interested?"

"Yeah."

"I thought you might be, seeing as nothing's gone in since yesterday morning. I'm happy to do that. However, as always, I'll need something in return."

"What you want?"

"I want to bring in medical. I want the hostages checked out and I'd be happy to treat any inmate who needs it as well."

"No." The word was swift and final.

"I guess you're not as hungry as I thought." Gemma kept her voice light. "I'll get in touch then when I hear from the DOC." Without allowing time for a response, Gemma cut the connection.

McFarland sat back in his chair and studied her. "That's an interesting tactic. We've been here ten minutes and you're already tired of dealing with him?"

"Not at all. He got what he wanted yesterday; I'm just making it clear I'm not going to waste time trying to convince him to take what we're offering."

"I like it," Chen said, nodding in approval. "They got breakfast yesterday, but nothing since and they must be starving by now. So instead of you applying pressure, you're going to let his own guys do it."

"I don't want him to feel we're at his beck and call. He's in control in there, but I want to take some of his control over the whole situation out of his hands. I want to leave him feeling a little less arrogant and a little more like he needs to depend on us."

"What made you think you needed to change tactics?" Williams asked.

"The fact that Rivas is now calling in. At first, he wouldn't pick up the phone, then he'd only talk if we contacted him. Now he's contacting us when he wants something. I'm leaving the ball in his court. I bet he'll get off the phone and someone will immediately ask him when breakfast is going to arrive, and he'll have to say it's not coming."

McFarland double-tapped his temple. "Smart."

Gemma pushed her empty coffee cup toward him. "Reward the smartness."

"When are my cookies coming?" He hefted his thermos off the floor, groaning dramatically.

"Yeah, yeah, I get the hint. You're waking at the crack of dawn to brew four pots of coffee for us, so the least I can do is bake until midnight as a thank-you."

McFarland unscrewed the lid and poured Gemma a generous cup. He motioned to Chen and Williams to pass their cups across as well.

Chen leaned toward Williams. "I like this. He brews, she bakes, we score." His stage whisper was clearly audible across the table.

"Hey," McFarland protested. "Maybe you should be responsible for lu—"

The phone rang and all banter instantly ceased as they snapped back into work mode.

Gemma waited until they were ready and Chen had his pen poised over his pad of paper, then she picked up. "Good morning."

"Fine." The single word was flat with a heavy helping of resentment.

Gemma couldn't help the smile but worked hard to keep it out of her voice. "You'll accept breakfast in exchange for a visit from the med team?"

"Yeah. On two conditions."

"You don't get to set the conditions, Mr. Rivas. That's my job."

"I'm setting them this time. First condition, no team. One doc only. Second condition, I know the docs here. They're not going to do jack shit for us."

"I assure you, this one will."

"Yeah, he will. Because you're going to bring him."

Gemma stiffened in her chair, her gaze shooting across the table at Williams, who was already shaking his head.

The golden rule in hostage negotiation was to avoid face-to-face negotiations at all costs. The only hostage negotiators killed on the job had died meeting with hostage takers in person. It was why 99 percent of hostage negotiation was done via remote communication, usually by phone or bullhorn.

Gemma had defied Garcia's direct order during the City Hall crisis. She'd felt there was zero chance the hostages would survive otherwise when the suspect had offered to release all the hostages in exchange for her. Garcia had ordered her to stand down, but she'd laid down her gun and shield and walked into City Hall with only her wits to protect her. He'd later backtracked on his decision and returned her gun and shield, and the entire incident was largely unknown except to her family, Garcia, Taylor, McFarland, Logan, and Lieutenant Sanders, the A-Team commander that day.

Gemma turned her head to meet McFarland's eyes. His head tilt paired with a flat stare told her he was thinking the same thing she was: Garcia had to approve this or it couldn't happen.

Don't do it again. There won't be any second chances.

Her father's words after he'd reinstated her rang in her head. She had to play this one by the book. "That's not how we negotiate. What you and I are doing, *this* is how we negotiate."

"If you send in a doc, he won't help us. None of them ever help us. They might even try to screw us over. But they won't if you're there."

"You know I can't send a doctor in there on his own. The A-Team will have to accompany them."

"I figured that. That makes it worse. Look, you wanna help the hostages. We need food. I'm tryin' to meet you in the middle."

"This isn't my call to make. Negotiating is one thing. Putting myself in there with you is something else."

"Scared?"

The sneer in his tone didn't touch her. "Not at all. But out here in the real world where we respect the hierarchy, sometimes it means we need to consult with our superiors. I can't agree to this without running it by my lieutenant. If he says yes, I'll be there."

"Ball's in your court." Rivas hung up.

Gemma dragged off her headset and met McFarland's eyes. "Well, *that's* unexpected."

"I'll say. Garcia is going to be *pissed*."

"I imagine so. But we need to run it by him."

Williams fixed her with a curious stare. "He let you go in the last time. This time will be even safer because you'll have Cartwright and his men. He allowed it before, so there's no reason why he wouldn't now."

Gemma didn't miss a beat. "Every situation is different. And if the DOC and Rowland are giving him a hard time, he may be less willing." She pulled out her cell phone, dialed Garcia's number, and put her phone on speaker so the entire team was part of the discussion.

"A little busy here, Capello." Garcia sounded harried. "Is it an emergency?"

"Yes."

"Give me a minute." His voice went muffled as he excused himself. There was a long pause and then his voice returned, full strength. "What's going on?"

"Sir, you're on speaker and the team is here with me. Rivas has made us an offer."

"I don't like the sound of that, especially if you need to clear it with me before proceeding."

"I got him to agree to exchanging food for a visit by a doctor accompanied by the A-Team to check out the hostages."

"What's the catch?"

"Remember the list of demands you're mediating? They don't trust the docs here. They say they won't be treated fairly. They want me to go in with them."

There were several seconds of silence which Gemma assumed was Garcia slowly counting to ten . . . and not making it all the way. "Whose idea was this?"

"His."

"And you'd be willing to do it?"

"Yes. Cartwright and his team will be right there. I'd

be surrounded at all times, as would the doctor. Nothing would happen. But I need your approval on this."

More silence. Then, "Williams, you're our most experienced officer. What's your read?"

"He reads as genuine. The anger in his voice sounds rooted in honest-to-God neglect. I don't think he's putting on a show or trying to trap Capello in the ESH. The A-Team would never let it happen anyway. He honestly thinks the medicals won't treat them."

"Chen?"

"I agree," the younger man said. "I don't think it's a trap. Yes, they have weapons, but they're homemade close-quarter weapons, and Capello doesn't need to get within ten feet of anyone."

"McFarland?" Garcia drew the word out.

He's really asking for McFarland's opinion in light of Boyle.

"Let her go, sir. Cartwright won't let anything happen to her." McFarland met Gemma's gaze. "And we know she can handle herself even if everything goes to hell. Which it won't."

The background noise filtering through the phone told Gemma Garcia was pacing, as he so often did when weighing a decision. "Okay, you have my approval. I want you and the doc to get body armor from the A-Team. If anything looks off—*anything at all*—you pull back."

"Yes, sir." The knot in Gemma's gut loosened slightly.

"Williams, you're going to be monitoring Cartwright's helmet cam. I want to be kept in the loop by text. When they go in. How it's going. When they come out. If it goes to hell, you call me directly."

"Yes, sir."

"Good luck." And Garcia was gone.

Gemma tucked her phone in her pocket. "I honestly didn't think he'd go for it."

"Ditto," McFarland agreed. "And now you may have the tougher lieutenant to convince. Cartwright is *not* going to be happy."

"Davis won't be either," Williams said. "You're taking in one of his medical staff."

Gemma pushed back her chair. "Let's divide and conquer. McFarland and Chen, go find Davis and tell him to find a doctor from one of the other jails who'd be willing to go in to treat anyone in the ESH who needs it. Make sure the doctor knows to bring anything needed to treat any variety of unknown injuries. Williams, you stay with me. We'll get Cartwright in here and talk him through it."

"And if he objects?"

"We'll just have to convince him. This isn't about him or us or Rivas. This is about the hostages. They need us, and we're not going to fail them now."

CHAPTER 18

*C*artwright, Logan, and Johnson turned to look at Gemma when she stepped out of the negotiation room.

"Are we ready?" Gemma asked.

"Waiting on the doc," Cartwright said. He pushed aside his cuff to check the time. "He's late. I'm going to check and see what's going on." Without a backward glance, he clamped one hand over the butt of his carbine to hold it steady against his chest and strode down the hallway in the direction of Davis's office.

Gemma stared off down the corridor after Cartwright, keeping her eyes fixed on the end of the hallway even after he disappeared through Davis's doorway. She could feel Logan's eyes on her but refused to meet them. Shifting her gaze to Johnson, she found him glancing quizzically from Logan to herself and then back again.

Awkward, party of three.

She swallowed the sigh of frustration that threatened to break free. *Why did it have to be Logan on this incident?* Especially while her irritation with him was still so fresh. A year from now, maybe she could look at him without feeling resentful for the meaningless loss of life.

When the silence hung heavily for a full ten seconds, Johnson attempted to bridge it. "So . . . how's it going in there? He seemed surprisingly calm when he talked to Coulter."

"That's because he's showing his best face to the world. That's not the guy I'm talking to. That guy is a lot more argumentative and a lot less stable."

"You've probably handled worse though," Logan said.

Gemma didn't look at him, just away from Johnson and down the hallway.

Out of the corner of her eye, Gemma saw Johnson draw breath as if to say something then stop.

Cartwright needs to get back here.

From behind her, Logan gave a low curse and moved in close to clasp her arm. Before she could react, he pulled her with him across the hall and into the conference room.

"Hey!" Stumbling and off balance, Gemma couldn't get her feet under her until he stopped in the quiet of the dimly lit room. The lights were off and only daylight filtering through the dingy window glass brightened the space. She yanked her arm out of Logan's grasp and took a step away. "What are you doing?"

"Making you talk to me. Something you won't do on your own. I know you're angry. Let's have this out so we can start working together."

"We *are* working together."

His laugh carried a harsh edge. "Hardly. We've been

'working'"—he put the word in air quotes—"together for days and I don't think you've looked at me more than once."

Even knowing he was goading her, she turned to face him. "Better?"

"Yes." He unsnapped his chin strap, pulled his helmet off to reveal his short-cut blond hair, and tossed his helmet and safety glasses onto the nearest chair. "This has been coming for a while. So clear the air. Get it all out."

"That seems . . . unprofessional."

"What's unprofessional is the wall you've put between us."

"There's no wall between us." She looked at him through lowered lashes as if he was beneath her notice. "There's nothing between us."

"Wrong, and you know it. If there was nothing between us, you wouldn't be angry. This is all about Boyle. You know I was following orders. You heard Sanders give them. But it's still eating at you. Why?"

Fury licked through Gemma as she half turned away from him, averting her face so he couldn't read the expression she knew said more than she wanted to reveal. Even though part of her recognized some of that rage was from her frustration at the current situation, she couldn't push it back down and tuck it out of sight. She walked away several paces, her hands curled into fists, trying to fight the rising tide.

Crouching in the cemetery behind a headstone as her brother ghosted behind another grave marker. Closing in on their target in a desperate bid to save his life. Knowing instinctively he wouldn't go quietly, that he'd rather die than go to prison. Trying to connect with Logan, stories overhead, a rifle in his hands and his sights locked on a retired cop. Banking on their shared past, their shared connection, as she implored him to listen to her. Pleaded with him to save a life. The shock of hearing the shot echo through the August night.

She spun to face him as the tide overflowed. "You didn't need to kill him. We had him contained. I *begged* you to save his life. You totally discounted my read on the situation. Me, the one person who'd been with him for hours and had gotten to know him. You disregarded that knowledge."

Color suffused Logan's face as he stepped toward the force of her anger. "So I was supposed to just sit back and hope you were right when your brother's life was on the line? When Boyle jumped off that tomb, he locked his weapon on Alex." He kept his voice low so they couldn't be heard in the corridor, but temper snapped in his eyes. "Did you think after everything you'd been through that day, after everything you'd been through as a child, that I'd risk Alex's life, especially while you stood *right there?*"

Gemma froze, stunned into silence by the words he didn't say, yet she heard loud and clear.

From feet away, you watched your own mother be shot to death by a bank robber while he held you hostage. You barely survived that experience. Boyle would have killed your brother right in front of you in exactly the same way. Would you have survived it a second time?

It never occurred to her that his ulterior motive had centered around anything other than the suspect and the scenario. Eyes wide, she could only stare at him, her snappy retort drying to ash in her mouth.

"Yes, I had my orders," Logan continued, his eyes locked

on hers and his words terse. "But Sanders told me it was my call to make. I made it."

She struggled to reorganize her ordered image of the scene, now confounded by this new reality. "You made it to protect me?"

"To protect Alex."

"But for me."

"Well . . . yeah." Logan's temper ebbed and his tone was quieter. "Boyle killed Willan. Then he shot Coulter. He was clearly willing to take any life that stood in his way."

"But Sanders and his men had him surrounded. He knew he'd lost and there were only two choices. He didn't want to go to prison for the rest of his life, which left only one choice. I knew that."

"It wasn't a chance I was willing to take. You'd gone through enough."

In the months since the City Hall standoff, while her anger at Logan had festered, she'd never once considered that his decision to kill Boyle as he launched himself at Alex had been anything other than an officer following an order from his superior. Even though she was angry he'd ignored her personal plea—*Sean, don't do this*—the cop in her had always recognized he'd done what his commanding officer had asked of him. The idea that Logan had killed Boyle not only to save Alex's life, but to spare her the grief of not only losing her brother, but witnessing his murder, had simply not occurred to her.

It was a stunning realization. She knew from experience how an officer was forever marked from a death at his or her hands. Even from a sniper's distance, there was still an emotional toll when a life was taken. It was a permanent scar on the soul. That Logan had willingly and voluntarily accepted that scar for her sake took her breath away.

"I don't . . . I don't know what to say." Her voice was only a thin whisper.

"You don't have to say anything. Just keep in mind next time that a person's motives may not always be as clear as you assume." He turned toward the doorway, toward their next task. Away from her.

"Wait." Struck by the weight of regret in his eyes, she reached out to stop him, closing her hand over his where it gripped the butt of his rifle. His hand was warm, the skin where her fingers wrapped around his was rough with calluses from hours spent target shooting. "I'm still sorry Boyle died. To this day, I still don't think he would have killed Alex. We'll never know if I was right or not. But if I wasn't, the price of my arrogance would have been too high. I love my brother. If he'd died because he came when I asked, I'd never have been able to live with myself." She unblinkingly held his gaze for several seconds. "You knew that, didn't you?"

A half smile tugged one corner of his lips. "The woman I knew years ago wouldn't have been able to live with it. That kind of character doesn't change. It's chiseled in. So yeah . . . I knew."

So many assumptions and so much anger directed at him. Yet the representation of him she'd held in her head was entirely wrong. The hot burn of guilt flickered in her chest, and while she wasn't sure a few words would be able to balance the scales, she owed him at least that. "Thank you. For making sure I didn't have to weather that grief." She gripped his hand tighter. "And for my brother."

For a moment they simply held gazes, the unspoken connection from years before still humming between them.

Movement in the corridor pulled away Gemma's attention. "We'd better get back before Cartwright starts bellowing." She dropped her hand from his.

Turning, he grabbed his glasses and helmet, putting them on and sliding back behind the shield of his professional persona. He held out a hand toward the door. "After you."

Gemma stepped into the corridor to find Cartwright striding toward them, a man in scrubs and a white coat scurrying to keep up.

Even with the pressure of the medical visit looming ahead of her, her spirit felt lighter than it had in months.

CHAPTER 19

*C*artwright looked over his shoulder at Gemma. "Ready?"

"Ready."

"Dr. Peltier?"

"Um . . ." The young man's gaze skittered from Cartwright to Johnson to Gemma. "As I'll ever be?"

They stood gathered in front of the ESH door. Cartwright had called in a unit of the Rikers ERSU to take the place of his own men while he took them into the ESH. The ERSU officers stood ready just out of sight of the doorway at Cartwright's order, who was mindful of the Ninja Turtles drawing the ire of the men inside. The A-Team stood as a cluster around Gemma and Peltier. Both wore the same heavily armored vest as the officers around them. The A-Team had brought extra gear and uniforms in case they were needed, but this time Gemma wore the armor over her own clothes as she was going in with the inmates' full knowledge. Cartwright suggested she carry a weapon, but she'd turned him down.

She needed to be the mediator, the peacekeeper. The body armor already implied that she considered them to be a threat—she'd passed on the offer of a helmet simply for optics—but she needed to not be lumped in with the offensive team. The inmates had to see her as standing in between the A-Team and themselves. They knew she couldn't be entirely neutral, but if she walked in with a rifle, it would claw back every bit of progress she'd made with them.

She would have to depend on the A-Team officers for protection if something went sideways.

So would Dr. Peltier, who was clearly terrified to go in by the slight twitch in his left eye, but was doing his best to hide it. Relatively new to Rikers, and currently stationed at the nearby Anna M. Kross Center, he was selected because he'd never treated anyone from OBCC and could be considered a blank slate with inmates who had strong feelings about their mistreatment by the medical staff. Gemma had to give him credit—as scared as he was, he wasn't running. He might have a white-knuckled death hold on his duffel bag of supplies and be breathing rapidly as he bounced his weight from foot to foot, but he was there. More than that, he was willing to step into the ESH.

What was it FDR said? That courage is not the absence of fear, but rather the assessment that something else is more important than fear. That's Dr. Peltier.

"Let's get on with it then." Cartwright turned to the ERSU commander. "Open the door at my command, but then close it behind us. Keep watch and be ready to open it again at the first sign we need to pull back." He tapped the small oval with a dangling fob attached to his vest. "We each have a personal alarm. If any of us gets into trouble, we'll pull the rip cord and you won't be able to miss the alarm even through the door. It's like standing beside an ambulance with full sirens on. If you hear that, open the door immediately and be ready to infiltrate. But listen for a command from me, Detective Logan, or Detective Capello, in case I'm unable to give it. I don't want you coming into the facility except as a last resort, but we may need the door open as we pull out."

The commander of the ERSU was a big man, his broad frame made bulkier by his body armor, and tall enough that even Cartwright had to look up at him. "We'll be ready."

Cartwright turned to his men. "Form ranks around Detective Capello and Dr. Peltier and be—"

"No." Gemma cut Cartwright off. "I need to go in first."

"That sounds like a great way to get yourself killed."

"I didn't say I need to go in thirty feet in front. I just need to go in first. They need to see that I don't think they're a threat to me."

Cartwright's laugh was harsh. "Do I need to remind you about Evans's condition?"

"I remember just fine, thanks. But if I go in surrounded by you, the trust I've built with Rivas is going to chip away. I need to be able to show him I'm not scared of him and I don't think he and his men are such a threat, so much so that I'm willing to go in unprotected. I *know* they're a threat. But I'll make them an even bigger one if I piss them off the second I walk through the door."

"It's a risk."

"It's an acceptable risk. You'll be right there."

"Sir," Logan interjected. "We'll be able to see through the open doorway how far away they are. If it's optics we're going for here, we can make it look like Detective Capello is on her own but be ready to close in in seconds. If they're too close to begin with, she can ask them for more space."

"I'll also remind them that the food they want so badly won't be provided unless this is a successful medical visit. Coleman will be coming in about thirty minutes and the food won't be going in until we're out. We have leverage here." Gemma rapped her knuckles on the bulky vest. "And I'm not going in without protection. Not to mention, I'm damned good at hand-to-hand. And I have all of you. So let me go first, then you come through with Dr. Peltier."

Cartwright faced his team. "Sims, Mulgrew, and Johnson, you stay with Dr. Peltier. He's going to need to pay attention to his patients, so you'll pay attention to everything else for him. Unless it all goes to hell, then you stick with him like glue. Logan, Hill, and Peterson, you watch the inmates and you watch Capello. Stay close, but not so close you're hanging over her. Form up!"

The men fell into position in a rough circle around Peltier. Cartwright was positioned directly behind Gemma with Logan to her left and Peterson to her right. They held their rifles at the ready and Gemma could only hope the officers were being overly cautious and firepower wouldn't be needed.

It would all go to hell if it was.

Gemma studied the cell block through the strip of glass at eye level in the door. Beyond, the ESH stretched out before her. The cell block still looked like the riot had taken place only the hour before, from the clothing and garbage strewn over every flat surface to the noose still hanging from the second-floor railing. The front section of the facility was deserted. However, there were several men lounging on the steps leading to the mezzanine and another leaning on the center railing that bisected the half flight of stairs. Rivas was nowhere in sight. But there was room to get in and announce themselves.

"Open the door please," she called to the ERSU commander.

"Yes, ma'am."

With a metallic scrape the door slid open and as soon as she cleared it, Gemma stepped through to the other side. She sensed more than saw the A-Team officers move through behind her, maintaining a set distance between them.

The smell hit her first and she had to force down the urge to gag—a murky combination of stale sweat, human waste, rotten food, and vomit. She knew for a fact that the airflow hadn't been turned off for exactly the reasons they'd given Rowland—because it would put the hostages at risk. But this was simply the sheer scope of odor and of men leaving their mark in rage and frustration for someone else to clean up.

Gemma worked to keep her face in neutral lines and concentrated on breathing through her mouth.

She scanned the men on the stairs, each of whom had shot to their feet. "Gemma Capello, NYPD. We're here to do a medical visit with the hostages and anyone else who requires attention."

"We don't want no cops in here." A tall, lanky man swaggered down the steps, his dark eye fixed on Gemma, his hands balling into fists as he headed right for her.

Drunk on freedom and a sense of power. Enough to confront six armed men.

To her right, Peterson stepped sideways, clearing his way for an unobstructed shot if the inmate kept coming.

"Moreno. Back off."

Gemma looked left at the familiar voice, and a second later, Rivas rounded the corner of the mezzanine and into view.

"We don't need their kind here." Moreno had stopped, but he leaned forward like a runner ready to burst from the starting blocks.

"They have my permission. They come in, we get food." Planting a hand on the other man's chest, Rivas shoved him hard enough to stumble back toward the stairs, his comrades laughing at his clumsiness, earning a black glare. "We let them come in, do what they need to do, and go. Then we eat."

Moreno mumbled something vicious under his breath but marched up the stairs to reclaim his place in the group.

Rivas watched him silently for a moment, then turned to Gemma.

"Mr. Rivas. Thank you for allowing us access to the hostages."

Catcalls and whooping came from the group. "Show the lady who's boss!"

Gemma kept her eyes firmly on Rivas's. "As I said, we're happy to look at any of the inmates as well as the hostages."

"We good."

I highly doubt that. But if you tuned someone up, you might prefer they continue to suffer. Someone like Burk.

"Think about it. The offer remains open. I have Dr. Peltier with me. Can you take us to the hostages, please?"

Rivas glanced from Gemma to the man surrounded by a phalanx of officers. "Don't know that doc."

"I know you've had trouble with the OBCC docs, so I brought in someone new." She turned around to look past Cartwright to Peltier, who gave a nervous smile and held up one hand in greeting.

Rivas nailed the doctor with a steady, cold stare. Peltier's smile wobbled, then disintegrated as his hand fell back to his side.

"The hostages, Mr. Rivas?" The cold stare slid sideways to her and she felt the stab of it as if he'd physically touched her. *Never forget he's dangerous. He's making nice to get something from you, but he'd cheerfully kill you if it suited his purpose.*

"Follow me."

He skirted one of the toppled tables and led the way toward the cells lining the right-hand side of the facility. Gemma followed behind, giving him sufficient space to ensure she'd have at least a second of warning if he turned around and went for her. The long corridor stretched ahead of them, a chute of concrete blocks split by pairs of blue doors, the railing of the mezzanine rising above the half wall on their left. Garbage and dark, odorous puddles lined the floor. The A-Team fell into paired ranks behind her, the space just wide enough for two men in body armor; if any action was needed, the men would have to break into a staggered single file.

Gemma threw a quick glance over her shoulder, long enough to catch Cartwright's stony, lock-jawed expression, his gaze constantly on the move, watching for any oncoming threat. It was confirmation of what she already knew—Cartwright wouldn't like this position. They were simply too enclosed, even with the men likely spacing out in pairs behind her and around Dr. Peltier. They were penned in by concrete—from the floor to the walls to the ceiling riding directly overhead—and only the upper portion of the left wall opening into the mezzanine gave them an escape route. But that same gap could also be used for an incoming attack.

Gemma let the A-Team watch for oncoming threats and turned her attention to the men and the facility. She was getting used to the stench, even though it lay so heavily in the air, it pooled as a sour taste in her mouth she couldn't swallow away. Blocking it out so it didn't distract her, she concentrated on every other aspect around her: The shouts of men in the background overriding the echoes of their footfalls. The corridor, scattered with refuse and stained, tattered bedding, the floor scuffed and worn. Her first glimpse inside a jail cell, no longer the spare, freshly painted compartment in the pictures Davis had provided, but a bleak cage with a grimy window, a rusted, flickering fluorescent fixture overhead, a patched concrete floor, and a sagging sink and toilet, as if someone had tried to rip them from the wall.

She'd known the stories were true, but now she could see in full color how Rivas's demands were based in mistreatment here.

Imagine spending up to seventeen isolated hours a day closed into that cramped, dirty, rotting piece of hell. Imagine being in there twenty-four hours a day whenever there's a lockdown. It would be enough to drive you mad . . .

She took a deep breath to force down the rage simmering just below the surface and turned her attention forward.

"Hey, *chica,* how about you forget about the fucking COs and come deal with me?"

The catcall drew her gaze through the horizontal bars of the railing and into the mezzanine, though she was careful to only track the caller with her eyes so he wouldn't be able to tell from so far away that he had her attention. Three men sat on the top of several tables in the open space, leering at her, and one of them grabbed his crotch. A series of snappy responses rose to her lips, but she swallowed them all. Now was not the time. But if he came at her, she'd be happy to put him in his place—flat on the floor, gasping for breath as she walked away from him.

Rivas slowed, drawing her attention when he stopped in front of the closed door of cell 20. "Some of them are here." He pointed across the mezzanine. "The rest are over there."

"Where is Officer Keen?"

"Here."

"Open the door please."

"Open twenty!" Rivas called toward the control room.

There was a pause, then metal ground against metal as the door slid open. She half turned to the men behind her. "Dr. Peltier? In here, please." She stepped through into the cell, trusting Peltier would follow and Cartwright and his men would ensure they didn't get trapped inside.

Inside the room, the smell only intensified, the rank odor of stale sweat and a splatter of vomit where someone had tried to get to the toilet but missed.

Everyone's reaction to being terrorized was different. And, often, it was even worse when those used to having all the power, now had none.

Three men and one woman occupied the cell, wearing uniforms stripped of their badges, name IDs, and their utility belts. One man lay on the bed, his face bruised, his lower lip puffy and split, and his left eye blackened and bloodshot. A male and female CO perched on the edge of the bed, and a third man sat on the floor between the bed and the short jutting slab of table.

"They beat me half to death, is that what you want to hear?"

"Do you need medical assistance?"

"Probably."

There was no *probably* about it. The man on the bed had to be Vic Keen. And from his pallor and the sheen of sweat on his brow, Gemma wasn't at all confident about his claim that his injuries weren't life-threatening. His eyes were open, but they focused blearily on the ceiling above the bed, likely not really seeing anything.

Had they arrived just in time to save this man's life?

CHAPTER 20

"*L*et me by." Peltier had clearly also appraised Keen from a distance and shared Gemma's concerns. He sidled past her in the narrow space, his bag bumping against her knees as he passed. The nervous twitch had disappeared the moment he'd seen his patient, and his voice was sure. He knew what he needed to do now, and his entire concentration was on the job. "Excuse me." As the two COs squeezed out of his way to stand against the wall, he glanced at the floor, shrugged, knowing there was nothing else for it, and dropped his bag on the grimy concrete.

Nowhere in the cell was clean. He'd have to make do with what he had.

"Officer Keen." When Keen didn't respond, Peltier bent over him so he was directly in his field of view. "Officer Keen."

Keen blinked a few times and tried to muster a smile. "Just Vic . . ." His voice sounded gravelly.

"Sure, Vic. I'm Dr. Reg Peltier and I'm going to take care of you." He pulled on a pair of purple nitrile gloves, and then rummaged in his bag and extracted an infrared thermometer which he pointed at Keen's forehead. "One hundred point three. I thought you said he'd only been beaten? There's an infection going on here."

"That's all he told me. Non-life-threatening injuries that could use medical assistance. Could he be sick?"

"Check his left arm." The man on the floor stood, backing against the sink to give Peltier room to work. "One of them jabbed him with something during the fight." His tone for the words "one of them" was full of disgust.

"A shiv?" Peltier bent over him and carefully picked up his wrist.

Keen moaned.

"That would be typical of them. I'm Jake Garvey," said the CO. "That's Andrea Montgomery and Dewayne Jackson. Keen was fine for the first few days, but this morning he woke up feverish. We tried to get their attention"—Garvey threw a dark look toward the doorway—"yelled and pounded on the door, but they don't care. No one came."

Moving closer, Gemma could see now the navy-blue shirt was washed slightly darker halfway up the forearm, and the material was unnaturally stiff.

Peltier glanced up at her. "That's dried blood." He unfastened the cuff and turned the sleeve back to reveal an angry, open gash about an inch long with ragged edges oozing pus over puffy, splotchy skin. A foul odor drifted up from the wound. Peltier swore under his breath. "This is why he's running a fever. Officer Keen, did you receive this wound on the day of the riot?"

"Uh-huh."

Peltier glanced around the cell, his lip curling in disgust at the filth and disrepair. "What are the chances we can get him out of here?"

"We'd have to give up a pretty big concession to do it. I'll do my best to make it happen if his life is in danger, but they'll swing for the fences as soon as they know we want something time-dependent. Any concession of that magnitude is likely going to have to go through Davis and the DOC."

"So don't count on it."

"I'll do my best if you need it." She studied Keen's sweaty face. "If *he needs* it. But there's a bigger problem with that. Any hostage we draw attention to runs the risk of further mistreatment because the inmates will know they have a specific point of leverage."

"Good to know. Let me see what I can do here with the arm, but this looks like cellulitis."

"What's that?"

"A deep-tissue infection caused by a penetrating wound. It doesn't look that bad on the surface—it's not a huge gash—but I suspect whatever was used came in at an angle and penetrated the muscular part of the forearm. I need to clean and irrigate the wound, close it, and get him started on antibiotics."

"Can you do that here?"

"Sure can. That's why I brought such a big bag. I tried to pack anything I might need. But I can't work on him like this. We need to turn him around so I have full access to the arm. Just let me examine him first to make sure there isn't anything else that needs treatment."

Peltier took several long minutes examining Keen, making sure there were no skull fractures or any other broken bones or lacerations. "They beat him badly, but it's all soft tissue damage and a chipped tooth. The arm is the worst. Garvey, Jackson, can you give me a hand? I need to turn him around to get clear access to his far side."

"You bet."

Gemma and Montgomery stepped back in the snug space, nearly crowding out the door in an effort to give them room to maneuver. Gritting his teeth, but trying to help, Keen worked with the three men to lever up, turn around, and lie down again.

Keen let out a hiss of pain, his face even paler than before.

"Everything all right in there?"

Gemma turned around to find Cartwright and Logan peering in through the doorway right behind them. "Officer Keen requires medical attention. We're resettling him so Dr. Peltier can work on him."

"Call if you need a hand," Cartwright said.

"Will do." Gemma swung around to find Peltier bending over Keen's arm while the other three looked on. "What can I do to help?"

"I need a work surface. You'll do. Sit down." He patted the edge of the narrow bunk.

Gemma did as he asked, perching on the edge beside Keen's knees, not quite sure what Peltier needed. But she understood when the doctor unfolded an absorbent drape over her lap and then laid Keen's forearm and hand on it.

"Vic, can you move your fingers for me?" Peltier asked.

Keen slowly straightened his bent fingers and then let them curl in again.

"Very good. Now, can you bend your wrist?"

Keen made a strangled noise in the back of his throat but managed to bend his loosely clasped fist up and then down again.

"Excellent. That might have hurt like hell, but you have better motion than I hoped. I don't think we're looking at any serious nerve or tendon damage. Muscle damage for sure but that will mend. Vic, I need to deal with this wound. Do you know what you were stabbed with?"

Vic shook his head.

"I didn't see anything either," Garvey said. "But they had weapons. The place is in such lousy shape, they can rip a metal strip off an air vent and grind it down into a shiv against the floor or any other hard surface. Or shave down a toothbrush handle. Or rip a piece off the chain-link fence outside, straighten it, and wrap one end to use as a handle. They can be pretty . . . creative." From his tone of voice and curled lip, Garvey's description was anything but a compliment.

"And then Rivas had a goddamn switchblade," Jackson added.

Gemma looked up at him. "We heard about that from the officers who got out that day. Where on earth did that come from? How did someone smuggle it in past the metal detectors?"

"Because it wasn't metal," said Montgomery. "They keep us locked in here with the door closed, but it's not totally soundproof. We've taken turns, sitting at the door, trying to catch bits of conversation so we knew what was going on. 'Ear hustling,' as the inmates would say. On one of my shifts, I heard them boasting about it. It's 3D printed plastic. Folds in half, opens with a button. It's even got an edge. Not the stability of a metal knife, but it's good enough to do damage." She studied the putrescent wound and grimaced. "Might have done that."

"We'd be lucky if it did this." Peltier didn't look away from his examination of the wound and palpation of the surrounding tissues. "I suspect it was some sort of modified metal weapon. A dirty metal weapon, which is why the wound is such a mess. Vic, I'm going to have to get in here, so I'm going to freeze the wound. After that, you won't feel it." He handed Gemma a pair of gloves and waited while she put them on. "I need you to hold him like this." He wrapped her hands around Keen's wrist and rotated the arm so it was exactly where he wanted it. "And don't let him move. Once the first couple of shots of lidocaine are in, he'll be better." He pulled a syringe and a small bottle of clear liquid out of his bag, and then drew a measure of fluid into the syringe. "Hold him tight. If he's going to buck you, it's going to be now, Vic." Peltier raised his voice slightly. "You need to hold really still. I can clean this out for you, but I need to freeze it and the first couple of jabs will sting. Hang in there." He carefully inserted the needle into Keen's skin a fraction of an inch from the wound and dispensed some of the lidocaine.

Vic sucked air in through his teeth but held admirably still.

Peltier pulled out the needle, moved to the far side of the wound, and inserted it again. "It should be going numb." He inserted the needle again. "Can you feel that?"

"No."

"Perfect."

As Peltier continued carefully freezing the entire wound

site, Gemma pushed the story a little more. "So by the time of the riot, the knife was inside the ESH. Any idea how they got it in here?"

"We pieced the story together from what we heard, so if we ever get out of here, we can report how they did it to keep it from ever happening again. Rivas's lady visited and brought their baby."

"ESH inmates have visitation privileges?"

"Limited, but yes, they do. This isn't solitary confinement."

"So how did they pass off the knife? Assuming his partner brought it with her."

"She'd hidden the knife down the back of the baby's diaper. She passed through the metal detectors without a problem because it was all plastic, and when they searched her purse and the baby bag, there was nothing to find. They never thought to strip down a fussy infant to look for weapons."

"No wonder it was fussy, if it was lying on a folded switchblade," Gemma said. "Then at some point during the visit she must have passed it to him, or he slipped it out when he was holding the baby."

"He palmed it while he held the baby and managed to slip it out of sight. Then he hid it in his cell when he got back."

"I thought cell searches were standard. It was one of Rivas's demands—that searches not be done in the middle of the night, stripping them naked and having a half-dozen guards searching." A derisive snort from Garvey had Gemma looking up. "Is that not how it goes?"

"It can. Look, some of these guys are animals. You go in there and start rooting through their stuff and they go berserk. So a team has to go in."

Gemma refrained from pushing further. She wasn't here to mediate between the prisoners and the COs, simply to get the COs and any vulnerable inmates out. From that point on, it was up to the DOC to navigate the treacherous waters between its staff and Rikers detainees. But there was one relevant point. "Why wasn't the knife found?"

"Fair question," said Dewayne.

For the first time, Gemma noticed that Dewayne stood slightly apart from Garvey, even in the cramped confines of the cell. The only person of color in the room, it made her wonder if there wasn't some bad blood between Dewayne and Garvey, especially when it came to the treatment of inmates of color. "You'd have expected it to be found?"

"I would hope it would be found. That might depend on how much time was spent roughing up the inmate and throwing his stuff around versus actually searching."

Garvey took a threatening step forward. "Just because you—"

"*Hey!*" Trapped under Keen's arm as Peltier worked, all Gemma could do was throw out a hand toward Garvey. "We're not doing this now. If you two have a problem, take it up with your commander when you get out of here. For now, we pull together as a team so I can get you out safely. Is that understood?"

Garvey stepped back, saying nothing, but from the set of his shoulders and the line of his mouth, he was still angry.

Apparently, inmate/CO conflict isn't the only issue in here.

A movement at the doorway caught her eye and she looked over to find Logan with one foot into the cell, watching the two COs. He, too, had sensed the oncoming confrontation and was about to intercede. She caught his eye, and gave a tiny shake of her head. *It's okay. But thanks . . .*

He gave a single nod and turned to face outward, continuing his surveillance of the ESH.

"That should do it for the freezing." Peltier discarded the needle into a tall, narrow sharps container in his bag before pulling out more materials. "This is where things are going to get messy." He glanced around, looking for anywhere to put his equipment, then shrugged and laid another drape open on Keen's chest. He unpacked sterile gauze, a bag of saline, tubing, a needle, a stopcock, and a fat syringe.

"What's that for?" Gemma asked.

"I need to irrigate the wound, but I need to do it field-triage style in here." He leaned in and pulled the lips of the wound slightly apart, trying to visualize the injury in the uneven light from the fixture above. "I'd love an X-ray to make sure there isn't anything solid in there, but we'll just have to go for it."

"Go for it?"

"I need to irrigate the wound with saline with some force and hope we can bring out any particulate matter embedded in the wound." He quickly set up the irrigation system with the stopcock as the central pivot between the bag of saline, the syringe to provide the driving force, and the flexible catheter to deliver the liquid.

"I'll irrigate the wound, and then once it's as clean as I can get it, I'll clean the outer edges." He bent over the wound, carefully angled the catheter, and pointed a steady stream of saline into it. After the first round, he asked, "Vic, you hanging in there?"

"Yeah. Can't feel a thing."

"Perfect."

Peltier bent over Keen's arm and directed another jet of saline into the open wound. Thick yellow-green pus, speckled with dark bits of clotted blood and debris, sluggishly spurted from the opening to soak into the drape.

The foul, sulfurous odor of rotting flesh wafted from the puddle causing Gemma to turn her face away, clenching her jaw and holding her breath as her stomach rolled.

"Doing great. Hang in there." Peltier kept his gaze locked on the wound, but Gemma was certain his words were as much for her as for Keen.

Gemma turned her attention away from the procedure and to the other COs. "How are you holding up?"

The COs exchanged glances.

"As well as can be expected," said Montgomery. "For the most part they leave us alone. I think they know simply holding us in here gives them the leverage they need and any more damage than has already been done"—her gaze flicked to Keen—"will only reflect back onto them."

"They know that, or is that direction coming from the top?"

Garvey sharply looked up from where he was watching Peltier work. "There's a top?"

"Yes. Eduardo Rivas has been running the show since day two, at least. We don't know what happened on day one. We weren't able to get through."

"Goddamn Rivas. Of course, it would be him."

"Because . . . ?"

"Because he's an arrogant son of a bitch. Cool as a cucumber. Hard to shake."

"He's lost his temper with me."

"Really?" There was genuine surprise in Dewayne's voice. "I've seen COs and inmates get right in his face and he doesn't blink. He must have been rattled."

"This whole situation may have shaken his bravado," Gemma said. "But that's good info to know. I'll see if I can use it." She met Montgomery's eyes. "You're in a different kind of danger from the men. They haven't gone for you?"

"No."

"They'd have to go through us to do it," Garvey stated.

At Peltier's murmur of satisfaction, Gemma glanced over to find the wound finally running clean with only blood-tinged saline. "I'm glad you're standing up for each other. Hopefully this won't last much longer. What about food? Have they delivered food and water?"

"We have a sink. That's our water source. And yeah, we got a little food from yesterday's delivery."

"I'll make sure it's understood that some of the food coming this morning is to go to you if they want more to come for the rest of them beyond today."

Montgomery sagged. "There's going to be another day?"

"I'm sorry. I can't say for certain either way. We're working as fast as we can, but your safety is paramount. I'll make sure your families know we've seen you and you're well. And we'll update Officer Keen's family about his condition. Doctor, how is he doing?"

"The wound washed out well. If I can get all the detritus out, that greatly decreases the odds of the infection worsening."

"How are you going to close it?" Jackson asked.

"I'm not, or at least not totally. It needs to drain, so I'll use Steri-Strips to partially close it, then dress it." He met

Gemma's gaze. "If we can't get him out, what are the chances of me getting in here tomorrow?"

"I'll have to negotiate for it, but I can try."

"I'd like to be able to change the dressing tomorrow."

"Can you leave supplies here with us?" Montgomery asked. "We can do it if you show us how."

"That's a good idea. I can always bring more in if we can get access. If not, you can do it. Vic, how you doing, buddy?"

"Hanging in." Keen sounded slightly more coherent, likely an effect of the grinding pain in his arm being replaced by blessed numbness.

"Excellent. Detective, can you lift his arm slightly, please?" He slipped out the saturated drape, wadded it up, jammed it in a plastic bag for disposal, and laid out a fresh one over Gemma's lap. "Now, you can lower it down again. Like that. Thank you." He used Steri-Strips to close the middle of the wound, leaving the edges open for drainage, and then covered the wound with a sterile dressing, sealing the edges in an attempt to keep the wound clean in the filth of the cell. He packaged some extra supplies, which he handed to Montgomery. "Vic, any idea when your last tetanus shot was?"

Keen thought for a moment, then shrugged.

"We'll update that too." Another vial and another syringe came out of the bag and he quickly made up and delivered the injection. "Any drug allergies? Specifically, to any antibiotics?"

"No. Do I need 'em?"

"You have something called cellulitis. I need to treat it with antibiotics. I have amoxicillin-clavulanate on hand, which would do nicely, as long as you won't react to it."

"I've taken amoxicillin before. No problems with it."

"Excellent." He pulled out a bottle of pills, counted out nine, and put them into a small plastic bag, and added that to Keen's medical supplies. "This is in case I can't get in here tomorrow. He needs one in the morning and another at night." He helped Keen sit and offered him another pill with a bottle of water and waited while he swallowed the antibiotic. "Give it about twenty-four hours, but you'll feel better after that." He turned to the other COs. "Do any of you need treatment?"

"No, we're okay," Montgomery said. "They threaten harm, but they've mostly left us alone after that first day."

"That's when Rivas took charge," said Gemma.

Jackson stepped back to lean against the wall. "I'm not sure how that's going."

"What do you mean?"

"Even if no one is listening at the door, sometimes things get loud and you can't miss the conflict. The gangs are shaking things up out there. If Rivas is the one holding control, then I think things are getting rocky. He would have the Filero Kings behind him, but I can see everyone else starting to break rank by now."

Gemma exchanged an uneasy glance with Peltier. "A gang war is about the last thing we'd want. We don't need any more injuries and I don't want it spiraling out to the COs."

"They're angry. They're hungry. They're mean. And they have no respect for human life, unless it's in their own gang," said Garvey. "You're running out of time."

Stress curdled into a tight ball in Gemma's gut. "Understood." She turned to Peltier. "Let's go treat the hostages on the far side. Then maybe we should think about offering the inmates treatment. Rivas says no one needs it, but that's likely a lie. And it might win us some good favor with the larger inmate population."

"I planned to treat them all along. And I have meds for some of them." Peltier grabbed his bag. "Not to mention, if what we're hearing is true, we're going to need all the goodwill we can muster."

CHAPTER 21

*T*he second cell of COs proved to be a much faster visit. The three men had no major medical issues, though it was clear from various abrasions and bruising that each one had been involved in the initial riot. Two of the men wore their navy uniforms; however, the third wore a pair of orange prison pants and a black T-shirt, likely what was left from his own uniform, the rest of which had been put on Rush when they disguised him as a CO.

Peltier treated the men while Gemma talked with them, inquiring about their mental welfare, listening to their concerns, and doing her best to allay them while making sure they understood how hard the team was working for them outside the ESH. They were stressed, exhausted, suffering from cabin fever, and desperate to see their families, but they understood she was balancing their safety against the need to end the situation.

Gemma left the cell feeling the quiet gnawing of guilt for not being able to move the process along faster entwined with the relief of knowing that they were safe.

Now to keep it that way.

Outside the cell, they rejoined the A-Team who closed ranks around them.

"You're done?" Cartwright said.

"No. I want to see if there are any inmates that need care." At Cartwright's raised eyebrows, Peltier looked over at a group of inmates watching them with suspicion from the mezzanine. "Let's go up there. It's an open space where we can have anyone who needs care come to us."

"I don't like it."

"It's why I'm here." There was steel in Peltier's tone now. The nervous doctor of forty-five minutes ago was gone; in his place was a man who knew why he was here and was determined to carry out that mission. "Let's go." Peltier tried to push through the officers to head to the front steps, but immediately hit resistance. He turned around and looked pointedly at Cartwright.

Cartwright muttered something under his breath about medical professionals and gave the hand signal to his men to proceed back down the corridor. Logan and Mulgrew led the group toward the front of the facility, stepping over trash and around piles of bedding, but then looped around and climbed the six steps to the mezzanine level.

The mezzanine stretched out before them in what was originally double rows of four-man tables marching down each side of the space toward a matching set of stairs at the opposite end. Now, however, two of the tables lay drunkenly on the floor below. About ten men stood or lounged at tables in groups of two or three. But that was only a fraction of the total number of inmates in the facility. Gemma scanned the upper level, counting the men who stood above them, tracking their every move, but also watching for threats. In front of her, Hill did the same, likely making the same calculation as she—that a man could vault over the railing on the second floor to land on the tables below with little risk of injury, but with a clear path to leaping on anyone standing on the mezzanine. Put a weapon in the hand of that man, and it could be a deadly situation.

"Doctor, that's far enough," Cartwright barked from behind them. "Take that first table on the left. If anyone wants treatment, they can come to you. A-Team, defensive positions but leave the center corridor clear. I'll take these stairs."

Mulgrew took the forward position with Logan on the opposite side and back several feet. Sims and Peterson flanked Gemma and the doctor and Johnson and Hill took up positions bracketing the staircase. They were now guarded on all sides.

Gemma glanced at Cartwright who stood a few feet away from the center of the top step, his eyes constantly scanning. Like the rest of his men, he held his rifle pointed at the floor, one hand clasping the barrel, the index finger of his other hand resting along the trigger guard. He kept the butt of the weapon near his right shoulder, so at the slightest sign of threat, the weapon could be raised, braced, and aimed in under a second.

Cartwright and his officers knew from experience that death could come in only scant seconds. The only way to survive in their job was to be constantly ready for attack.

Today, inside this facility, their caution wasn't an over-reaction.

Peltier set his bag down on the table and stood, hands on hips, looking up at the inmates ringing the upper reaches of the facility. "I'm Dr. Peltier," he called.

"Who gives a fuck?" The shout came from toward the rear of the facility, but Gemma couldn't identify the speaker.

"Some of you might," Peltier continued, seemingly unperturbed. "It's entirely up to you, but Detective Ca-pello worked to get me in here so I could attend to anyone with medical needs."

An older man stepped out into the central corridor to-ward the rear of the mezzanine. "Why start now? We know how docs work at Rikers."

"You don't know me. I don't know what kind of care you received in the past, but it wasn't from me or you wouldn't have that complaint. Some of you may have in-juries. Some of you may be off your meds. I brought meds with me, so I can help there too."

Cartwright's head jerked around toward Peltier at the mention of drugs and he took a half step closer. Meds could be a real problem. Desperate men might do any-thing to get their hands on them.

"I don't have pain medication," Peltier clarified, and Cartwright relaxed fractionally. "But many of you are on regular medications for a range of health problems. I have a list and am happy to deliver doses to you. And I'll treat any injuries. No questions asked."

The scowls and suspicion of the men around them lightened slightly. *Score 1 for Reg Peltier.*

Peltier unzipped his bag and pulled out a folded piece of paper. "I can be here as long as you need me. Anyone who'd like attention please come forward. Though I would like to see these men first barring anyone with critical injuries." He proceeded to reel off a half-dozen names.

Peering over his shoulder, Gemma could see at least one drug listed beside each name.

Peltier put down the list. "I'm happy to see you, one at a time. Officers, please step back so the men can pass through."

There was a pause as every officer looked to Cartwright for confirmation. On his nod they all stepped back a pace.

For a moment, there was silence while no one moved, and a sinking feeling of failure settled around Gemma. But then the older man who'd questioned Peltier's care walked toward them. He didn't give the A-Team officers even a passing glance, but walked to Peltier. "Ray Santino."

"Mr. Santino, thank you. Please sit down. I have some medications for you."

The man sat at the far side of the table, perched on the edge of the seat as if ready to fly at any moment, but Peltier continued as if he didn't notice the man's discomfort, asking questions about his health while he readied a small baggie of prescriptions for him.

Some of Gemma's tension eased slightly. Maybe this was going to work out after all.

With Peltier surrounded by six officers, Gemma stepped

away, moving farther into the mezzanine but still keeping a healthy distance between herself and the men. She had a little time on her hands now and wanted to get a better lay of the land, to be able to use that inside knowledge to her advantage.

The divisions between the inmate population was immediately evident once she took the time to truly observe versus simply scanning for threats.

Age skewed young, likely having more to do with the population of individuals perpetrating crimes, but race appeared to be a defining factor. The men congregating on the mezzanine—*marking their territory?*—all had the medium coloring of those of Latinx origin, whereas the majority of the men hanging over the railing were black. White inmates were in the minority, with a few mixing into the other groups but more either peering solitarily through cell doors or in a small group at the back of the facility on the ground floor, near one of the emergency exit doors. Past the clear racial boundaries, there was a commonality of appearance. The men wore orange prison pants, but nearly all had stripped off the regulation orange prison shirt for plain white T-shirts or to simply be bare-chested. A plethora of tattoos were on display as a result, from skulls, to ferocious animals, to faces, to messages for other gang members or to ward off opponents.

But there was one face she had yet to see—Burk. She knew his face from his ID photo, but no one on the mezzanine, or the walkways, resembled him. Certainly, no one was showing the facial defects Burk must have.

Is he lying low? Doesn't want to show his injured face? Doesn't trust the medical staff enough for treatment? Or had Rivas or his guys finally been successful?

"Detective."

Gemma turned at the sound of a familiar voice to find Rivas at the bottom of the stairs, one foot on the lowest step and his eyes locked on Cartwright, Johnson, and Hill. Rivas held his hands up, palm out and fingers spread, making it clear he carried no weapon. "Lieutenant, please let Mr. Rivas come up. I'll be . . ." She looked from officer to officer. "Fine."

Cartwright's reluctance was clear in his prolonged hesitation, but then he stepped back a pace, keeping his eyes on Rivas as he mounted the steps.

"Mr. Rivas." Gemma stepped away from Peltier and toward the stairs to meet him.

Rivas climbed the steps and strode toward her, but Cartwright stepped forward when he was still five feet away. "That's far enough."

Rivas threw him a dark look but stopped.

When he turned to Gemma, she felt the full blast of his icy fury.

"I said we didn't need medical attention."

"Dr. Peltier and some of the inmates disagreed with you. They need care. More than that, they need their meds. Or you may have bigger problems on your hands than what you have now."

"That wasn't part of the arrangement. You lied."

"I didn't. Dr. Peltier insisted."

The look on his face said he didn't believe her. "Why has no one answered our demands?"

"The DOC and city officials are discussing them now."

He spat on the floor about a foot from her boots. "That's what I think of the DOC and the city officials."

Hill took a step toward Rivas, but Gemma motioned him away with a flick of her hand. "You may not like them, but they hold the power."

"We hold the power, not them."

"I'll give you part marks. You both have power in different ways." She took a step forward, feeling the stab of Cartwright's stare as she partially closed the distance. But where Cartwright saw the opportunity for attack, Gemma saw a chance to demonstrate her trust in Rivas. If Rivas perceived a lack of response to his demand as a rejection, she needed to build him back up. "You're angry."

"You're goddamn right, I'm angry. You're ignoring me."

She met his furious gaze with calm surety. "I'm not ignoring you. If I was ignoring you, I wouldn't be here. I'm doing everything I can to move this along."

"And in the meantime, we're starving."

"There will be food arriving shortly. You know the deal we made. The medical visit for food for everyone. Including the hostages. Do I have your word on that? Their care is in your hands. Their well-being, or lack thereof, could alter the conversation being had as we speak."

He simply stared at her, shaking his head slightly.

"You think I don't hear you, but I do." She took the chance to take her eyes off him, only four feet away, to gaze around the facility, looking past the garbage and scattered belongings to the filth and disrepair under it. "Now more than ever. I can't agree with the actions taken that brought us here. As you might imagine, I'm a firm believer that conversation and compromise build more bridges and solve more problems. But I understand some of the frustrations that brought you to this point." She would have liked to have taken another step forward but suspected that Cartwright would tackle her to the ground if she dared. And would have been absolutely correct in doing so. There was too much fury radiating off Rivas and no real grounds for trust. "You have to believe me when I say they're working on it. It's not simply a matter of accepting or not accepting your demands. They'll make a counteroffer for you to consider. And, in doing so, they'll have to let loose a little of the control they hold. You need to give them time to make that mental shift. Especially considering you asked for immunity. That means there are legal hurdles as well."

"You jus' giving them cover to not take us seriously."

The laugh slipped free before she could stop it, but, in retrospect, she knew it showed Rivas exactly how absurd his statement was. "Not at all. They're taking this entire situation *very* seriously. In fact, if they weren't taking it seriously, you'd have heard back last night. Time is a good thing. You'd be smart to give it to them. But, with that in mind, I'll follow up with them as soon as I leave here this morning and I'll let you know how it goes, whether it's good news or not. Will that satisfy you?

"It's better than nothin'."

"Agreed. I'm walking a fine line with them. If I push them too hard, or contact them too often, I could interrupt their negotiations and ruin their progress. Trust me to deal with them and to push as hard as I feel I can, but then I'll have to pull back." She waved her index finger between the two of them. "But open communication between us. If I learn anything, I'll pass it on as soon as I can. Deal?"

"Don't have much choice, do I?" He turned and strode

away down the stairs and over to the corridor on the far side.

Gemma watched him stride away, only murmuring "You're welcome" when his back was to her and she was out of earshot.

She turned to Peltier to find him with a different inmate, applying a tensor bandage to the man's wrist.

They stayed for another twenty minutes as Peltier bandaged minor wounds and doled out prescriptions. But the inmates were getting restless, knowing food was coming, and the doctor moved rapidly through the last few men. None of whom were Burk.

Peltier was closing his bag after finishing with the last man when there was a sudden pounding of feet along the mezzanine. Gemma's head jerked up as she pivoted, her hands automatically coming up to meet whatever threat approached. The man headed directly for her was tall and wiry, and moved with speed and agility, leaping onto the tabletops to keep himself separated from the A-Team officers. He held something narrow and pointed clenched in his leading fist.

A homemade shank. But just because it was homemade didn't mean it couldn't be deadly.

The 120-decibel scream of a personal alarm blasted through the air.

Mulgrew was closest to the runner but was on the opposite side of the aisle after giving the men room to walk between the tables to Peltier. He lunged for the man as he went past, stepping onto a bench seat and then the floor. His hand grabbed the man's sleeve but couldn't hold on to it.

Gemma had a fraction of a second to recognize the inmate as one of the Gutta Boys, when Logan stepped directly between them, already raising his rifle. But the *crack* she anticipated never came. Instead he released the carbine from its single point sling with the press of a button and grasped it like a staff. Pausing for a fraction of a second for the man to get closer, he brought the barrel of the M4 down on his outstretched arm, catching him at the wrist, forcing it down and knocking the shank from his hand. He then continued the motion, bringing the stock up to catch the inmate under the chin. The blow knocked the man backward and right off his feet to slam to the floor, gasping and fighting for the breath that had been knocked from his body. Logan and Mulgrew were on him then, flipping him over and cuffing him before standing, leaving him wriggling facedown on the floor as the alarm suddenly shut off.

"ERSU! Hold!" Cartwright's booming command would have been easily heard in the hallway by the Rikers team.

The other inmates on the mezzanine backed away, surely realizing that if they weren't careful, the mezzanine was about to become a war zone and the only men with long-distance weapons were the NYPD officers.

Logan turned around, his gaze finding Gemma, then shifting behind her to where Peltier stood, and then back again. "You okay?"

"Yes. You never let him get close to us."

He gave her a nod and rounded on the man Mulgrew had on his feet.

"Fall back!" Cartwright's command was sharp, the fury in it unmistakable. He hadn't wanted time with the inmates for exactly this reason.

As a group, they backed toward the stairs, Logan and Mulgrew marching the attacker between them, keeping their gazes on the inmates until they'd cleared the tables knowing Cartwright stayed between them and the door ensuring a clear path. They covered the distance quickly and then were down the stairs and moving as a unit to the door the ERSU already had open.

As soon as they cleared the door, Cartwright gave the command to close the door. Only then did they collectively relax.

"What just happened?"

They turned to find Nya Coleman and another DOC officer standing by the far wall with carts loaded with food.

Coleman marched toward them, but her gaze was locked on the man who'd run at them. "Lafferty, what the hell did you do?"

"Tried to attack an NYPD hostage negotiator and one of your docs with a homemade shank," said Cartwright. "Luckily my guys got in the way."

The inmate grunted with pain as he tried to pull away from Mulgrew who simply tightened his hold without changing his expression. "You broke my wrist," he snarled at Logan.

Logan pinned him with a flat stare. "I didn't, but even if I had, you'd be lucky that's all you got."

"Serves you right if he did," Coleman snapped, drawing the man's startled gaze. "What were you thinking? You didn't give him any choice if you were running at him with a shank. You're lucky that's all that happened." She turned to her own ERSU commander. "Roberts, you and your men take Lafferty to the Bing. We'll figure out what to do with him once he's contained."

The A-Team officers handed Lafferty off to the ERSU and then watched as he was marched down the hall.

"I'm sorry." Coleman laid a hand on Gemma's arm. "I'm glad he didn't hurt you."

"I knew the risks going in. I'd like to talk to him later if that would be allowed. I'd like to know exactly why he attacked. He might also be able to provide some information. Rivas has kept that entire unit locked up tight. What's Lafferty's gang affiliation?"

"Outside of Rikers, he was Murda Gang. But inside, he joined the Gutta Boys."

"So possibly a member of a gang Rivas hasn't let speak. Maybe things in there are rougher than we think."

Coleman glanced down the corridor when Lafferty had disappeared. "I'll clear that interview with Davis."

"If things are rougher than we think, it may be time to seriously consider a tactical solution," Cartwright said. "It's already not looking great four days in. How long do you want this to go on?"

"Until we know negotiations aren't going to work. We're not there yet."

"Unless things start to move significantly, we're going to hit that wall soon."

"Maybe, but we're not there yet." Gemma enunciated the words slowly knowing she had to be emphatic but, at the same time, not rile Cartwright because he had the final say on when the operation went tactical.

"Are we still sending in this food?" Coleman asked.

"No," Cartwright snapped.

"Yes," Gemma insisted. "That was part of the deal. They let us do the med visit we asked for. Now they need the food we promised. Remember, it's not just for the inmates. It's for the hostages too. And they need it. We keep the bargain we made, or else I'll lose ground in the negotiations. Rivas is already angry because he thinks he's being stonewalled by the DOC. Let's not give them an excuse to not trust us." She looked through the glass slats into the ESH. "The DOC itself is already pushing them in that direction. We definitely don't need to add to it."

CHAPTER 22

"What happened?"

Gemma looked across the table at Chen as she sat down. "I assume you followed along through Cartwright's helmet cam?"

McFarland paused with his coffee cup almost to his lips. "We tried, but when things got hairy and everyone converged, it was hard to see exactly what was going on. But we knew it at least ended well. It looked like some guy took a run at you?"

"One of the inmates rushed Peltier and me brandishing a shank."

McFarland looked her up and down. "I saw him on the floor afterward. You're clearly okay, so did you flatten him?"

"Didn't need to. We were surrounded by A-Team officers. Mulgrew lunged for the guy and missed, but then Logan got in between him and us."

"We didn't hear a shot."

"That's because Logan never fired. He did something interesting though. Popped his rifle off the sling and used it as a stick." Gemma mimed holding a stick horizontally in two hands, then raising one side, then the other. "The barrel took the weapon out of the guy's hand. The stock caught him in the chin and took him straight down to the floor."

"Nice." McFarland was nodding in appreciation with a triumphant grin. "Neutralized the threat without it turning into a war zone."

"If Logan's smart," said Williams, "and I haven't seen anything to prove otherwise, he likely knew that firing the first shot would encourage another officer with a stronger tendency to do the same and then you'd have a real problem. Only one inmate posed a danger, so he dealt with only him."

"And it was fists or the rifle, so he used the rifle, just not how I thought he would," Gemma said.

"Peltier's okay?"

"It happened so fast, Peltier was standing there with his jaw on the floor. We pulled out, and the next thing he knew, he was standing in the hallway with the door to the ESH closed."

"I bet. How was the medical visit?"

"Overall, it went well, but Officer Vic Keen is *not* in good shape."

McFarland's gaze shot to the list of CO names and details on the wall. "He's the one who said he'd been beaten?"

"Yes."

Chen stood, a marker in his hand. "What do we need to add?"

"He was shanked with something during the riot." Gemma rubbed her left forearm in the same spot as Keen's injury. "Ended up with a gash about an inch long, which wouldn't have been that bad, but whatever the shank was made of—and no one knows what it was—it went deep."

"He didn't see what happened?" McFarland asked.

"It was utter chaos at the time and the inmates were carrying weapons they'd jury-rigged out of whatever they could get their hands on. And areas of the facility are falling apart. It was likely some rusted piece of metal ripped off of a light fixture or an air vent. But it's created a hell of an infection in there. When Peltier rolled back his sleeve, you could smell the wound. But hopefully Peltier has that under control now. He had this giant duffel of supplies which had anything he might need. He put together an irrigation system and blasted the pus and gunk out of the wound, then bandaged him and put him on antibiotics. Actually, Peltier was solid in there."

"You didn't think he would be?"

"He looked terrified before we went in, but the moment he had a patient to focus on, he got right into the zone, and was calm and competent. If we need to go in again, I want him. He was a good choice."

"Do you need to go back in for medical?"

"Keen should have that arm looked at daily. But that might be a pipe dream, especially after that inmate, Lafferty, tried to go after us today. Some of the COs told me the inmates are on edge in there."

"Considering the standoff, did you expect anything else?" Williams asked.

"It's not because of the hostage situation—we'd expect them to be on edge because of that—but because of gang friction. At least they're eating now. Hunger does a great job of dialing fury up to eleven, so hopefully this will calm some of them down. But one good thing came out of today's attempted attack."

"What's that?"

"Coleman's going to get me a sit-down with Lafferty. They took him to solitary confinement, but hopefully I can get in there later today or, more likely, tomorrow. I might be able to get some inside information out of him about how things are actually working in the ESH."

"What about making him a deal?" Chen suggested. "There will be additional charges because of the attack. Maybe you could get more out of him in exchange for lower charges?"

"That's above our pay grade, but I'll talk to Garcia about it. He could take the request to the Bronx DA to work out a plea deal in exchange for information. Actually, someone from the DA's office is in the group to begin with." Gemma pulled her cell phone out of her pocket. "I need to call him now anyway. I promised Rivas an update on the demands." She marked the time on the clock on the wall. "I figure we should give them an hour to distribute the food and eat. Hopefully I'll have answers for them at that time. Let me call him."

She dialed his number, then put her phone on speaker and set it on the table in front of her.

"Garcia."

"Sir, it's Capello. I have you on speaker with the team. Can you talk for a few minutes? The inmates are getting restless and I told them I'd try to get an update on your progress."

"Hang on."

Dead silence came over the line, telling Gemma Garcia had muted them as he pulled out of the meeting.

A full minute passed before Garcia came back on the line. "Sorry. Told everyone to take fifteen. They could use it too. Gives everyone a chance to take a breath."

"Is it confrontational in there?"

"We were doing okay. Hitting some bumps, as expected, but we were getting somewhere. Then Rowland showed up."

Gemma didn't need to hear McFarland's curse. She could read lips well enough. Besides, a similar curse filtered through her own mind, only in Italian.

"I assume that was the end of cooperation?"

"To a large degree. The DOC sent the first deputy commissioner again. Because the Board of Corrections oversees the condition of Rikers as well as physical and mental health processes, they also sent the BOC chair. Davis is here because he runs the OBCC."

"I can see Davis providing a lot of pushback."

"You'd be correct. He's definitely hardline. The inmates are here as punishment and should take their knocks accordingly."

"Except some of these men are detainees waiting for trial. They haven't been found guilty. Unless he sees the fact they're still inside the ESH as guilt."

"That's definitely his opinion. One he's not afraid to share."

"Except when the riot happened, we know some guys got trapped in there when they might have preferred to leave. Davis could be unfairly coloring them with the same brush. Is there anyone from the Bronx DA's office?"

"Assistant DA Pattesell. He's reporting to DA Farrow as needed because she's not free to come down currently. But she'll make herself available if we need her."

"We may." Gemma quickly updated Garcia on the medical visit and the attack. "I think we may have some leverage there if the DA will play along."

"Agreed. Let me sound out the assistant DA on it."

"Also, I think we have something with Dr. Peltier. He's newish to the island, completely new to the OBCC. No one knew him, so there were no simmering resentments, and he seemed genuinely interested in the men. I think he may be our way in to better medical care for the inmates if the DOC will allow it."

"I'll take it back to them. Peltier . . . how do you spell that?

"P-e-l-t-i-e-r. But back to Rowland. Did he not send anyone?"

"He sent the new first deputy mayor, but Rowland's twitchy about hostage situations, so then he surprised everyone by showing up himself."

"How disruptive is he being?" McFarland asked.

"About as much as you'd think. And that's part of the problem. We had most of the group coming together on a number of points, but Rowland is fighting some of it, mainly their request for immunity from prosecution."

"He's going to be sensitive about that," Gemma said. "After losing First Deputy Mayor Willan the way he did and then missing out on the chance to prosecute his murder, he may be looking at this as an opportunity for justice. But if that request isn't met, we may not get anywhere with them. There's a historical precedent for immunity. They're detainees and inmates, but that doesn't mean they don't know anything. Rivas mentioned Attica specifically by name. He may not know the details of the amnesty, he may just know it was given."

"My gut read on it is Rowland wants to see them pay."

"All of them? We don't know who's responsible for what. We'll never be able to prosecute until we get more reliable testimony or evidence to prove who committed which crime. That could have been a gimme."

"Preaching to the choir, Capello."

"Right. Sorry, sir. Can you give me anything else so I can pass something along to Rivas and his men to help keep things calm?"

"You'll have to be vague because until we have a final document, nothing is written in stone."

"Understood."

"Then pass this along." Garcia proceeded to quickly outline several points, then excused himself because he needed to keep the room on task.

Gemma hung up and pocketed her phone. "Well, some of that is promising."

"And some, not so much," said Chen. "You're going to call to pass that along?"

"As much as I can. I don't want to lead them on, but I want to give them enough hope to keep things calm in there." She slid her headset into place and then checked to make sure everyone else was ready before calling through.

It took three rounds of calling before anyone picked up the phone, which Gemma took as a positive sign that everyone was so involved in eating, they weren't hanging over the phone.

"I have an update for you, as promised," she said when Rivas answered.

"Yeah?"

"Keep in mind they're still discussing your demands, so nothing is final yet, but there are some good signs."

"Like?"

"The men seemed to like Dr. Peltier, and I didn't see anything in his care that wasn't sincerely focused on his patients. I've asked my lieutenant to see about getting him moved to OBCC, or, at least, getting you access to him."

"He's better than any of the OBCC docs."

"I was impressed by what I saw today. Your point about fair pay. That's a state statute, but there's a state legislator who's been talking about a bill setting a higher minimum wage inside correctional facilities."

"What do you mean, a higher minimum wage?"

"Possibly between three and four dollars an hour." Rivas made a derisive sound, but Gemma kept going. "That might not seem like much compared to minimum wage outside, but that's forty times what you make now. Also, remember, there's no way they're going to rubber stamp every demand, so compromise is important."

"What about immunity?"

"I don't know."

"You don't know, or you're not saying?"

"Remember how I told you I'd never lie to you? When I say I don't know, I don't know. Of everything you asked, that might be the demand that will meet with the most resistance."

"Who's deciding this?"

"I can't give you names, but it's members of the city administration and the county DA's office." She paused, considering, then decided that moderating expectations was the wisest course of action. "And representatives from Rikers."

"Representatives . . ." Rivas trailed off. "Shit. That's gotta be Davis." His voice took on a razor-sharp edge. "Coleman was here this morning with the food. With Coleman, we'd have a chance. Davis will happily screw us."

"He'd be doing it in front of his boss from the DOC." Gemma skipped over the part that it was the first deputy commissioner and not the commissioner herself in attendance, but Frye stayed fully informed about the negotiations. "He's going to have to be reasonable. If you think he has it in for you personally, or for some of you, he'll have to justify his opinion and won't be able to. And my lieutenant is there personally to mediate the discussion. Let him do his job."

"Yeah . . . we'll see. Call me when you actually have news." He hung up.

Chen laid his pen down on his pad of paper. "He asked for an update but seems unhappy he got one."

"I guess it was supposed to be the update he wanted, not necessarily the real one." She sat back in her chair. "So now we wait until we have more to say to him."

The next few hours were spent reviewing notes, brainstorming scenarios, and trying to wait patiently for more news from Garcia.

But when the phone rang next, it wasn't Garcia.

"Capello."

"Get over here. *Now.*" It was Cartwright's voice, full of strain and tension. "We're going to have to go into the ESH."

Gemma surged to her feet. "You can't do that unannounced. They might hurt the hostages. Or worse."

"I doubt that. They're too busy trying to kill one of the other inmates. Get down here before they succeed."

CHAPTER 23

*G*emma and Williams went in at a run.

Leaving McFarland and Chen behind on the slim chance anyone called in, Gemma took Williams, the team member with the most experience, with her for support, and tore out of the room, sprinting down the hallway. If it was as bad as Cartwright implied, seconds could be the difference between life and death.

Rounding the corner, she found the A-Team officers gathered around the door. "What's going on?"

Cartwright ducked a little lower to peer through a slat of glass, pointing into the ESH as she stopped beside him. "That."

Shorter than Cartwright by several inches, she didn't need to stoop to see through the glass. Men were gathered on the mezzanine, in the entrance foyer, and on the second-floor walkway. But more alarmingly, a young man in inmate garb was perched facing outward on the outside of the second-floor railing, his hands behind his back and the bedsheet noose looped around his neck. Two other inmates held his arms, pinning him against the railing. That and the inch of flooring under his heels were all that kept him from a potentially neck-snapping fall. There was no mezzanine below at that point, just a full-story drop to the first floor. Lots of space to fall paired with a short bedsheet was a very bad combination.

And there, finally, was Burk. He didn't have Rivas's height or breadth, but he looked like he was all compact muscle. He wore his dark hair in short springy twists and sported heavy tattoos on his arms and the slice of chest revealed at his neckline. But his most notable feature was the vicious gouge on his right cheek—swollen and crusted with blood, it looked angry and painful. And like it most definitely should have been tended by Peltier earlier.

Burk stood behind the young man, surrounded by a group of mostly African-American men. Fifteen feet down the walkway, Rivas, backed by a small cluster of his own men, faced off against the group, held in place by a large inmate wielding a wickedly sharp metal shank dangerously close to his throat.

She could hear Rivas and Burk screaming at each other through the door over the shouts of the men around them. "*Gesù Cristo.*"

"Open the door and take our chances?"

"They're not leaving us any choice."

"Didn't think so. Hill! Open the door!"

The moment the door rumbled free, sound exploded from inside the ESH. Gemma darted for the widening gap, but Cartwright seized her arm.

"You need a vest."

She yanked her arm free. "No time." She slipped through the slice of doorway and into the ESH. "*Stop!*" But no one could hear her over the roar of voices: Rivas and Burk bellowing at each other, the men on the walkway jeering at the inmates below, and the men on the mezzanine yelling for "Vega."

Alvaro Vega. She recognized him from his prison record.

Maybe only twenty-one or twenty-two, Vega was one of the youngest men in the ESH. Perhaps that was why he was the target—strike at the youngest to hit the hardest. Dressed in prison pants and a dirty white T, his dark hair was cut short with sharp corners at the temples. Both arms were tattooed with full sleeves and a band of script climbed his neck from behind the slack noose. His Adam's apple bobbed, sliding through the script and then back down again to disappear under the twisted rope of sheeting. He was holding absolutely still, clearly recognizing that any kind of struggle could send him over the edge without help from the men who'd put him there.

Time to get everyone's attention.

Whipping around she reached for the closest A-Team officer—Detective Sims—and, instead of pulling his rip cord, she drilled an index finger into the button on his personal alarm. A high-pitched, pulsating siren blasted out and Gemma gave it three full seconds before she released the button.

The facility was silent with every eye locked on her.

Now that Burk was still and facing her instead of Rivas, she recognized the distinctive symbol under his Adam's apple from his Rikers intake photo—the letters *G.B.* on a flowing ribbon, bisected by a broadsword. *The gang version of "Live by the sword, die by the sword."*

"Mr. Burk. I need you to bring Mr. Vega to the other side of the railing."

"Fuck off. You got no business being here."

Logan and Peterson stepped up to flank her on either side, both with their rifles ready in case the inmates turned on them.

"That's not what it looks like to me. Whatever's going on, we can work it out."

"Disagree. We didn't need your help outside. We don't need it inside. We can settle this ourselves."

"By threatening a man's life?" A quick glance down the corridor to the right showed several inmates standing in the doorway of the cell where some of the hostages were held. *Have to play this very carefully or the hostages will be the ones to pay.*

"Why not? They killed one of mine. And you're helping them to get away with it scot-free."

The blood-streaked face of Tyrell Rush as he lay on the floor outside the ESH filled Gemma's mind. Whether he'd died in the initial riot or afterward wouldn't matter to the gang mindset. They'd lost one of theirs, so it was only fair to repay the favor.

An eye for an eye.

The fear in the eyes of the young man with the noose around his neck telegraphed he knew it too. He was right to be terrified; if they pushed him, even if Gemma and the A-Team could get him down, there was always a risk depending on how the noose was tied that it would snap his neck. Then there wouldn't be anything anyone could do.

She had to take her chances they didn't know how to tie a proper noose. They were gang members, and while many of them likely felt like they were born with a gun or a knife in their hands, knots were unlikely to be one of their skills. In a worst-case scenario, that could buy them, and Vega, some time.

Always the truth.

"There's no guarantee they're going to get away with it, Mr. Burk. The team meeting about your group's demands is struggling with that particular aspect of the list." Gemma kept her eyes fixed on Burk, but out of the corner of her eye she saw Rivas's head whip toward her. She hadn't lied to him but had tried to spin the negotiations as positively as possible. That spin might come back to bite her in the ass, but that was a later problem. Right now, she just needed to keep this man alive. "Any actions that happen now, that happen in front of NYPD officers as witnesses, would have very different ramifications."

"And if we walk away, where does that leave us? Rivas has cut off communication. My men don't fucking *eat.*"

The rage in Burk's voice had every man in the A-Team raising their rifles an inch. Without looking at Cartwright, she lay a hand on both Logan's and Peterson's forearms. Turning her head slightly to the side, she kept her voice low but just loud enough that every officer could hear her. "Do *not* shoot. The moment you do, they'll let go of him. And then probably go after the hostages as well. Defensive posture only. You may have live ammunition, but if they rush us, there is no positive outcome." She looked to the men on the walkway. "What do you mean they don't eat? I sent food in this morning."

"None of my guys got any of it."

The gangs are shaking things up out there. If Rivas is the one holding control, then I think things are getting rocky. He would have the Filero Kings behind him, but I can see everyone else starting to break rank by now.

Jackson had been right. The uneasy coalition between the inmates that carried them through the first few days was shattering before her eyes. Rivas was slowly starving out his competition, and it was getting mean.

Williams had called it yesterday. Rivas had played both ends against the middle, trying to look like the group leader and spokesman to the outside world, while enforcing gang dominance inside the ESH so the uneasy truce had shattered under pressure.

The mutiny was playing out before their eyes.

"Mr. Rivas, that wasn't our arrangement. The arrangement was for everyone to eat, including the hostages. Or did they go without as well?"

Rivas's smirk answered her question before he even spoke. "No, they ate."

The man with the shank let out a guttural curse and took a swing at Rivas, who jumped away from the arc of the blade.

Four days without food. No wonder it's all going to hell. This is exactly what we were trying to avoid. "Burk I can arrange to get you food."

"Why would I believe you?" Behind Burk' was the weight of authority letting him dow time after time.

"Because *I* don't lie." She let her emphasis on the personal pronoun carry the full effect. *I always held up my end of the bargain. I delivered food in good faith. It was forces other than myself that barred you and your men from that food.* "But all bets are off if you hurt Mr. Vega. I negotiate in good faith. Bring him in and I'll personally ensure you and your men are fed."

Burk waited for a long count of five before he stepped closer to the railing and met her eyes. "*I* don't negotiate." Holding her gaze, he shoved Vega with both hands.

Vega gave a startled scream as he fell, his body twisting in midair for the fraction of a second he was unsupported. Then the sheet snapped tight, grotesquely jerking his body to a stop before swinging slowly back and forth while Vega thrashed violently.

The moment Vega's feet were airborne, Gemma and the A-Team officers moved as one, sprinting across the foyer. Sims got there first, wrapping his arms around the flailing legs, barely avoiding a violent kick to the temple, and lifted Vega, taking some of the weight off his windpipe. Overhead, Vega gasped for air, his face turning a sickly purple-red.

"Cover us," Logan barked, throwing a look over his ⟨...⟩ remaining officers moved for⟨...⟩ ⟨...⟩ng a protective barrier from the ⟨...⟩

⟨...⟩, pushing it on the sling behind ⟨...⟩pen a pocket in his cargo pants ⟨...⟩em, your hand!"

⟨...⟩ out automatically and he

words
time after

He locked gazes with her. "Thomson's live-fire training exercise."

She looked down at the folded tactical knife he'd pressed into her palm. And with that, she had his entire plan.

Back in the academy, where they'd been competitors, but had occasionally worked together as a winning team.

Sergeant Thomson's role-playing scenarios, where the recruits were thrown into real-life situations to stop a crime, save a life, arrest a suspect.

They'd been sent into the state live-fire training facility for a scenario with an aggressive suspect who was barricaded in a second-floor apartment. But instead of going through the door together as every other team did, Logan had the idea to divide and conquer. Instead of following standard protocol, he'd tossed Gemma high enough that she could stand on his shoulders to boost herself over the balcony. He'd gone in the front, she in the back, and they contained the suspect with no injury to anyone involved.

She turned her back to him and bent her knees so she'd have extra spring. "Don't miss."

"I got you." His voice was right in her ear as he stepped in close, bending his knees behind hers. His hands closed on her waist, gripping tight. "One . . . Two . . . *Three!*"

Keeping her gaze fixed on the line of sheeting, Gemma pushed off as Logan lifted, throwing her vertically into the air, but catching her boots and sliding them onto his shoulders as he straightened, pushing her upward the last foot or so. Catching the bedsheet, she quickly found her balance, depressed the button on the side of the knife, and the blade sprang free. Hands reached for her from between the railings, but Logan sidestepped them away, keeping her out of reach as she sawed at the bedsheet, the material parting easily under the tactical blade. Just a few seconds and she cut through the sheet, Vega's body falling limply into Mulgrew's waiting arms. Mulgrew and Sims jogged Vega out of the ESH with Johnson.

Gemma pressed the back of the blade against her thigh, reseating it in the handle so she wouldn't stab herself or Logan on the way down. As soon as Logan released her ankles, she jumped off, his hands catching her before she slammed into the ground, and then they were sprinting for the door of the facility where Williams waited for them, Cartwright, Hill and Peterson covering them as they pulled back.

Gemma paused in the corridor, taking in the scene. Burk looked furious—his prize had been snatched. All of the risk, none of the payoff. Rivas and his men had pulled back, retreating quickly now that their man had been pulled from the facility. But he cast one glance her way and they locked gazes, his cold, hers unreadable.

She couldn't give away her fury. She thought they'd connected, but while he'd played fair with her, he'd been playing a different game in the background. One that could have led to more deaths.

Or had it?

She spun out of the entryway, the metal-on-metal grind of the door closing behind her, to find Vega sitting against the wall, gasping and coughing. The noose lay in a tangled pile on the floor and his arms were still tied behind his back.

They'd been in time.

Logan stepped up behind her to study Vega over her shoulder. "He's alive."

She craned her neck to look up at him. "Thanks to you and Sims. That was smart shorthand, by the way."

"I knew I wouldn't have to spell it out for you. You'd understand instantly and would roll with it because anything longer than that might have killed him."

"Thanks for the accurate throw. That could have gone sideways."

"Could have, but we got lucky."

"I'll take lucky. I'm sure it didn't look very graceful, but it got the job done. I don't think Burk was counting on you carrying a knife. Or anything that might cut fast enough to get Vega down before he died. He probably bet on the fact that by the time we figured out how to get Vega down, it would be too late."

"He doesn't know tactical officers and their suite of tricks, then. We're trained to think on our feet."

She grinned and held out his knife. "Thank God for that."

"Anytime." Returning her smile, he took his knife and dropped it in the pocket of his cargo pants.

She was pretty sure he hadn't noticed, but when seconds had counted and he didn't have time to think, he'd appealed to her with the name he'd once called her only in their most intimate and connected moments. The one his gut said would get her attention. And had.

As she looked toward the ESH, her smile faded. They might have won this round, but it was going to put her argument with Cartwright to stave off a tactical solution on thin ice. Now that she knew Rivas was making a power play inside the facility, she had a bad feeling the situation was spiraling out of control and there wasn't going to be anything she could do about it. Negotiation as a tactic required both sides to compromise. She had done that and had thought he had. But he'd lied.

It was the kind of bad faith that could tank a negotiation.

Attica. Waco. Ruby Ridge.

She didn't want Rikers added to that list of failures.

CHAPTER 24

When the knock came at the door, Gemma was pulling a pan out of the oven. She glanced at the clock on her stove and realized there was only one person it could possibly be at this hour. "My hands are full," she called. "Use your key!"

There was a pause, followed by a slight scratching at the door and then the dead bolt shot back. The door opened and her brother Alex strolled in.

Only a year younger than Gemma, Alex was her closest sibling. They'd always been close—her brother Teo was only a year older than her, but he didn't have much interest in the family's only girl child, instead choosing to follow two-years older Mark and three-years older Joe around. Gemma and Alex had been natural playmates, but following the death of Maria Capello when they were nine and ten, they became inseparable. Gemma had taken on Maria's mothering role for Alex, a small boy who now had no mama to run to in times of trouble, and Alex had become protective of Gemma, who was traumatized not only by their mother's death, but because she had witnessed it. They had clung to each other in those early days, and though they led separate lives now, they remained more firmly entwined than any of the other siblings.

Calling on Alex for help during the Boyle case had only partly been because as Internal Affairs, he was the only Capello not already actively involved in the case. A larger part of it was she knew he might be the only one able to take the few scant clues she was able to leave and still deduce the message.

She'd been correct, and it had been the combined forces of Gemma and Alex that had nearly brought Boyle in alive. Logan knew how close she was to Alex—even in her academy days, it was already established Alex would be following in three of his siblings' footsteps into the NYPD—and now it was clear to her how that knowledge had possibly altered the outcome of the Boyle case. Alex had been as furious as she about the conclusion of the case. She wasn't sure if he'd be grateful or even more furious now that the reason for Boyle's death had been revealed to her.

Alex closed the door behind him and turned in to the kitchen. Similar in height and coloring, he shared her curly hair, but he kept his trimmed short on the sides and only let a bounce of curls spring free over his forehead.

Carrying a brown paper bag, he strolled into her apartment as if he owned the place. Considering he lived in the same building and easily spent as much time in her apartment as his own, he always said it felt like an extension of home. "Hey, I know you're in the middle of this Rikers thing, but I wanted to check in to see how . . ." His voice trailed off as he took in her kitchen counters. "Exactly how bad is it on the island?"

"It's not good." Gemma followed his gaze over to where she'd laid out cooling racks loaded down with the results of her evening. Rows of crisp, pale swirled droplets of *biscotti con mandorla*, their tops sparkling with a crust of sugar, sat next to a pan of semicircular pastries, artistically dusted with icing sugar.

He tossed the bag on one of the tall stools lining her breakfast bar. "Did you get off at eight?"

"Yes."

He marked the time on her stove. "You must have started this the moment you walked in the door."

"Pretty much."

"Did you eat dinner?"

"Wasn't hungry."

He gave her a squinted side-eye to tell her that answer didn't satisfy him whatsoever. "You're making me hungry." He reached over the counter and grabbed several cookies and extended one to her. "It's not the greatest of dinners, but start with this to get something in your stomach. Then I can make you one of my famous omelets."

"Breakfast for dinner?" She took a bite of cookie, nodding in satisfaction at the crisp crunch of the shell contrasting the fluffiness inside, all overlaid with a sweet punch of almond.

"It's what all the cool kids are doing." Alex popped a whole cookie in his mouth. His eyelids fluttered half-closed and he let out a hum. "You're sending some home with me, right? You can't eat all of this."

"I wasn't planning on eating it all. McFarland specifically requested those cookies." She picked up a small sieve half-full of icing sugar from a bowl beside the oven and started dusting the pastries fresh out of the oven.

Alex's bark of laughter conveyed what he thought of his sister baking at ten o'clock at night for a coworker. "That's an excuse if I ever heard one. You're not baking for him. This is stress baking." He looked more closely at the pastries she was putting the finishing touches on. "Ooh, *cassatelle*. Which ones did you make?"

"Ricotta with cinnamon."

"Marsala in the crust?"

She simply raised a long-stemmed wineglass covered with greasy fingerprints—she'd been enjoying while she baked—and took a sip, watching him over the rim.

"Now you're just buttering me up. What do you want?" Alex selected one from a cooling rack. He gave a delicate sniff, groaned in satisfaction, and took a bite. "Whatever it is, it's yours." His words were muffled by his full mouth.

Gemma set down her glass, wiped her hands on the towel she'd tossed over the counter, then wiped the glass clean, a smile tugging at the edges of her lips. She needed this. Needed to connect with family away from the stress of Rikers, needed to connect with Alex most of all. "How about that omelet?"

"For Sicilian desserts, you can have almost anything your heart desires."

"You need to find yourself a woman who can cook."

"I need to find myself a woman who can *bake*," Alex countered. "The way to my heart is right through the dessert tray. You're going to be a hard act to follow though. You done so I can get in there?"

"In a minute. I need to finish off these *cassatelli*." She set down her wineglass and picked up the sieve again.

"Speaking of *cassatelli* . . ." He lobbed the paper bag gently to Gemma. She caught it in her free hand and then set down the sieve. The bag was marked with LA CASSATELLA in its familiar red script. Simply seeing the familiar logo made her smile. "You stopped at the bakery?"

La Cassatella was a bakery-café in Little Italy run by Francesca Russo and her father. Gemma had grown up with Frankie, the sister Gemma was never given by birth, and they remained close decades later.

"Popped in just before closing."

Gemma double-checked the time. "Just before closing? Did you get lost on your way here?"

"Frankie had me pull up a stool while she closed the bakery and, the next thing I knew, half an hour had gone by, and I had to hustle if I wanted to catch you before bed." He looked pointedly at the baked goods. "Of course, if I'd known you were baking, I'd have taken my time."

"You could have." She opened the bag to find a tightly wrapped package of coffee beans inside. She looked up sharply. "You didn't."

"I sure did. Knew you'd probably need a pick-me-up so I asked Frankie for some of that dark roast you like. Nice and fresh, roasted this morning."

"You're a miracle. If you tried some of the coffee at Rikers, you'd know exactly what this means to me."

"I live on cop coffee. I know what it means to you."

"Rikers coffee makes station coffee taste gourmet." Gemma pulled out the bag, held it to her nose, and pulled in a long breath. "So good." She set it down beside her coffee grinder. "That will make my morning tomorrow considerably brighter." She turned around to lean against the counter. "You know, speaking of a woman who can bake . . ."

"Yeah, yeah, I know. You won't let me forget."

"She runs a bakery for God's sake."

"And thinks of me as her little brother. I'm not getting burned on that fire."

Gemma shook her head at his stubbornness. "All you have to do is ask her."

"And when she says no, it will be weird between us forever. Nuh-uh, I value her friendship too much."

"You're making a mistake." At her brother's pointed stare, she shrugged, took up the sieve again, and went back to tapping it gently against her open palm over the pastries, enveloping them in a sweet cloud. A few passes up and down the pan and she was done. "There we go."

"Clear that stuff out of the way and let me in there. We both won't fit."

Gemma's apartment was in Alphabet City on the Lower East Side. It was modest—a one-bedroom on the eighth floor with a small balcony that overlooked D Street and out beyond the buildings across the street to the East River. The space had been newly upgraded when she moved in, with new appliances and polished wood floors. The super was so happy to have an NYPD detective in-house that he'd approved her request to paint the stark white walls a warm, neutral mocha. She'd filled her living room with a couch and chair around a glass-topped coffee table opposite her wall-mounted flat-screen TV. But rather than formal, her living room was comfortable, a space where you could nap under the fuzzy hand-crocheted afghan currently draped over the cushions, or relax with family with your feet up on the coffee table.

When Alex had been looking for an apartment, it had

been Gemma's relationship with the super that netted him an early shot at an apartment in the building. He now rented a studio apartment a few floors down, saying that was all the space he needed, but he tended to gravitate to Gemma's space more than his own, which was strictly functional versus comfortable. It wasn't just for her cooking—he'd also learned from their grandmother how to cook; he just didn't get the same comfort from it she did. For him, for both of them really, the Sicilian roots went deep, and home was family, not simply a space to be on your own. Someday, when either of them had a live-in partner, that would change, but, for now, his presence in her space suited both of them. He came and went as he pleased, and she always had the right to tell him to go away, not that she often did. It worked for them. Which was why it wasn't strange for him to spontaneously drop by at ten at night, or to be at home in her kitchen.

A soft meow attracted their attention as a vibrant black, white, and orange calico cat wandered out of Gemma's bedroom.

"There's my Mia." Alex walked over to meet the cat, an adult, but so tiny, it was as if she'd never completed her kitten growth. He scooped her up, tucking her into the crook of his arm and scratching under her chin and behind her ears. She immediately started to purr and butted her head against his jaw. "I wondered where you were."

"Napping on my bed, I'd imagine." Gemma smiled fondly at both Alex and the cat. When she'd left her father's house to live downtown to be closer to work, she'd found the space, while charming, empty and lonely. She'd rescued undersized and underweight Mia from a local shelter, they'd immediately bonded, and the cat had quickly settled in. Gemma had initially worried her sometimes long and erratic hours wouldn't be good for the cat, but Mia was independent and enjoyed not having to compete for resources in her new space. A water fountain and supplemental food on a timer put Gemma's mind at ease for when she was trapped on the job. Though Alex always stood by to feed and hang out with the cat, if needed. Gemma suspected Mia was also part of why he preferred her apartment to his. On several occurrences, she'd found them stretched out asleep in the sun on her couch, Mia curled into a compact ball on Alex's chest as they snoozed. Alex also had a tendency to slip her food during meals to "fatten her up" when caught red-handed. Gemma had suggested to him a few times that he get a cat for himself, but he said he already had one and his girl wouldn't like him coming in smelling like some other feline. It would be like cheating.

Alex gave the cat a kiss on the top of her head and set her on the floor where she wandered in the direction of the cat tree tucked into the corner of the living room between two windows where she had a whole city to watch. "Okay, you, out of my kitchen."

"*Your* kitchen?"

"For the next fifteen minutes it is. Out. And I'm stealing a glass of your Marsala while I cook."

"Help yourself."

They changed positions, Gemma settling on a stool at her breakfast bar after organizing the baked goods to give her space at her counter. Alex washed his hands, poured a glass of wine, and then picked through her fridge and cupboards, pulling out eggs, roasted red peppers, sundried tomatoes, goat cheese, and herbs. He moved through the kitchen like he owned it, easily finding the bowl and pan he needed.

He started breaking eggs into the bowl. "So, what's going on that brought on the baking?"

"It's that obvious?"

"It is to me." He scanned the rows of sweets. "Probably would be to the entire family. Was it a specific event, or is it just days of frustration?" He set her abandoned wineglass down in front of her, then picked up his own.

"Thanks." She took a sip and let out a sigh, her shoulders slumping as she braced her forearms on the counter. "It's days of frustration topped by an event." She set down her glass and massaged her forehead with both hands.

He started beating the eggs with a fork. "Headache?"

"Low-grade. It's been nagging at me for hours."

"Did you take something?"

"Yes, Dad. Not really touching it though."

"Did the baking help?"

"Actually, yes."

"Then you, me, and McFarland all win." He pulled out a cutting board and chopped the red peppers and the sun-dried tomatoes into smaller pieces. "Tell me what's going on."

As he crumbled cheese and then melted butter in a pan before pouring in the eggs, she caught him up on the overall situation, including the players on all sides. As she talked, he deftly put together her omelet, making sure everything was perfectly seasoned and cooked through. She was finishing the summary of the morning's attempted attack when he slid the omelet onto a plate and set it in front of her with a fork.

"Thanks. It smells divine." She grinned. "Suddenly I'm hungry."

"Me too." He picked up another *cassatelle* and bit in. "My compliments to the chef."

"Ditto." She cut off a piece with her fork, popped it in her mouth, and chewed. "Mmm. Really ditto. That's amazing. Put us together and we make an outstanding full meal."

Alex let out a burst of laughter. "Now you're just being kind. You don't need my help for that in the least." He leaned against the counter and took another bite. "I've been staying out of your way because I figured you needed decompression time when you got home, but there's obviously more going on here."

"I have to admit this case is already one of the worst I've ever dealt with. A high-profile hostage situation with heavy media attention and the DOC and the mayor of New York City breathing down our necks."

He waved the *cassatelle*. "You said there was an event. I assume that's what got you baking."

She ate another piece of omelet, taking her time in chewing and swallowing. "I'm losing control of the situation and I'm not sure I can get it back."

Alex whistled and put down his pastry. "That would bring on stress baking. What are you leaving out?"

"It's what happened later today. There are serious cracks forming and I'm not sure I can talk my way out of it a second time." As she ate, she told him about the attempted hanging. "We only barely saved the guy's life. At least I think we did. I'm pretty sure he's going to make it, but depending on how long his oxygen was cut off, there might be some permanent damage." She shook her head, her lips pursed. "The battle lines drawn here were put into place long before I got onto the scene."

"If you ask me, those lines were drawn out there"—he pointed out the window in the general direction of Brooklyn—"long before they got to Rikers. I'm not sure how you can mediate that kind of long-standing hatred. I'd say what you pulled off today is notable all on its own."

"I don't know about that." She put her fork down on her empty plate. "That was great. Thanks."

He carried her plate to the sink to rinse. "You're welcome. I accept payment in any and all forms of sugar and flour." He returned to the counter. "You're worried about tomorrow."

"Yeah. It's not just us against the hostage takers with the hostages in the middle. It's us against at least two factions inside the ESH with the hostages at risk from all of them, and with the DOC on the outside not wanting to give any ground because of the precedent it would set. They know word gets around and they don't want to look weak. The DOC is fighting its own internal battles with CO brutality and dysfunction, but they don't want to take away, or worse, lose, any of their authority because of this situation. We're being pulled in every direction and failing in all of them."

"I disagree."

"What? How?"

"You're looking at the glass as if it's half-empty. Now try looking at it like it's half-full. You've kept a verifiably terrible warden out of the picture because he'd only make it worse, leaning on his deputy when needed because you see her as the asset she is. You're four days into this and you haven't lost a single hostage. You've successfully negotiated the release of one of the hostages and you've negotiated for the safety of the others for the time being. One inmate is dead, but it's likely he died during the initial riot or shortly thereafter, before you were involved, so it can't be put on you or your team."

"But if I don't have control of the situation—"

"Control is an illusion and you know it. You present that illusion, but you have a facility of inmates and detainees who are already there for various crimes. Some of those inmates are on their way to life sentences and know they have very little to lose. That's where the real control rests." He met her eyes, nodding at what he saw there. "You know it, and that's why you're baking."

"I guess." She soothed herself with another sip of wine. "A successful negotiation is always the goal, but I have a bad feeling on this one."

"You think you're going to have to hand it off to Cartwright? I know a tactical conclusion is never your choice."

"No, but sometimes it's where we end up. I just need to remind myself that it isn't about me and the HNT. It's about the hostages. Yes, a negotiated surrender is always our goal, but sometimes it's simply not possible and that doesn't mean we failed. It means in this situation, that strategy was unsuccessful."

"Also, in this case, the hostages aren't only the COs. You have unidentified hostages in the form of other inmates. Without cameras inside the ESH, you can't tell what exactly is happening, and who's at risk."

She swirled the amber liquid in her glass, watching light sparkle through it. "And I can't protect a group I can't identify."

"It sounds to me like the clock is ticking down at this point. Prison riots have gone on longer, but there's a war going on inside the ESH. The situation can't be allowed to deteriorate further. All you can do is your best to bring as many out alive as possible. It's not a failure for the HNT. You've bought time, you've saved lives. You'll save as many more as you can." He emptied his wineglass and set it beside the sink, then gave her a sideways glance. "By the way, it sounds like you and Logan worked well together this afternoon. Have you let him off the hook?"

"It's funny you'd ask that . . ."

Alex waited for a few beats before pushing again. "Because . . . ?"

"He and I had it out today."

"Really?" He bent over the counter and braced his elbow on it to rest his chin on his hand. "Do tell."

"This is totally bringing out the eighth-grade girl in you."

"Adult men can be nosy, too, you know."

"Oh, I know. Anyway, this is the first op Sean and I have worked since August. I guess he got tired of my ignoring his presence—which I'd been doing since day one—because he pulled me into a conference room and confronted me."

"You didn't knee him in the balls and put him on the floor?"

Four brothers had individually made sure she knew how to handle herself with men from her teen years onward. "I could have. But I never felt physically threatened. In fact, he basically told me to let him have it . . . so I did."

"Did he justify the death?"

"In the end, yes. And, really, I guess, neither you or I can complain about his reason."

"I'm not sure I'd complain. I was mad because I thought we had him. *You* thought we had him, and that was good enough for me. But Sanders told him to take the shot. He was following orders."

"The order gave him cover, and he could have not

taken the shot. But he wasn't willing to take the chance that Boyle was bluffing. I was certain he wasn't, that Boyle had too much respect for the badge itself to kill another officer, especially one who was blameless of any wrongdoing. His respect for the badge is what started everything in the first place. Not that Sean knew that because there wasn't time to explain. But that wasn't the deciding factor."

"It wasn't?"

"No. You were."

"Because there was a chance he was going to kill me?"

Gemma shook her head. "Not exactly. If I'd had another officer with me, I'm not sure what he would have done. But it was you."

Alex stared at her in confusion for a moment, and then the light came into his eyes as he deduced the rest. "It goes back to Mom." When she nodded, he continued. "He couldn't stand by and watch you lose someone else. Watch another Capello murdered in front of you. So he added to his own body count to safeguard me. And through me, you." He straightened. "Damn, I didn't see that coming."

"Me either."

"What did you do when he told you?"

"Stopped him from walking out and thanked him for watching out for us. It's still not the resolution to Boyle's case I wanted, but now I understand what happened, and I can't fault him for it. He had a split second to make a decision."

"And he went with his gut, even if that meant ignoring your request."

"Yeah."

"Well, if that helped build a bridge between you, the result was the life you saved together this afternoon. That's a definite plus." He looked over his shoulder to check the time. "I'd better get going because you're going to have to head to bed pronto to be as fresh as possible for tomorrow. Let me help you pack all this away."

"And carry some of it out of here while you do."

"If you insist."

That drew a laugh from her. "I wouldn't have it any other way. I'll pack a container for you and one for the team tomorrow. That will make the guys happy. And if I'm lucky, really lucky, maybe it won't all go to hell the moment I walk in the door."

CHAPTER 25

Gemma set the tin canister on the table in front of McFarland. "You're welcome."

McFarland snapped away from a conversation with Shelby to stare at the container. "You didn't."

"We had a deal. You bring the coffee, I bring the cookies. You've been bringing coffee for days."

"I didn't actually think you'd go home to bake after the day we had yesterday." He popped open the lid, bent over, and drew in a slow inhale of rich, sugary almond. "I think I've died and gone to heaven."

"Are those your famous almond cookies?" Shelby snuck a hand in under McFarland's nose and snagged a cookie.

"Hey!"

"You snooze, you lose." She took a bite. "I stand corrected. We all win." She pinned Gemma with a pointed stare. "You did these last night? After the medical visit and the attempted hanging?"

Gemma half shrugged. "Yeah."

"I guess everyone needs an outlet for that kind of a day and stress baking is a legit outlet." She grabbed another cookie. "This will power me on my way home to bed."

McFarland grabbed two cookies. "And me for this shift. Along with probably a half-dozen more."

"I need to talk to Garcia about his team selection." Corbitt helped himself to a cookie. "Next multiday stand-off, *I* get Capello."

The teams passed off with an update of a quiet night from Taylor and then it was just the day squad left in the negotiation room.

McFarland set a cup of coffee in front of Gemma and then saluted her with his. "Amazing, as always."

"Thanks. You should be glad I got a container's worth to bring in. Alex dropped by last night and raided the stash first. I had to cut him off."

"He can eat your baked goods anytime. We have to wait until Garcia schedules us in with you." His gaze drifted past her to the far wall and the names and maps posted there. "They've been out of touch all night. We better call them. They'll know it's you."

"I'm not sure Rivas is going to be as interested in talking to me now that I know he's been jerking us around. Unless I have some news. Has anyone heard from Garcia?"

"Not me." Williams snagged a cookie, tipped his head to her in thanks. "Maybe we should call him."

"Let me text him. I doubt they're at it yet, but just in

case, let's not interrupt them." Gemma pulled out her phone, zipped off a quick text, and was rewarded with a reply within a few minutes. She read the message and then looked up to find three pairs of eyes locked on her. "He says they're almost there. He'll be over this morning with their answer and we can present it then. Maybe knowing an answer is coming will convince him to talk to me because, clearly, there's a lot we don't know still."

"That can't be a surprise," Chen said.

"It's not. I'm not his family. Not his friend. I'm the enemy. I thought we'd been able to build a bridge over some of that. But he's playing both sides against the middle, and one of his own guys nearly died because of it."

"Maybe that got the point through to him?"

"We should be so lucky. Let's find out."

Ten minutes later, Gemma disconnected the call for the fifth time. "They don't seem interested in picking up today." She slipped off her headphones and tossed them onto the table in front of her. "Let's give them fifteen and then try again. We need to get through long enough to tell them Garcia will bring—"

A pulsating alarm went off, stopping her midsentence. It sounded like it came from every direction, but from miles away, a faint, strobing *whoop-whoop-whoop* in the distance.

Gemma's head snapped up to stare at McFarland in alarm. She'd heard that sound the day before. Twice.

The personal alarm of one of the A-Team officers.

Gemma pushed back her chair with a screech. "The ESH!"

The men were also on their feet. "Go!" said Williams. "I'll watch the phone."

McFarland got to the door first and wrenched it open, then Gemma, McFarland, and Chen sprinted down the corridor. From a distance, nearly inaudible over the growing wail of the siren, an anguished scream cut the air. Gemma nearly stumbled when Johnson, his face set in stone and hardly sparing them a glance, sprinted by them in the opposite direction.

Something is very wrong . . .

They ran faster.

They sprinted past the courtyard and around to the entrance to the ESH. McFarland jerked to a halt so quickly, Gemma nearly ran right into him. She sidestepped and might have staggered if he hadn't grabbed her arm to steady her.

"Oh my God."

A writhing man dressed in a CO's uniform lay on the floor in front of the door to the ESH, like a grotesquely animated incarnation of the dead inmate only days before. The A-Team officers were gathered around, a few still on their feet, most of them on their knees around the man. Cartwright faced Gemma with his gloved hands pressing down on the man's belly, trying to hold him still.

His blood-covered hands.

The strain in Cartwright's face told her how much pressure he was applying. The kind of pressure needed to save a life slowly leeching out of your grip.

The alarm shut off abruptly as Sims snapped his rip cord back into the device.

"Hold him still," Cartwright ordered. "Logan, Peterson. Get his shoulders. Sims, Hill, his legs."

Gemma closed the rest of the distance, stopping short momentarily when she identified the man on the floor.

"Officer Garvey?" The men shifted slightly and she knelt down on the opposite side from Cartwright. Garvey lay on his back, his eyes open and glazed, his pale face washing toward gray. His navy-blue uniform shirt had turned black over his torso, the material saturated with blood that followed gravity to drip onto the floor in a slowly spreading puddle.

So much blood.

"Jake, it's Gemma Capello." Gemma rose up on her knees, leaning forward into his field of view. "I need you to hang on. We have you. And more help is coming."

His response was lost in a pained gurgle.

Logan knelt beside Cartwright, one hand holding Garvey's shoulder against the floor, the fingers of his other hand pressed to Garvey's throat, his eyes unfixed as he stared at the floor counting heartbeats. Gemma didn't like what she read in his set expression. She looked back at Cartwright. "What happened?"

Cartwright kept his eyes on the blood that oozed out from under his fingers. "We're not sure. They shoved him out the door like this."

"This isn't going to do it. We need medical."

"Johnson went for prison admin to raise the alarm. We need staff from the island. They know how to get them here quickest. We need to hold him until they get here."

Gemma studied the blood flow with a critical eye. NYPD officers were trained on advanced emergency first aid as they were often first responders at a scene; even the limited training she had told her Garvey was losing too much blood. "You're not getting enough pressure. McFarland, give me your jacket."

Without questioning the loss of his suit jacket, McFarland stripped out of it, quickly folded it into a thick pad and knelt beside Gemma. "Ready? On the count of three. One . . . two . . . *three*."

Cartwright lifted his hands just long enough for McFarland to slide the pad over the wound, but in that quick second, blood welled fast and dark. Cartwright pressed down hard and Garvey moaned, his eyelashes fluttering. But the anguished screaming of only a few minutes ago now seemed past him and his face, tipped toward her, was slack. Unconscious? That would be a blessing, unless he was slipping away.

Garvey was losing too much blood, and they, in turn, were losing him. She couldn't tell under his shirt if there was arterial spray, but if there was, they could be standing in an OR and it still could be too late.

Gemma looked up at the men towering over her. "Who has gloves?"

Both Hill and Peterson dug into a pocket in their cargo pants. Peterson got there first, pulling out a pair of blue nitrile gloves and handing them to Gemma. She pulled them on—too big for her small hands, but they got the job done—and placed her hands around Cartwright's, pressing down hard. This time there was no response as Garvey's blood slowly soaked into McFarland's jacket, warming Gemma's cold fingers.

"Pulse rate is climbing. He's going into shock." Logan said. "Where the hell is the medical team?" He froze for a moment, then bent down, his ear over Garvey's mouth and one palm flat against his chest. "He's not breathing. We're losing him."

"Start CPR." Maintaining pressure, Gemma turned around to look over her shoulder and down the hallway.

Logan shifted slightly, lay the flat of one hand over the other on Garvey's sternum beside Gemma's right hand. Straightening his elbows and leaning over Garvey to center his weight over his hands, he started rhythmic compressions. Garvey's body jerked with each compression and Gemma had to fight to keep her hold when her hands slipped on the wet fabric.

Pounding footsteps behind them heralded the arrival of help.

Gemma glanced back in time to see Peltier and Johnson running toward them.

"What happened?" Peltier was out of breath and blowing hard.

"They tossed him out already bleeding." Cartwright spoke as if through clenched teeth, his body rocking with the compressions. "Looks like they stabbed him in the gut."

"I thought you worked in another building?" Gemma asked.

Peltier dug in his bag and fished out a pair of angled shears. "I came in this morning to see about getting in to see Officer Keen." Peltier's head cocked in the direction of the doorway. "I was heading for Davis's office with my medical bag when your officer stopped me." Peltier yanked a plastic box out of the end pocket of his bag. "Stop compressions."

As soon as Logan's hands were off Garvey's chest, he quickly cut the shirt open to bare Garvey's blood-splattered chest but left the abdomen alone to continue the pressure. He opened the case and pulled out two adhesive pads on the leads, stripped off the backing, and slapped one pad on Garvey's upper right chest and a second on his lower left chest, curving down his side. "Everyone off . . . Clear!"

The moment Gemma and Cartwright lifted their bloody hands into the air, Peltier hit the button. The machine measured Garvey's heart rate and quickly delivered a shock. Garvey gave a slight spasm, his shoulders lifting into a shrug, then he lay still. Peltier murmured something under his breath and adjusted the settings. "Clear!" And hit the button again, staring at the numbers on the screen. Shaking his head, he made another adjustment. "Clear!" and pushed the button.

Gemma knew they'd lost before Peltier spoke. Lost the battle, lost the war from a negotiation standpoint. Lost an officer who went to work one morning, only to never go home again.

It was every cop's greatest fear.

"He's gone." Peltier checked his watch. "Time of death, oh-eight-twenty-four." Peltier tugged off one pad, then the other, pulling them off their leads, pressing them together. "He simply lost too much blood. He could have been on the table in the OR and I still likely wouldn't have been able to save him." He dropped the pads into a clear bag, then pulled on a pair of gloves. He lifted the saturated coat, holding it aloft so he could look underneath. The shirt was held in place where it was still tucked into his pants but above the belt buckle and to the left there was a jagged tear in the shirt. "A single puncture wound. Considering the placement and the blood flow, it likely severed the mesenteric artery. He never had a chance." He set the jacket on Garvey's abdomen. "Someone needs to find Davis. This is now a crime scene so he's going to want to call in the NYPD." He glanced at the officers surrounding him. "Homicide. And the DOC. We all need to step back."

Gemma stripped off her gloves, dropping them on the floor as part of the evidence, stood without touching anything around her, and stepped away to stare at the body.

A hostage was dead. There was no coming back from this.

"We need to call Garcia."

McFarland's voice pulled Gemma from her unhappy contemplation. "Yeah. He's coming down here to bring the counteroffer on the demands."

"Those aren't going to be relevant anymore."

"No."

"I'll go to the office and update Williams," Chen offered. "And I'll contact Garcia."

"Go update Williams, but I'll contact Garcia. He left me here as primary. It needs to be me." She pulled her eyes from the body to look past it, through the slats of glass and into the ESH. There were men on the mezzanine, and she could see legs on the upper walkway, but no one was near the door. No one watched to see the results of what someone inside had done.

Because they'd already seen Garvey's death as a foregone conclusion. *Nothing to see here.*

A crescendo of voices attracted her attention and she looked over in time to see Cartwright stalking around Garvey's body toward her. Fury etched deep lines in his forehead and around his eyes, and his lips were compressed into a tight white line.

"We're done, Capello. Do you understand me?" He closed the distance between them fast. "Done! I don't care what Garcia says. This just became a tactical operation." Cartwright leaned in so close, the hot breath of his fury fanned her cheek. "You had time to sort this out, but that isn't going to happen now. This op is mine." Spinning on his heel, he stalked off down the hallway, swearing under his breath.

She'd fought for time to work out a compromise. The odds had been against her, but she'd held out hope for a Hail Mary.

She'd lost.

CHAPTER 26

She pushed through the door, swinging it wide as she unloaded her frustration onto it, and strode through into the sunny October morning.

The large courtyard was paved in concrete, a sheltered space completely contained on all sides by the different wings of the OBCC. A cluster of picnic tables lined the far end and several basketball nets were mounted over the windows lining every side. A number of faded basketballs studded the concrete where they'd rolled to a stop following the last pick-up game.

The courtyard was quiet now. No basketball during lockdown.

She pulled her phone out of her pocket and sent a text to the one person she knew had a professional interest in her case but would likely be out of the department loop because he wasn't officially involved—Joe.

It's done. They killed a CO. Cartwright is taking over.

She slid her phone away, jammed her hands into her pockets, and struck out in ground-eating strides for the far side of the courtyard, trying to burn through some of the fury and grief roiling in her gut.

Who had killed Garvey? Was it Rivas, making a point? Was it Burk, retaliating for the prize she'd snatched away from him yesterday? Or was it someone else entirely, someone tired of the power struggles and trying to break through the noise?

The time of the attack wasn't lost on her either. By this time, days into the standoff, they knew the regular shift times of the two teams by whose voice was on the end of the line at what time. They knew the teams switched off at 8 a.m.

They timed killing Garvey until she was in the building so that she'd be there to see the results of their handiwork. Whoever was making the point, was making it, loud and clear, to *her*.

She looked down at a basketball on the concrete decking, gave in to her rising temper and sense of helplessness, and kicked it as hard as she could toward the far wall. It struck with an echoing *thump,* but she found that taking her anger out on the ball eased none of the smothering weight. She considered another ball a few feet away, but, instead of kicking it, picked it up, its surface cool and pebbly under her fingers. She started bouncing it, each bounce harder than the last, feeling the satisfaction of the push-away as well as the stinging slap as she caught the ball with her open palm, held it for a moment, and then slammed it back onto the concrete. She hadn't played basketball since high school gym class, but what she remembered said her dribbling technique was all wrong. But really, this wasn't the light touch of dribbling; this was the equivalent of short repetitive volleyball spikes, each one a driving effort to expunge everything that happened that day. There was no finesse, only brute force.

She glanced over at the sound of the door behind her swinging shut to find Logan standing on the far side of the courtyard, unsnapping his chin strap and taking off his helmet. Setting the helmet upside down near the wall, he dropped his safety glasses and gloves in before starting toward her.

She watched him with cold eyes as he approached. "Aren't you supposed to be guarding the door to the ESH?"

He raised an eyebrow at her whiplike tone. "Cartwright told us to take thirty once homicide arrived. He called in the ERSU to spell us at the door and told us to take a walk. I was taking that walk when I saw you through the window kicking that basketball into next week."

"It's a big courtyard. Take your walk over there." Turning her back on him, she continued to pound the ball into the ground.

"I'd rather take my walk over here."

"Fine. Then I'll go over there."

She turned away from him, but he reached out, snagged the ball midbounce, pivoted toward one of the baskets, set up his shot, and took it. The ball sailed through the net, cranking her temper even higher. The only thing that made her feel slightly better was that it hit the rim before going in. Not quite a perfect shot.

She pinned him with a glare that could have melted steel. "Really?"

He shrugged. "High school varsity team. I'm a little rusty."

"That's hardly rusty. Did you come out here to get under my skin or just to show off?"

"I came out here to get some air and to see how you're doing. You know as well as I do what this means."

"Of course I know what this means!" Gemma's control slipped a notch, both her pitch and tone rising higher. They'd just entered into a fragile peace; was it his intention to toss it all away? She threw up a palm toward him in the universal gesture of "stay," turned on her heel, and strode toward the picnic tables at the far end of the courtyard.

She needed ten minutes of peace to gather her thoughts and to push down the kind of raging emotion that could be deadly in a negotiation— for the hostages, the hostage takers, and, sometimes, even the negotiator.

She didn't get fifteen feet before the rhythmic bounce of a ball rang out behind her. But instead of moving away from it, the sound followed her. She sped up; she just needed some space, and some silence, and why did that ball keep going *slap . . . slap . . . slap . . . ?*

She spun around and found him close enough she could grab the ball out from under his hand. She pulled back and hurled it at the side wall. It arced through the air, falling short by several feet to bounce harmlessly off the concrete three times before rolling to a stop near the wall.

Gemma hung her head and blew out a long breath.

"Feel better?"

"Not particularly." She walked over to a picnic table and sat down backward on the bench, spreading her arms wide to rest her elbows and forearms on the tabletop. She leaned back against it and tipped her face skyward, eyes closed, the warmth of the sun on her face. And gave herself a moment to breathe.

Wood creaked as he sat down on the end of the tabletop, followed by the clunk of his heavy boots on the bench.

The silence between them wasn't uncomfortable and didn't leave her with the need to fill it to make herself feel better, but after a few minutes, she felt centered enough to attempt to put her thoughts into words. "It's been going downhill for days. I knew it, but I thought I could hold it together."

"You knew from the start the deck was stacked against you."

"Prison riots are always dicey because of who's involved. In this case, the internal gang structure maybe meant we never had a chance. But I thought I had it. I thought I had a feeling for Rivas and could leverage the hostages out."

"You got Evans out. That was no small thing. He might have died given another day or two."

"But we lost Garvey. The point is to get them *all* out alive."

"You know that's not always possible."

She tipped her head forward and opened her eyes to stare down the long run of concrete toward the shallow gray building at the far end. She found it particular to the OBCC—so much of it was done in tones of gray, like the lack of color was the best way to suck the life out of everything associated with the facility. "Oh, I know. And they've made it clear to me that they know. Message received. Loud and clear."

"You realize that none of this could have anything to do with you? What if it's just that Garvey was an SOB who roughed up prisoners? What if someone outside of the main conflict chose this moment to get some of his own back? Have you pushed that possibility to the bottom of the list because you're so focused on the main players and the conflict going on in there you can't control?"

"I've already thought of that. But no matter who did it, they waited until just after shift change to make sure I was there to see him die."

Her phone vibrated in her pocket and she pulled it out to find a text from Joe.

I'm sorry. You did everything you could. Even with everything I know about them, I couldn't have gotten through to them either.

A pause, then a second message arrived.

Cartwright and his men are good. Give him a chance to pull it out of the fire.

They better be, or it's going to be a massacre.

"You think Garvey was a message to you?" Logan asked, dragging her back to their conversation.

"I think it's not so much me personally, but the voice on the line. I speak for the team and I've been in the facility with them twice. They don't know the rest of the team. They think they know me. They could have attacked Garvey last night and tossed him out for Taylor to find. They didn't. They waited for shift change. They're telling us that as far as they're concerned, they're in charge."

Logan's laugh was dark and razor-sharp. "They can think that all they want. Their little world is about to implode." He looked over at her. "You did everything you could, and you did it by the book. With some groups, it might have worked. Even if this group hadn't jumped the gun this morning, it might have worked. They threw it away, not you."

Knowing you have to go back to that way of life, and probably worse because you just put a giant target on your back as far as the COs are concerned, what would convince you to surrender?

Gemma recalled her own statement from days before. She'd known then her chances of success with these men were small. But even knowing that, she'd built her own expectations impossibly high and was now crashing back to Earth.

"But your negotiation gained us valuable information on the facility and the inmates inside, which will lead to a safer tactical op," Logan continued. "You know it wasn't a waste, right?"

"Yeah. At least the logical side of my brain does. That's why I'm sitting out here. I'm giving the rest of me time to catch up."

"Cartwright's making the right call."

"It's what he wanted all along."

"Yeah, but he knew from the get-go that it's all about the hostages. At the beginning, any incursion would have put them at too much risk from inmates who were working together against a common enemy."

"They were too much of a united front then. But the way they've splintered . . ."

"There are enemies all around. Us, the DOC, the inmate in the cell next door. And Rivas no longer has control, which means it's now a bigger risk to leave the hostages inside versus the risk of incursion, as Garvey's death showed. Cartwright gave you time to resolve this without a siege, but the inmates had to work with you to get there. In the end, they chose not to." His gaze drifted toward the door at the far end that would lead him back to his team and to what now had to be a tactical end to the standoff. "Now the only goal is to get those six COs out alive. And God help anyone who gets in our way."

CHAPTER 27

Gemma entered the small interview room and stopped just inside the doorway, wrinkling her nose at the heavy odor that hung in the room—dank moisture, mildew, and . . . was that weed? Probably. She, too, had heard the stories of COs who turned a blind eye to inmates who smoked weed in their cells because taking the smuggled item away from the inmate would likely require the use of force, and it simply wasn't worth it to get written up for nothing more than a joint.

Like everywhere else in the facility, the walls were dingy slate-gray, this time with chips and gouges along the far wall where the back of a metal chair had scraped across it countless times. The two chairs that comprised the room's only furniture were identical metal slat-backs, likely once silver but now a dull gunmetal. They were on opposite sides of the small space, the far chair positioned next to the wall where an iron bar was bolted at the level of the top of the chair. Glancing at her watch to confirm the time, she sat down in the chair in the corner farthest from the door, crossed her legs, and set the clipboard and pen she carried on her knee.

Tactical incursion planning was going to start shortly, and Cartwright was bringing in additional teams and commanders to assist with the assault. The A-Team officers were highly trained, but a team of six was simply not enough to ensure a safe dynamic entry into a closed incarceration facility. Negotiations were over, for all intents and purposes. They'd still try to get Rivas on the phone to downplay any suspicions he might have about their next steps, but she didn't trust herself to talk to him right now, not with a thick layer of fury coating her every thought.

Williams was acting as primary for now, but just because she didn't trust herself to talk to Rivas right now didn't mean she couldn't help in other ways.

With an incursion upcoming, they needed every bit of intel they could get. They had the blueprints and staff information about how the facility usually functioned, but this was anything but business as usual. What they really needed was an inside scoop. And who better for that than an inmate with an ax to grind.

Her original intention had been to interview Lafferty. But with the news that Vega was stable after the attempt on his life, she changed tactics. She wanted to hear from someone who'd lived inside the ESH post-riot, someone who knew about the power structure and the inmate affiliations. Lafferty would know all that, but considering he'd tried to attack her, he'd be an unwilling witness when time was of the essence.

Vega was a different story. He had nothing against her.

In fact, he owed his life to Logan, Sims, Mulgrew, and herself for cutting him down. He might even be feeling a touch of gratitude for their actions.

She was willing to play that card to get the information she needed.

She heard the voices coming down the hallway through the open door, two voices, low and indistinct. Then Vega came through the doorway, his hands cuffed behind his back, steered by an unfamiliar CO who entered the room behind him.

Vega was in unrelieved Rikers orange, the scrub-style V-neck shirt revealing not only his tattoos but the ugly evidence of his attack. Angry splotches of black-mottled purple spread over his throat, obliterating the details of his neck tattoo.

"Over to the chair," the CO ordered.

Vega complied and the CO unlocked the handcuffs from one wrist only, and then secured the free loop to the metal bar on the wall. "Sit down." The guard waited for Vega to sit, one arm suspended from the bar, before moving to stand against the wall.

In the small space, Gemma could read his nameplate with a quick glance. "Thank you, Officer Perry."

For the first time, Vega looked up to meet Gemma's eyes. Recognition dawned.

Closer now, Gemma could see the bruising at his throat was overlaid with red abrasions stretched taught over swollen skin where the sheet had rubbed his throat raw as he thrashed. Still, as long as there was no serious internal damage, given a few weeks, he would heal.

It had been a near thing.

If it hadn't been for Cartwright's alarm, Sims's speed, Logan's quick thinking, and their connection that allowed her to instantly understand her role, Vega wouldn't be facing her now.

"Mr. Vega, it's good to see you up and about."

"Guess I need to thank you for that." His voice was slightly raspy, likely the result of swollen or damaged vocal cords. "They told me you cut me down."

"Working with the A-Team, but yes, I was the one with the knife. There was no time for anything else. Even if we'd been able to get through the inmates on the second level, by the time one of the officers got there, it would have been too late." Her gaze dropped to his throat. "That looks painful."

His left hand jerked against the metal cuff as if to move to touch the injury before he remembered he was restrained. "It's getting better."

"I'm glad to hear that. Now, I asked to meet with you because I wanted to talk about the ESH standoff. I need your help."

"With what?"

She normally wouldn't share police procedure with a prison inmate, but in this case, it was one who was entirely cut off from the situation and who had the kind of knowledge that would make or break the operation. And save lives.

"This morning, everything changed in the standoff. Someone killed one of the COs. He died on the floor in the hallway outside the ESH."

Vega's eyes flared wide in surprise, but he remained silent.

"This leaves us with little choice," Gemma continued. "The standoff will end in the next twenty-four hours before anyone else gets hurt. We'd like your help to ensure that."

His gaze shifted from hers to the side wall and he shook his head slightly.

Perry made a move to push away from the wall, but Gemma raised her hand slightly to stay him. He stopped, but kept his eye on Vega.

"You don't seem willing, Mr. Vega."

"I just got attacked. I don't need it to happen again."

"You're concerned about retribution. Who'd know you're here?" She looked up at the CO. "Officer Perry, did you verbally indicate where you were bringing Mr. Vega when you escorted him off the cell block?"

"No, ma'am."

"Thank you. You have no concerns then, Mr. Vega. If anyone asks, you were brought to see Dr. Peltier who wanted to examine your injury. If anyone is concerned that you were away too long to justify that, tell them Peltier had a medical emergency and you had to wait in the clinic. I understand the need to keep yourself safe. We can give you cover."

Vega shifted uncomfortably, his reluctance writ large.

Time to try a different angle. She contemplated the bright tattoos on his forearms. "You're one of the Filero Kings, I understand."

"Yeah."

"Isn't part of being in the group that you look out for your Kings at all times? You watch their backs just like they watch yours?"

"Yeah."

"Your help here will allow you to do exactly that. Our primary goal is to retrieve the hostages without any more bloodshed." She pressed her fingers to her own throat. "There's been enough of that already. The more of an advantage going in we have, the better the chance we can contain the inmates without anyone getting hurt and without the hostages suffering further retribution. You help us, you'll help keep the Filero Kings safe."

Vega remained silent, his jaw clenched tight, but he started to rock back and forth slightly, like he was vibrating.

Getting through.

"Do you know what my main goal as a hostage negotiator is?"

He shrugged carelessly.

"To keep everyone alive. *Everyone*. We took a risk coming into the ESH to get you. We risked ourselves, we risked the hostages' lives, but you were going to die so we had to take the chance. We got you out—alive—and the hostages were untouched. But the price of your life may have been the life of one of the COs."

Rock, rock, rock. "Who died?"

"I can't say until next of kin is notified." Gemma knew it wasn't a strong argument, but she only needed Vega to believe it. If he, too, had a grudge against Garvey, he might be so satisfied with the outcome he would choose not to help. She had to hope he might have enough of a connection to any of the other COs to not want to risk their lives.

"What's in it for me?"

"Besides knowing you'll be helping your brothers, I don't know. I'm not a prosecutor, I can't make you a deal." Vega's scowl had her pushing onward. "But I can tell you this—having a cop in your corner to testify to your assistance in closing down a five-day standoff can only help during your next court date or parole hearing." She met his hard, dark eyes. "I'll do that for you. You help me, I'll stand up for you to testify to it. That will only make your life easier later." She sat back in her chair, crossing her arms over her chest. "Surely that must be worth something when you're weighing helping your brothers versus sticking it to the Gutta Boys for what they did to you."

"What's going to happen to them?"

"The ones we stopped from killing you?" She leaned forward, holding his gaze. "They'll be prosecuted, and they'll be found guilty. Nine NYPD officers witnessed the crime." She gave him a sly smile, letting a touch of her own fury slip through. "Look at it this way. In saving their lives during the raid, they'll have longer to live out their soon-to-be extended sentences."

The light behind his eyes warmed as a satisfied smile curved his lips. "I could live with that."

She opened her clipboard to reveal a smaller version of the blueprint on the wall of the negotiation room and pulled her chair in a little closer. "Let's go through the entire facility a room at a time. People, placement, weapons, habits. Tell me everything you know."

CHAPTER 28

Gemma slipped into the meeting a few minutes after it began. Located in the same room where DOC staff and the NYPD teams had met that first day, the space was once again standing room only. She quickly scanned the crowd, finding her team as well as Taylor's night-shift team brought in so they'd be available to take part. She knew how a lack of sleep could drag you down, but she also knew that, if it was her, she'd want to be involved. Caffeine was a blessing; adrenaline would do the rest to get them through. They could always sleep tomorrow.

She ignored the possibility that the op could go wrong and, like Garvey, some of them wouldn't be going home tonight. For a cop, focusing on the negative was the best way to fulfill that prophecy.

Cartwright stood at the front of the room, describing the ESH layout for the newly arrived teams. A-Team officers lined the rear wall, standing with their rifles pointing safely at the floor. Logan and his team stood together, joined by what looked like three other full teams, and Gemma recognized a number of officers she'd worked with often, including Lieutenant Sanders. That would put their number at approximately one officer for every two inmates in the facility. They would be at a disadvantage by sheer numbers but would have surprise on their side. And with the design of the facility, specifically the narrow corridors of the second-floor walkway around the mezzanine, too many men could actually be a disadvantage. Lean and efficient sometimes beat overplayed and heavy-handed. Men trapped in position on a catwalk would be no use at all. Worse, they could become targets.

Spotting Chen, she wound her way down the side aisle to where the HNT teams sat together in the third row from the back. Chen motioned her over and pointed to the empty seat beside him. She mouthed her thanks and slid into the chair. McFarland leaned forward, lifting his hands in silent question. She held up an index finger— *wait for it*. Cocking his head, he studied her quizzically, but then returned his attention to Cartwright.

Gemma continued to scan the crowd from her seat, looking for and finding her father once again in the front row beside Commissioner Frye and down the row from where Garcia sat. She knew he'd be here. The chief had started the standoff with them; he'd be there at the end as well. His teams were involved, so his place was in the building to make any snap decisions required on the fly.

To take responsibility if anything went wrong.

He raised a single eyebrow at her, holding her gaze, his *Why were you late?* crystal-clear. She held the clipboard against her shoulder, tapped it twice, and then looked from him to Cartwright. He gave her a single nod, understanding her shorthand that she had information for Cartwright.

"The entrances to the facility are here." Cartwright walked over to the image of the facility projected onto the front whiteboard, broken into upper and lower levels. "The front entrance, controlled from both inside and outside the facility. The emergency exits, one on each level on the west side, at the north end of each corridor." As he talked, he pointed out each individual location. "Controls for those doors are located in both the main security room inside the ESH and from the stairwell that runs up that end of the building. Here, here, and here. All facilities in that wing have the same emergency exits joined by a single staircase that opens into the fenced area on the ground floor in case of fire blocking the main exit. We will use all three doors as our points of incursion.

"There are currently thirty-nine inmates inside the facility, down from the original forty-two. There are six hostages, down from the original eight." Focused on the upcoming op, Cartwright skipped past the decreased body count. The only thing relevant to him and the teams was who was inside the ESH now. "From several forays into the facility, it's clear gang lines have been drawn and territories formed. The two gangs involved—the Filero Kings and the Gutta Boys—don't encompass everyone inside the ESH. There are a handful of inmates who don't seem to have an affiliation for one group or the other. But that doesn't make them any less dangerous. Sometimes it's the lone wolves who feel they have no one to protect, and no one to protect them, and therefore nothing to lose."

Walking over to a laptop on a small desk against the

wall, Cartwright hit a key and the projected image changed to a front-facing picture of the facility. It was the same image the team posted on the wall of the negotiation room, showing the ESH from the main door, the mezzanine stretching toward the classroom and rear windows, and the second-floor walkway circling the space. In the distance, on the left, two bright red emergency doors were located at the end of the west walkway, just to the left of the two-story bank of window slats.

"Here's the facility as it looked when it opened years ago. It's a little rough around the edges now but the layout is the same. The center mezzanine with two rows of four-seater tables flanking a center aisle. The cells that circle the facility in pairs on both levels. The classroom used for programs and teaching. There were originally cameras in these locations"—he quickly indicated those spots—"but depending on the installation, they have been ripped down or destroyed. Either way, we have no internal eyes into the unit. One other note about this unit relevant to the operation is that the inmates trashed it during the initial riot. There's garbage and clothing and broken equipment scattered throughout that could make for a significant trip hazard. Also, these two tables, the first one on the right and the third in on the left, have been removed and tossed into the entranceway. Be aware of your surroundings." He moved to the next image. "This is what each cell looks like, or the mirror image of it. Built-in bed under a small reinforced window, small built-in table, a couple of plastic bins for their belongings, assuming it and the belongings haven't already been tossed out of the cell in the first place. Metal sink, toilet and mirror installed on the diagonal wall, so no corners to worry about. You won't need to enter the cell to clear it. You can see the entire space from the doorway. Now, when we went in yesterday the hostages were located in cell numbers five and twenty."

Gemma stood up. "Sir, I've just received updated intelligence. My apologies that I didn't have time to bring it to you before the meeting started."

"Who from?"

"Inmate Alvaro Vega, who you and your team removed from the facility yesterday after the attempt on his life. I just left him after requesting an interview through Warden Davis. One of the things I learned is that the hostages have been moved."

Cartwright looked unimpressed his briefing was being interrupted and he was being caught off guard, but he extended a hand toward the floor beside him. "You better come and update us then."

"Be right back," Gemma said under her breath to Chen and rose. She made her way to the front of the room and opened her clipboard. "When I sat down with Vega, I informed him of the death of Officer Garvey, without actually telling him which officer had been killed. He was initially reluctant to help, but I appealed to his sense of honor to his gang brothers in the ESH. And I threw in an offer to speak at his next hearing, testifying that he had assisted the NYPD in ending this standoff. That finally convinced him to help us.

"When Dr. Peltier, the A-Team, and myself visited the ESH to tend to some of the hostages and the inmates, we found the hostages in cells five and twenty." Gemma pointed to the two cells on the image, midway down both corridors on the lower level. "However, after we left but before the attack on Vega, there was a discussion between the inmates about the location of the hostages.

Some of the inmates were uncomfortable that we knew their location."

"We knew that before we went in there," Cartwright pointed out. "We could see where they were guarding them."

"At the time, the inmates weren't trying to hide the location of the hostages. They were happy for you to see they were in the middle of the facility so you knew if you breached any door without their permission, you'd never get to the hostages before they'd be able to kill them, or at least threaten to. But after the med visit some of the inmates were concerned that while we were there, we'd had the chance to get a better lay of the land and would be able to formulate a plan to retrieve the hostages. There were also concerns that having the hostages in larger groups, even if there were two of them, would make it too easy for any incoming team to take control of a single room. Or both rooms, and they'd lose their leverage." Gemma flicked a glance at the rear of the room where the A-Team officers were whispering to each other. They were already ahead of her. "So they moved the hostages. And split them up. Now the six hostages are scattered around the facility. You may not have seen them make the move because they made the hostages change into Rikers orange. When the operation commences, all officers will have to know the faces of each hostage because it could be a split-second decision of how to react to what looks like an inmate but may not be."

"Smart move on their part. That definitely complicates things for us."

"It does, and increases the risk to the hostages significantly. Can we go back to the blueprint?" She waited while Cartwright switched to the previous image. "Thank you. I can't guarantee the hostages haven't been moved since yesterday, but these are the locations to the best of Vega's knowledge." She stepped to the board, picked up a dry-erase marker, marked down the numbers beside the projected blueprint of the facility, and then circled them on the board over the image. "Cells three and seventeen on the lower level, and cells twenty-nine, thirty-five, and forty-six on the upper. And he thinks forty-one, but he's not sure. It might be forty-two. What he did say though is that all the cell doors are open. They're operated by the control room, but they didn't want to take the chance that a closed door would keep the hostage out of their reach if they needed to use them for quick leverage, or that they might lose the control room and access to any hostage. The hostages are each guarded by one of the inmates inside the cell."

"By who?" McFarland called.

"Rivas was calling the shots and would only put his own guys in charge of the hostages. And this was where the problem started yesterday. The two sides mixed it up verbally."

"How did we miss that?" From his tone of voice, Cartwright was torn between anger and bafflement.

"Vega said they were in the classroom at the far end of the facility and partially blocked by the mezzanine. They know they're being observed through the main entrance, so they use the classroom for discussions they want to keep on the down low. Except this discussion spun out and then Vega was grabbed. He's the youngest inmate in the facility, the gang baby brother, so to speak. The Gutta Boys thought they'd have the best leverage with him.

And they wanted to make a show of it—a slow, agonizing death in full view of the Kings. Except their grandstanding caught your attention and then we acted on it."

"Is there anything else he gave you?"

"I asked him about routines, such as they are, since the riot. He says at the beginning they were taking turns, staying up all night so someone was always ready to sound the alarm if we went in. But by yesterday, things were starting to fall apart. Rivas doesn't have a hold on easily a third of the population, and even with his own guys, they're tired, hungry, discouraged, losing their tempers, and rebelling. But things do quiet down mostly at night, so your element of surprise is going to be in the wee hours of the morning." She flipped her clipboard shut and looked back at the blueprint, studying the hostage locations. "We can hope the hostages are in these locations, but in case they aren't, you'll need to adapt on the fly."

"Thank you, Detective."

She gave him a nod and returned to her seat.

"This new intel about hostage location allows us to do some fine tuning of the original plan. We will breach anytime after two a.m. when the facility is quiet. Five smaller teams will go in led by myself, Sanders, Barrow, Kirkpatrick, and Logan." He picked up the dry-erase marker and added to Gemma's drawing. "Barrow, Kirkpatrick, and I will take the main entrance." He wrote "B", "C", and "K" at the front door and then outlined each route with an arrow. "Barrow and his team will take the first level east corridor, retrieving the hostage in cell seventeen. I'll take my team up to the second floor east"—he sketched an arrow following the stairs to the second floor landing, moving over to the second level blueprint to continue the path—"to cells forty-one or forty-two and forty-six. Kirkpatrick, you take the mezzanine level and can provide cover from there to both the upper and lower walkways. You'll also clear the classroom at the far end of the mezzanine." He moved back to the lower level map, sketching in "S" at the emergency door. "Sanders, you'll come through the first level emergency exit by the classroom, covering the first level west corridor, taking cell three and then looping around to close any gap at the main entrance so no one tries to slip out." He added "L" to the second-floor emergency exit. "Logan, you'll take the second level emergency exit leading into the second level west corridor to retrieve the hostages in cells twenty-nine and thirty-five. Simultaneous, timed breaches, multiple flash bangs to disorient as we go in. The Rikers ERSU will be our backup between the ESH and the rest of the OBCC from the main entrance and the stairwells in case anyone gets past Sanders and his team. Avoid lethal force unless you're given no choice to save your lives or the life of a hostage or vulnerable inmate. We'll learn the hostages' faces before we go in because it will be snap decisions. Deputy Warden Coleman is currently organizing moving inmates out of the identical unit two floors above ESH1 so we'll have rehearsal space. As soon as they're out, we'll drill this operation until it's seamless. Any questions?"

The room was silent.

"Good. Lieutenant Garcia."

Garcia traded places with Cartwright who took his chair. "Hostage negotiation teams, it's our job to make this look like any other day. Regular teams at scheduled times. We will attempt to bargain with them about their demands and the DOC concessions. In no way can they know they crossed the line this morning. They may expect it. It's our job to make them think we're still pinning all our hopes on a negotiated surrender because anything else would be a media circus the NYPD is determined to avoid." He looked over the heads of DOC personnel to his teams at the rear of the room. "It's going to be hard, but you can't let them know the hammer is about to fall. Lean on your active listening skills, stay calm, and buy the A-Teams the time they need to make this a successful operation where everyone goes home tonight."

The meeting ended shortly thereafter, the groups breaking up to discuss among themselves. Taylor and his group excused themselves to head home for a bit of shut-eye before their shift at 8 p.m., and Gemma and her team were about to head to the negotiation room when a familiar voice spoke from behind her.

"Detective."

Gemma turned around to find her father saying goodbye to the DOC commissioner. "Sir?"

"A word."

"Yes, sir."

She followed him to the back of the nearly deserted meeting room and took a seat beside him, not flinching when his searching gaze gave her the once-over.

"How are you feeling about this op?"

"Cartwright has it well in hand. He's solid and so are his men."

"This wasn't the end you wanted."

She gave him a look that only a daughter would give a father, not a detective her division chief.

"But you're okay with it?"

She nodded. "What I'm not okay with was what happened to Garvey. There was history between him and some of the inmates. Maybe I should have seen that more clearly and bargained for his release."

"Do you really think that would have happened?"

She looked toward the front of the room where the image of the ESH blueprint still shone on the whiteboard and let out a sigh. "No. If we'd tried to single Garvey out, they'd have likely gone after him then and there. The only thing I could have done was gotten them all out faster."

"Which you were trying to do the entire time." When she looked at him quizzically, he said, "I read the reports. I follow what my kids are doing whether they're in my division or not. I've been closely following this situation from the beginning even if I wasn't physically on-site. Garcia doesn't find fault in how you, Taylor, and your teams have handled it, and neither do I."

"It's Garvey that bothers me. Rush's death likely happened before I was on the island. But when Garvey was killed, I was trying to keep a lid on the situation."

"As you said, there was a history that went back months or more. He wasn't a random hit."

"Logically, I know that. But try convincing the emotional side of my brain."

"Are you going to be able to do what you need to do in there?"

"Of course, I am." She could hear temper edging her words. She knew her father, knew that's who'd asked the question, not her chief. "Sorry. I didn't mean to snap." She rubbed at her forehead with both hands. "I'm tired and it's been a bit of a stressful day." Closing her eyes, she took a deep breath, held it for a slow count of three, let it out, and opened her eyes to face her chief. "Yes, I'm going to be able to do what I need to do in there." And then at eight o'clock when her shift was over, she'd stay, catch an hour horizontal in a dark room somewhere, and would be there for the op whenever it went down.

She needed to be there in case they needed her as the primary negotiator at some point. But more than that, she needed to be there to see it go down. For Garvey. For Evans. For Rush.

She'd see it through.

CHAPTER 29

*T*hat evening, Gemma stood with Garcia, her father, and Commissioner Frye to observe the tactical rehearsal again and again.

While the NYPD and DOC had come together to discuss strategy in the meeting room, Coleman had orchestrated teams of COs in transferring the inmates in the second ESH that stood two levels above the hijacked facility to other housing units or jails for overnight. By the time the inmates were removed, one at a time, and the facility was empty, Gemma's shift was over.

Sometimes there was an edge to being a Capello. Usually, she didn't take advantage of it, but this time she did, joining her father against the mezzanine railing to watch the drills. She wasn't going to negotiate her way out of this crisis, but even though it was now out of her hands, she still felt ownership and genuine concern for the hostages and some of the inmates inside the ESH. This crisis wasn't of their making; they had simply been trapped in this hell. Now it was the NYPD's responsibility to do everything it could to get them out safely.

She'd spent the afternoon reaching out to the inmates in the ESH, but they shut her down. Call after call went unanswered, except for a single pickup and an unfamiliar voice at the other end that swore at her viciously and told her in no uncertain terms to stop calling.

She'd stopped calling. The last thing they needed was to aggravate the inmates to the extent they'd become violent. But that single answered call already filled in several gaps: Rivas was no longer in complete control; he hadn't answered her call. And the inmates likely recognized the response to their list of demands was now null and void because it had been dependent on them not harming anyone while they bargained in good faith.

The lack of communication terrified her. If the inmates had given up hope of a peaceful resolution to the crisis, the chances of hostages being hurt or killed increased exponentially.

Their options were now limited to waiting them out, storming the facility immediately, before the A-Team had time to perfect their approach, or take the time to rehearse the incursion and hope that no one died before then. Chief Tony Capello made the call—they'd wait until the scheduled time for a fully planned operation at the optimal time because the risk of loss of life and injury to his officers was simply too great if they moved too early. The inmates had already killed once that day; he hoped there would be a brief cooling-off period afterward. In the meantime, the A-Team would constantly monitor the facility with two officers standing at the door in full view at all times to observe the inmates. Usually they stayed out of sight to keep tempers cool, but now they used their presence to constrain the inmates inside. If things got hot, they would revise their plan accordingly and act; yet the hope was for a few extra hours to fine-tune the facility breach in order to keep everyone alive.

Once the inmates were out of the second ESH, the teams drilled their entry again and again, working with members of Rikers ERSU who stood in for some of the inmates. When a weakness was identified, they reworked the plan and ran it again. Repetition bred familiarity and gave the teams confidence that even if something happened— like losing the lights—they'd be able to successfully carry out their operation. They learned the geography of the facility and how to save steps to cover distance faster. Even though the ESH was purposely set up with only minimal corners and so most of the space could be viewed from a single position, there were still a few spots where inmates could hide—inside the classroom below the windows, behind the door, and under the tables; behind the wide support columns on the mezzanine; under the wide window of the control room overlooking the entire facility, or behind the control room door. By mapping out these danger areas, and assigning officers to specifically clear them, they greatly minimized risk.

This was no regular prison riot where rubber bullets and riot shields would be used. This was a rescue mission to reclaim the hostages and retake the cell block. The officers would be carrying live ammunition, and while it was a last resort, they would use it if lives were at stake.

"Let's run it again!" Cartwright's voice came over their earpieces from where he stood out of sight around the corner of the corridor with his team. "Are all teams ready?"

"Affirmative." The response came from Sanders, Barrow, Logan, and Kirkpatrick in unison.

"Affirmative," said one of the ERSU officers who was taking on the role of an inmate for the drill.

"On my mark then . . . *Mark!*"

Men streamed into the facility from three doorways. Dressed in black from helmets to boots, they moved in single file, in "snake" formation, the point man at the front taking all the risk and making all the spot decisions to alter any set plan of penetration depending on the environment in which he found himself and his team.

They came in crouched, sweeping their rifles from side to side, the blinding light on their rifle barrels flashing through the railing bars, bellowing, "NYPD! Get on the ground!" over and over. Boots pounded on the walkways overhead and ERSU members popped out of cells or around corners at them, only to be safely subdued facedown on the ground. The mezzanine quaked underfoot as Kirkpatrick and his team flowed up the stairs and over the floor to stake out preset positions and areas of responsibility covering the other officers. Sanders's team ran down the corridor opposite them, a man sequentially clearing a cell, then another man running past to cover the next cell. They covered the space in surprisingly little time until they got to cell 3 where a "hostage" waited for them, and where one man stayed behind to guard the hostage. The rest of the team moved forward to guard the entrance in staggered formation, covering the upper and lower levels from their location. On the second floor, Logan swung into a cell—*Clear!*—and Hill ran past him to cell 29, where he disappeared inside to where a hostage should be found later that night. Down at the end of the mezzanine, an officer appeared in the doorway of the classroom announcing, "Collins, coming out!" so any team member would know it wasn't a hostile inmate.

The room quieted down as each team reached the end of their planned route, having freed the hostages or subdued the inmates.

Tony Capello halted the stopwatch on his phone. "Best time yet. And seamless. They're ready," he said to Gemma. Pocketing his phone, he stepped forward. "Excellent work," he said, his voice raised to be heard throughout the cell block. "Good timing, smooth transitions, complete coverage. That doesn't mean there won't be any surprises tonight, but you're ready for them." He turned to find Cartwright above him on the catwalk. "Any other comments?"

Cartwright stepped forward to rest one hand on the second-level railing. "Watch your approaches. We're going to have guys popping out all over and they're going to outnumber us two to one. We're tight now, but that process is going to get interrupted. Some of these guys aren't going to go down easy." He looked down at Kirkpatrick's team. "Give us as much coverage up here as you can. We have twice the hostages and half the maneuvering room." He unsnapped his chin strap, the end swinging free. "Be flexible, trust your point man. If he deviates from the plan, know there's a reason for it and follow." His gaze moved around the unit to touch each of his men. "We're going to have this wrapped in minutes and, God willing, with everyone safe."

Gemma met her father's eyes, saw the confidence there, and the pride in his men.

They were ready.

CHAPTER 30

*T*he teams gathered in the meeting room at 1:30 a.m.

The building was quiet, the regular staff long having headed home, the overnight staff settled in for what they hoped would be an uneventful night. All except those who watched over ESH1.

The latest reports from the men stationed at the door said it had quieted down an hour before. As had occurred for each night of the standoff, the lights stayed on, ensuring no one could sneak into the facility under cover of darkness. Some men slept in the cells on a bunk, some simply curled up on a walkway floor, not wanting to spend any more time enclosed in that tiny space, and a few put their heads down on the tables in the mezzanine. One table had three men still sitting up, talking. Hopefully they would be asleep by 2 a.m. If not, they'd have to deal with Kirkpatrick and his men.

Gemma moved around the room, chatting with the officers she knew, answering any questions they had about the facility or the inmates, wishing them safe passage.

She had nearly completed a full circuit when she found herself face-to-face with Logan, his eyes shaded by the helmet and partly hidden behind his safety glasses. "You're ready?"

"Yes." The eyes that met hers were steady and sure. "It's going to go fine. You'll be home by three. You know, light traffic and all at this time of night."

"There's that A-Team overconfidence you guys are known for."

"When you're good, you're good. What can we say?"

"I can say good luck. This time it's you walking into the lion's den."

"Yeah, but I'm going in with body armor and a rifle. That's better than what you took into City Hall."

"True." She knew she didn't need to tell him outright to be careful. He'd been at the top of his academy class and his performance in the years since then had cemented his reputation as an outstanding officer. However, even outstanding officers were killed by forces outside of their control, and inmates fighting for their freedom fit that bill exactly. "Still . . . head up and eyes open." She repeated the daily mantra from their time as trainees at the academy under Sergeant Thomson.

"Always." His gaze cut across to the doorway as Cartwright stepped in. "Looks like we're getting ready to roll." He gave her a cocky grin. "See you on the other side."

As Cartwright called the teams to attention, she retreated to the far side of the room where both hostage negotiation teams were clustered along with NYPD, DOC and Rikers administration. McFarland was hunched over a laptop on the desk against the wall. When he straightened, Gemma realized she was looking at Cartwright's helmet cam as it streamed his men standing at attention. She glanced over her shoulder to see the same scene from the reverse angle.

When she turned back, McFarland waved her over. "We can't go in with them," he said, "but we can follow everything that's happening from here." A click of the mouse and Cartwright's camera feed shrunk to the upper left corner of a grid of streaming feeds. "Five teams, five point men, five cams." He pointed to the second grid location. "That's Kirkpatrick." Then the next. "That's Barrow. Sanders. And that's Logan. Once the teams are out, I'll project this on the whiteboard. We'll be able to track what's going on in real time."

"You're a handy man to have around."

"Maybe mention that to your father and hint that a raise is a great way to compensate my skills."

"Nice try. No cigar."

"Can't blame a guy for trying."

"Detective Capello."

Gemma turned at the sound of her name to find Dr. Peltier behind her, his medical duffel at his feet. "Dr. Peltier? I didn't expect to see you here."

"I offered to be on hand for the raid on top of the regular OBCC medical team. Your officers are carrying rifles and may have to use force if attacked, so I wanted to be here in case of injury."

"Good idea, thank you. I sincerely hope we won't need your services."

"Me too."

McFarland stepped away from the laptop and turned to where Garcia and Tony Capello stood deep in conversation. "Sir." He waited until he had both of their attention. "We're ready to go here."

"You have audio to go with that video?" Tony asked.

"Yes, sir. I have it muted for now. I'll have audio up on all cameras when it's time. It'll be a mass of sound, but we should still be able to pick up specific incidents that can be reviewed later if needed, as their units are recording as well as streaming."

"Good." Tony glanced at his watch and then across the room as Sanders led his team out the door. "The stairwell teams are moving right on time."

Logan and his team followed, and then the rest of the officers filed out.

The room settled into silence.

"Give me one second . . ." McFarland made a quick adjustment and then the grid projected onto the whiteboard and a steady drum of footsteps filled the room.

Sanders's feed showed him moving down an empty hallway, then up a staircase. Logan's feed showed Sanders going through the door, trailed by his team. They jogged up several flights of stairs and then broke out into the hallway just down from the ESH2 wing. They jogged through the deserted ESH and through the bright red emergency door which had been left unlocked for them.

As soon as they hit the stairwell, nearly all noises ceased—not a word and only the lightest of footsteps. It was imperative they arrive in position silently, not giving any advanced sign. Logan's feed stopped at a door that said ESH1 - 2. His head turned tracking one of his men who moved to a panel to the right of the door. "In position and ready to release the door." Logan's voice was only a whisper of sound.

Sanders's feed continued down another flight of steps

to a door stamped with ESH1 - 1. "In position and ready to release."

There was about ten seconds of silence as the other three teams got in position around the corner from the main door to the ESH1. Cartwright eased around the corner just enough to see the ERSU standing off to the side and two A-Team officers standing in front of the doorway, exactly as they had all day. An ERSU officer nodded in Cartwright's direction as if responding to an out-of-sight hand signal; then he signaled to one of his men who moved to an unlocked control panel and then turned to nod at Cartwright.

"All teams, go, no go for breach." Cartwright's voice was quiet but clear.

"Barrow, go."

"Kirkpatrick, go."

"Logan, go."

"Sanders, go."

"Ready the flash bang, pull the pin." Cartwright paused. "Doors open on my mark. And . . . *mark!*" The last word was a shout.

Action exploded on the feeds. At the emergency doors, a single man stepped into the camera's view as the door swung wide, tossed a grenade, and ducked back out of sight as the camera also turned away from the opening. As the main door rumbled open, three officers ran forward and tossed the grenades in three directions—right, left, and straight ahead—into the facility before they retreated.

A blinding flash of light washed over all five screens accompanied by a succession of blasts in stereo from both the laptop and straight through the hallway door. The flash bangs—175 decibels of deafening noise set off against a burning light that caused five to seven seconds of flash blindness and a disorienting afterimage—were the cover for the men to enter the facility avoiding lethal force.

As soon as the grenades went off, the men were on the move, snaking through the doorway through a thick layer of smoke.

"NYPD! Get on the ground!"

The teams moved fast. Kirkpatrick sprinted for the center stairs, leaping up the few steps, and then he and his team were on the five men on the mezzanine. Blinking with sleep and stunned by the noise, only one of them put up a minimal fight.

Sanders bolted for the staircase to the right of the main entrance, pounding up the steps and then swinging into the first cell. The inmate came at him fast, launching from the bed to ram him, until he saw the M4 pointed at his torso and stopped, his hands rising into the air.

Barrow was on the ground floor and just about to check a cell when an inmate roared out of the doorway. Barrow let him get one step outside the cell before he moved in, raising the butt of his rifle to ram him between the shoulder blades. The man went down, a metal shiv flying out of his hand to clatter over the floor. "Keep going!" He bellowed as he bent down to crank the man's hands behind his back and restrain them. His men moved past him, carrying on down the corridor.

"First hostage is secure." It was Logan's voice. "Cell thirty-five. Duran. Sims is with him."

"Second hostage is secure." This time it was Cartwright. "Cell forty-six. It's Keen. He's with Clarke."

"Let go!" The shout echoed around the facility, but it

was Kirkpatrick spinning around and looking up toward the upper walkway that identified one of Sanders's men in a hand-to-hand struggle with an inmate trying to topple him over the balcony.

Kirkpatrick raised his rifle. "Let him go!" he shouted. "He goes over, I will shoot you."

It only took that brief second of distracted hesitation for the A-Team officer to reclaim control of the struggle, wrestling the man to the floor and cuffing him.

"Close one," McFarland murmured.

"Too close," Gemma agreed.

Already things were coming under control, the volume in the facility dropping as men were surrendering. Cartwright had Burk and was muscling him down the second-floor walkway with a bit less finesse and a bit more force than necessary. Reading the anger in Cartwright's every clipped command, Gemma thought Burk was lucky that was the worst he was getting.

Logan stepped into a cell doorway, rifle pointed at the occupant curled on the bed, who cringed, throwing up her hands to block the light from his rifle as she cried out, "Don't shoot!" He instantly dropped the barrel, and Andrea Montgomery lowered her hands and smiled in relief.

"Warrick, come in and stay with CO Montgomery," Logan ordered. "Logan, coming out!"

It was when he cautiously swung out of the cell that he was blindsided.

The attack came from the unsearched cell to his right. Gemma caught a brief flash of motion, a burst of orange leaping out like a speeding freight train, the inmate pushing Logan's rifle aside where it would be useless in close quarters, his other forearm raised as he barreled into

Logan full speed, catching him below the level of the camera. Then everything was in motion as they struggled, but Gemma caught a hand upraised with a blur of white in it, and a face frozen in a snarl of rage.

She knew that face. Rivas had nothing left to lose and was making a last stand. And was using his switchblade one last time to do so.

For several terrifying seconds the camera view was just a blur as the two men grappled, then Logan loosed a grunt of pain, followed by the *crack* of his handgun and a scream. Logan fell back against the wall, panting hard, his breath whistling through clenched teeth, but when he looked down, the camera feed found Rivas writhing on the ground, clutching his side. Then two other officers were on him, blocking Gemma's view.

And then it was done. In only the course of a few minutes, the last six days of hell was finally over.

Everyone watching the raid ran down the hallway, past the darkened courtyard, around the corner, and straight into ESH1. A-Team officers were marching cuffed inmates out one at a time while others sat restrained to the mezzanine tables. Officers Jackson and Keen sat side by side on the mezzanine steps looking exhausted but relieved. Keen cradled his left arm in his right hand, but he looked better than the day before. Peltier's lavage and the antibiotics appeared to be working well for him.

A rap of metal on metal drew Gemma's gaze upward to find Johnson coming down the south staircase with Logan's right arm over his shoulder, supporting him as they descended. She couldn't see Logan's injury, but the black uniform camouflaged blood all too well. Johnson was being careful, but each step must have jarred Logan from his clenched teeth and what looked like a few choice curses. He'd been hit during Rivas's attack, but how badly?

Peltier ran over to them, stopped them at the bottom of the steps for a quick examination of Logan's left shoulder. He turned to Keen. "Officer Keen, please wait there for me. I want to look at that arm before you move around anymore. Detective Logan, come with me." He traded places with Johnson and walked Logan out of the ESH. As they went, she heard Logan's protest that he could walk just fine and Dr. Peltier's response that he'd be the judge of that.

Concerned about the extent of his injury, Gemma took a step to follow, but then movement above her attracted her attention. Looking up, she found Andrea Montgomery coming down the stairs with Peterson. She looked pale and shaky, possibly shocky. Gemma grabbed a blanket off a pile just inside the doorway and met her at the bottom of the stairs.

Montgomery was even paler up close, her dark eyes sunken and stunned, her lips dry and cracked from dehydration. Gemma draped the blanket around her shoulders and wrapped an arm around her, feeling the deep tremors that ran through her. "It's okay. It's all over. You can go home now."

Montgomery bit her bottom lip, her breath catching raggedly. "I just want to see my kids."

"You will. It's over now. Your kids are waiting for you at home."

"I can't . . . I just need to—" Montgomery's knees buckled and Gemma lowered her to sit on the bottom step. The CO buried her face in her hands and wept, but to Gemma's ears, they were tears of relief.

Rubbing a hand up and down Montgomery's back, she scanned the cell block and met her father's eyes across the mezzanine. His smile was tired but full of satisfaction. She grinned back at him.

A successful raid, no death, minimal injuries. Thirty-nine inmates contained, all six remaining hostages rescued.

It was a win after all.

CHAPTER 31

Gemma easily found the curtained exam room and rapped her knuckles on the doorframe. "Sean? It's Gemma. Can I come in?"

"Uh . . . sure." There was surprise in Logan's voice. He likely hadn't expected anyone involved in today's raid would come all the way to Elmhurst after an already long night.

She tucked the jacket she carried securely over her forearm and pushed aside the curtain in time to see him sit up on the gurney and swing his feet off the end. He was shirtless—his shirt was likely in ribbons in a trash can somewhere after they'd cut it off him to evaluate his wound—but still wore his tactical pants and heavy boots.

A neat white bandage covered the front of his left shoulder. But around the wound, his skin was stained red with blood in smears and rivulets that ran over one side of his chest and down his arm.

"It looks worse than it is," he said before she could ask. "They wiped down anything that hadn't already dried, but they're leaving it to me to clean off the rest."

Gemma tried not to stare. "It looks bad."

"It bled a bit."

"A bit?"

"Maybe a little more than that."

"Peltier said the blade of Rivas's switchblade broke off in your shoulder."

"Yeah, it wasn't quite as sturdy as Rivas thought. They had to fish out the blade once I got here."

"No wonder it bled."

"I've had worse. What are you doing here? It's five o'clock in the morning."

"And you said I'd be home by three." Her chuckle couldn't hide her exhaustion. "I was on my way home, but I wanted to check in on you if you were still here. And here you are."

"Is it all wrapped at Rikers?"

"As wrapped as we need it to be. The ESH is cleared out and Davis is sending in teams to clean up the mess. All the inmates have been moved to other cell blocks, and the major players have been transferred to solitary confinement."

"Meaning both Rivas and Burk?"

"And a few others, but yes, those two specifically. Burk directly there, and Rivas eventually after high-security treatment in the hospital unit." She paused, fussing with the jacket, twisting the blue fabric in her hands.

"That bothers you?"

"No, they got what they deserved. I just . . . I just had

higher hopes for my contact with Rivas. That I'd have gotten through to him even a little bit."

This had happened to Gemma before, and she knew she'd work through it given some processing time. But the act of negotiation—the crucial connection to someone on the other end of the line, especially when it was over days as it was during this crisis—created an inadvertent intimacy between the players. Even though she was satisfied with the final resolution by and large, the fact that she'd never penetrated Rivas's innermost layers was akin to a small loss.

"I'm not sure anyone would have gotten through to someone as hardened as Rivas. His life circumstances and his place in the Filero Kings wouldn't allow him to make a connection like that. Not with you. Not with Taylor. Not with anyone outside of his gang life."

"You're right. Still, you hope for better." She gave him a half smile. "And sometimes you get it. Just not this time. Anyway, Rivas is going to have lots of time to think about if he could have handled this differently. He'll have a host of new charges. As will the other men in the ESH. Some of those charges are obvious—we know who the players are—but some of them I suspect we'll never know. I wouldn't consider the inmates dependable witnesses since many of them have agendas with each other, so we can't trust they're truthfully telling us what happened. But hopefully we can get enough consensus because I really want to know who's responsible for Garvey's murder. Past all that, what's left for me now is the paperwork."

"That'll be no small task."

"It never is." Her gaze dropped to his shoulder. "Are you just about done here?"

"Getting close." He tried to roll his left shoulder and winced. "The doc will be back with a prescription for antibiotics. And he wants to update my tetanus because that facility was so filthy. Then they'll spring me."

"Were stitches sufficient?"

"Looks like it."

"What happened? It was hard to tell from the camera feed."

"Rivas clearly had the attack planned. Not for me, but for whoever appeared first. He knew whoever found Montgomery would pause momentarily, giving him a chance to get ready. I came out of Montgomery's cell and he jumped out of the adjacent cell. He led with the hand that pushed my rifle away from him, but he was already too close for it to be any use in such close quarters. He's big and heavy—probably has two inches and thirty pounds on me—so his entire plan was based on brute force. He rushed me, slammed me against the open cell door with his forearm to my collar, and went for my throat with that goddamn switchblade. In the struggle, I managed to pivot enough out of the way that he only caught my shoulder at the edge of my vest."

"That was lucky. You could tell just by looking at him that he spends a lot of time working out."

"Overpowering me was definitely his master plan. I could have done better against him if I'd been fighting with both hands, but I was only using one and went for my Sig with the other. That's the shot that took him down." He glanced down at the bandage on his shoulder. "That plastic knife was surprisingly sharp, but considering the force of the blow, it just wasn't strong enough, and the hilt snapped off. Then the tissues swelled and they had to dig around for the blade to pull it out. They froze it first, so I mostly felt a lot of tugging. Luckily it came out in one piece with nothing left behind. It missed anything major, though I'm pretty sure they dragged the blade over bone pulling it out."

Gemma winced. "Ouch."

"Let's hear it for the meds." His gaze dropped to the blue fabric draped over her arm. "What's that?"

Gemma dragged her gaze away from Logan's injury. "I thought you might like to borrow this." She shook out the material to reveal a navy zippered, hooded sweat jacket with NYPD emblazoned across the front in yellow block letters. "I assume your shirt is history?"

"Yeah. I think those nurses take some kind of perverse pleasure cutting clothing off a guy. They could have just taken the sleeve, but they cut the whole thing off."

"They needed access to the whole wound to clean it."

"That's what they all say." Logan's tone was dry. "That can't be yours. It's way too big."

"It's not. It's my brother Joe's. He left it at my place weeks ago, and it's been in my car waiting until the next time I saw him . . . which was unexpectedly at Rikers, so it never occurred to me to give it to him. I think you need it right now more than he does. Not to mention it's a zip-up and you might have trouble putting on anything else for a few days."

"At this point, I'd appreciate not having to go home in a hospital gown."

"I bet." She unzipped the sweat jacket and moved to his left side to hold out the empty sleeve for him.

Trying to move his shoulder as little as possible, he slipped his arm into the sleeve, holding still as she drew the cuff over his hand and then lay the jacket across his shoulders.

He slid his right arm in, fiddled for a moment with the fastening, and then zipped it closed with his right hand. "That's better. Thanks. It's a bit drafty in here."

Suddenly feeling entirely too close, she stepped back, searching for what to say next, but her mind went blank. She'd wanted to stop by to make sure he was okay, but their truce felt fragile as butterfly wings and she didn't want to do anything to shatter it. Awkward discomfort crawled through her as she tried to find a way out. "Well, I don't want to get in the way here so—"

"You're not in the way. Why are you so uncomfortable? You used to be able to talk to me."

She'd forgotten how direct he was. Other people would skirt a topic; Logan would simply go in for the kill.

"I *am* talking to you."

"Barely. Something's on your mind. You came all the way down here." He plucked at the sleeve of the jacket. "You brought me something to wear home. You could have just called, but you showed up. Why?"

"As I said, you were injured during my op, so I wanted to make sure you were okay."

"It wasn't *your* op. You were part of it, but Cartwright was running it with Garcia's and Chief Capello's approval. And it's just a stab wound to the shoulder, not the gut. My life's in no danger. So, what's going on?"

She closed her eyes for a moment, gathering her thoughts. She should have known he'd call her on her BS. He always had; why stop now? "I guess I felt we left part of our conversation unfinished."

"You mean the one we had after you tried to murder an innocent basketball?"

That raised the laugh she knew he wanted. *Keeping*

things from getting too serious. She could appreciate that. "No, not that one. The conversation when you told me why you took that shot. I wanted to apologize."

He recoiled slightly, his brow creased. "You don't owe me an apology for anything."

"Yes, I do. For never giving you the benefit of the doubt. For instantly suspecting your motives and assuming the worst. I was too closed up inside my own head by that point in the case. It's not an excuse, just an explanation."

"Don't beat yourself up about it. It's amazing you survived that day at all. When you left me to walk into City Hall, I honestly thought you were going to die."

"But you let me go anyway."

"There was no 'letting you go.' I had no right to stop you. I wanted to, but it wasn't my place. I also understood what you were trying to accomplish."

"You just didn't think I could do it."

"I didn't think *anyone* could do it. Clearly, I was wrong. And if it had been anyone other than another Capello in the cemetery with you that night . . ."

"I know. But Alex was the only one who fit the bill. A cop—a damned good cop in fact no matter what anyone says about him being IAB—"

Logan raised both hands in the universal gesture of *I surrender* and then winced at the pain in his shoulder. "I never said he wasn't a good cop."

"No, but most others do. Anyway, he was the only one who could help. A cop who knew my background intimately enough to receive the barest of messages and still be able to decode it and come running."

"And the two of you came close to bringing him in. But that's on Boyle, not you. He forced my hand."

She let out a sigh, practically deflating as her shoulders slumped and her head drooped. "I know. But I could have handled it differently."

"Hey." He waited until she looked up to meet his eyes. "Gem, that day was pure hell for you. It had to bring back all the worst memories of what happened to your mother, but you didn't let that stop you. So it set you off balance, and if focusing on me and what I'd done let you claw your way out, that's fine. Are we good now?"

"Yeah, we're good."

"Then let's close the book on it. You know that's the kind of case that can fester if you don't let it go."

"Can you let it go? You killed a man and even from a distance, that's not an easy weight to bear."

"I'm used to it."

"*Cazzate.*"

His eyebrows rose at her vehemence, but he said nothing.

"Every one counts. Every one is a memory you can't shake. So let's agree to do our best to close the book on it, but admit that parts of it will haunt us for a while."

He simply watched her for a few silent seconds. "Deal."

"Good." She looked away, wanting to escape the weight of his gaze. "Anyway, thanks for your help on this one. I'm not sure how I would have gotten through the situation with Vega without you."

"You would have. Any of the other guys would have stepped up if I hadn't."

"Maybe, but you did step up. And your quick thinking saved a life. So . . . thanks."

"Anytime. And that was good intel you brought us. It was smart to use Vega like that. Not everyone would have been able to coax that information out of him, but you did. It likely saved lives."

"Thanks." She took a step backward. "Well, take care of that shoulder."

"I will."

"I guess I'll see you around then." Another step in retreat.

"Yeah."

She reached out a hand for the curtain when a thought occurred to her, causing her to stop and turn back. "Wait a second, how are you getting home?"

"I'll grab a cab."

She let the curtain drop. "At this hour of the morning? That's not right. I'll drive you."

"You don't have to."

"I don't. But I want to." As she spoke, she realized it was true.

So many years had passed since she'd really known him. During their time in the academy, he'd been arrogant, stubborn, and competitive, but he'd also been dedicated, courageous, and honest to a fault. Their relationship had always been an oddly fluid sliding scale of friendship, rivalry, and sexual attraction during that brief oasis in their lives at the academy. But when they'd left the academy, she'd purposefully cut all ties. There were simply too many expectations, too much pressure to live up to the Capello reputation, and she didn't want a personal entanglement to break her single-minded focus. So she'd let him drift away.

His smile faltered. "You're sure? I know . . . I know you've been angry with me for a while. Hard to get over that so quickly."

The pressure of his gaze made her want to squirm, but

she forced herself to meet it. "I didn't understand your motivation, so I believed the worst of you. We've cleared that up now. Consider it a fresh slate."

"A fresh slate. I like that." He tapped the edge of his boot against the leg of the hard plastic chair beside the gurney. "Might as well get comfortable then. You know how slow ER docs are unless you're dying. Which I'm not."

"I sure do." Gemma pulled the chair closer to the gurney and sat down.

And started getting reacquainted with an old friend.

ACKNOWLEDGMENTS

It takes a village to bring a book to publication, and I've been fortunate to work with some very talented individuals on SHOT CALLER:

Shane Vandevalk, who once again assisted with plot and title brainstorming, and who was my consultant for all tactical and fight scene planning, and for absolutely anything related to firearms. Thanks for your constant patience with my gun flubs! On the bright side, I never make the same one twice . . .

My crit team—Jenny Lidstrom, Jessica Newton, Rick Newton, and Sharon Taylor—for tackling this manuscript in the middle of the pandemic lockdown, and for their usual insightful and detailed critiques despite the challenging work environment.

My husband, Rick Newton, who assisted with the considerable amount of research at the beginning of story planning.

Kensington Publishing and its various departments for all their work turning the initial manuscript into the polished finished product, including Louis Malcangi and his fantastic art department for another evocative cover, enthusiastic communications support from Larissa Ackerman, Lauren Jernigan, Vida Engstrand, Alexandra Kenney, and Alexandra Nicolajsen, and editorial support from Norma Perez-Hernandez.

My agent Nicole Resciniti, who is always supportive and available, be it for a quick phone call to touch base, or for longer communications to tackle more substantial issues. And the rest of the Seymour Agency support team—Marisa Cleveland, Lesley Sabga, and Leslie Nunez—for publicity and for helping to get your authors out into the world.

Last, but very definitely not least, many *many* thanks to editor extraordinaire, Esi Sogah, who helped steer the creation of this book at one of the most stressful times of my life. Esi was extremely understanding that my day job as a COVID researcher working under the challenge of launching two national clinical trials at the beginning of the pandemic wasn't a the-dog-ate-my-homework type of excuse for being behind in my deadline, and graciously gave me more than sufficient time to complete the manuscript with my sanity intact. Esi, your words of compassion, commiseration, and encouragement are always appreciated, but never more so than through the spring of 2020 as I was struggling for balance. Thank you for giving me the time and bandwidth to make this book everything it could be.

Want more of the Capello family?
Make sure to read
EXIT STRATEGY
The first in the new
NYPD Negotiators series
Available now from
Jen J. Danna
and Kensington Books
Wherever books are sold

Visit us online at
KensingtonBooks.com
to read more from your favorite authors,
see books by series, view reading
group guides, and more!

BOOK █▊▟▍ CLUB
BETWEEN THE CHAPTERS

Visit us online for sneak peeks, exclusive
giveaways, special discounts, author content,
and engaging discussions with your fellow readers.

Betweenthechapters.net

Sign up for our newsletters and be the first
to get exciting news and announcements about
your favorite authors!
Kensingtonbooks.com/newsletter